FABLEHAVEN

NONE
WHO ENTER
WILL
LEAVE
UNCHANGED

TRESPASSERS
WILL BE
TURNED TO STONE

FABLEHAVEN

BRANDON MULL

ILLUSTRATED BY
BRANDON DORMAN

ALADDIN PAPERBACKS
NEW YORK   LONDON   TORONTO   SYDNEY

✳ ✳ ✳

For Mary, who made writing possible

❧

ALADDIN PAPERBACKS
An imprint of Simon & Schuster Children's Publishing Division
1230 Avenue of the Americas, New York, NY 10020
Copyright © 2006 by Brandon Mull
All rights reserved, including the right of reproduction
in whole or in part in any form.
ALADDIN PAPERBACKS and related logo are registered trademarks of
Simon & Schuster, Inc.
Published by arrangement with Deseret Books.
The text of this book was set in Goudy.
Manufactured in the United States of America
First Aladdin Paperbacks edition April 2007
24 26 28 30 29 27 25
The Library of Congress has cataloged the hardcover edition as follows:
Mull, Brandon, 1974–
Fablehaven / Brandon Mull.
p. cm.
Summary: When Kendra and Seth go to stay at their grandparents' estate,
they discover that it is a sanctuary for magical creatures and that a
battle between good and evil is looming.
[1. Magic—Fiction. 2. Grandparents—Fiction. 3. Brothers and sisters—Fiction.]
I. Title.
PZ7.M9112Fa 2006
[Fic]—dc22
2006000911
ISBN-13: 978-1-59038-581-4 (hc)
ISBN-10: 1-59038-581-0 (hc)
ISBN-13: 978-1-4169-4720-2 (pbk)
ISBN-10: 1-4169-4720-5 (pbk)
0510 OFF

Contents

CHAPTER ONE

A Mandatory Vacation

Kendra stared out the side window of the SUV, watching foliage blur past. When the flurry of motion became too much, she looked up ahead and fixed her gaze on a particular tree, following it as it slowly approached, streaked past, and then gradually receded behind her.

Was life like that? You could look ahead to the future or back at the past, but the present moved too quickly to absorb. Maybe sometimes. Not today. Today they were driving along an endless two-lane highway through the forested hills of Connecticut.

"Why didn't you tell us Grandpa Sorenson lived in India?" Seth complained.

Her brother was eleven and heading into sixth grade.

He had grown weary of his handheld video game—evidence that they were on a truly epic drive.

Mom twisted to face the backseat. "It won't be much longer. Enjoy the scenery."

"I'm hungry," Seth said.

Mom started rummaging through a grocery bag full of snack food. "Peanut butter and crackers?"

Seth reached forward for the crackers. Dad, driving, asked for some Almond Roca. Last Christmas he had decided that Almond Roca was his favorite candy and that he should have some on hand all year long. Nearly six months later he was still honoring his resolution.

"Do you want anything, Kendra?"

"I'm fine."

Kendra returned her attention to the frantic parade of trees. Her parents were leaving on a seventeen-day Scandinavian cruise with all the aunts and uncles on her mother's side. They were all going for free. Not because they'd won a contest. They were going on a cruise because Kendra's grandparents had asphyxiated.

Grandma and Grandpa Larsen had been visiting relatives in South Carolina. The relatives lived in a trailer. The trailer had some sort of malfunction involving a gas leak, and they all died in their sleep. Long ago, Grandma and Grandpa Larsen had specified that when they died, all their children and their spouses were to use an allocated sum of money to go on a Scandinavian cruise.

The grandchildren were not invited.

"Won't you get bored stuck on a boat for seventeen days?" Kendra asked.

Dad glanced at her in the rearview mirror. "The food is supposed to be incredible. Snails, fish eggs, the works."

"We're not all that thrilled about the trip," Mom said sadly. "I don't think your grandparents envisioned an accidental death when they made this request. But we'll make the best of it."

"The ship stops in ports as you go," Dad said, deliberately redirecting the conversation. "You get to disembark for part of the time."

"Is this car ride going to last seventeen days?" Seth asked.

"We're nearly there," Dad said.

"Do we have to stay with Grandma and Grandpa Sorenson?" asked Kendra.

"It'll be fun," Dad said. "You should feel honored. They almost never invite anyone to stay with them."

"Exactly. We barely know them. They're hermits."

"Well, they were my parents," Dad said. "Somehow I survived."

The road stopped winding through forested hills as it passed through a town. They idled at a stoplight, and Kendra stared at an overweight woman gassing up her minivan. The front windshield of the minivan was dirty, but the woman seemed to have no intention of washing it.

Kendra glanced up front. The windshield of the SUV was filthy, smeared with dead bugs, even though Dad had squeegeed it when they last stopped to refuel. They had driven all the way from Rochester today.

Kendra knew that Grandma and Grandpa Sorenson had not invited them to stay. She had overheard when Mom had approached Grandpa Sorenson about letting the kids stay with him. It was at the funeral.

The memory of the funeral made Kendra shiver. There was a wake beforehand, where Grandma and Grandpa Larsen were showcased in matching caskets. Kendra did not like seeing Grandpa Larsen wearing makeup. What lunatic had decided that when people died you should hire a taxidermist to fix them up for one final look? She would much rather remember them alive than on grotesque display in their Sunday best. The Larsens were the grandparents who had been part of her life. They had shared many holidays and long visits.

Kendra could hardly remember spending time with Grandma and Grandpa Sorenson. They had inherited some estate in Connecticut around the time her parents were married. The Sorensons had never invited them to visit, and rarely made the trek out to Rochester. When they came, it was generally one or the other. They had only come together twice. The Sorensons were nice, but their visits had been too infrequent and brief for real bonding to occur. Kendra knew that Grandma had taught history at some college, and that Grandpa had traveled a lot, running a small importing business. That was about it.

Everyone was surprised when Grandpa Sorenson

showed up at the funeral. It had been more than eighteen months since either of the Sorensons had visited. He had apologized that his wife could not attend because she was feeling ill. There always seemed to be an excuse. Sometimes Kendra wondered if they were secretly divorced.

Toward the end of the wake, Kendra overheard Mom cajoling Grandpa Sorenson to watch the kids. They were in a hallway around a corner from the viewing area. Kendra heard them talking before she reached the corner, and paused to eavesdrop.

"Why can't they stay with Marci?"

"Normally they would, but Marci is coming on the cruise."

Kendra peeked around the corner. Grandpa Sorenson was wearing a brown jacket with patches on the elbows and a bow tie.

"Where are Marci's kids going?"

"To her in-laws."

"What about a baby-sitter?"

"Two and a half weeks is a long time for a sitter. I remembered you had mentioned having them over sometime."

"Yes, I recall. Does it have to be late June? Why not July?"

"The cruise is on a time frame. What's the difference?"

"Things get extra busy around then. I don't know, Kate. I'm out of practice with children."

"Stan, I don't want to go on this cruise. It was important to my parents, so we're going. I don't mean to twist your arm." Mom sounded on the verge of tears.

Grandpa Sorenson sighed. "I suppose we could find a place to lock them up."

Kendra moved away from the hall at that point. She had quietly worried about staying with Grandpa Sorenson ever since.

Having left the town behind, the SUV climbed a steep grade. Then the road curved around a lake and got lost among low, forested hills. Every so often they passed a mailbox. Sometimes a house was visible through the trees; sometimes there was only a long driveway.

They turned onto a narrower road and kept driving. Kendra leaned forward and checked the gas gauge. "Dad, you're under a quarter of a tank," she said.

"We're almost there. We'll fill up after we drop you kids off."

"Can't we come on the cruise?" Seth asked. "We could hide in the lifeboats. You could sneak us food."

"You kids will have much more fun with Grandma and Grandpa Sorenson," Mom said. "Just you wait. Give it a chance."

"Here we are," Dad said.

They pulled off the road onto a gravel driveway. Kendra could see no sign of a house, only the driveway angling out of sight into the trees.

Tires crunching over the gravel, they passed several

signs advertising that they were on private property. Other signs warded off trespassers. They came to a low metal gate that hung open but could be shut to prevent access.

"This is the longest driveway in the world!" Seth complained.

The farther they advanced, the less conventional the signs became. *Private Property* and *No Trespassing* gave way to *Beware of .12 Gauge* and *Trespassers Will Be Persecuted*.

"These signs are funny," Seth said.

"More like creepy," Kendra muttered.

Rounding another bend, the driveway reached a tall, wrought-iron fence topped with fleurs-de-lis. The double gate stood open. The fence extended off into the trees as far as Kendra could see in either direction. Near the fence stood a final sign:

Certain Death Awaits.

"Is Grandpa Sorenson paranoid?" Kendra asked.

"The signs are a joke," Dad said. "He inherited this land. I'm sure the fence came with it."

After they passed through the gate, there was still no house in sight. Just more trees and shrubs. They drove across a small bridge spanning a creek and climbed a shallow slope. There the trees ended abruptly, bringing the house into view across a vast front lawn.

The house was big, but not enormous, with lots of gables and even a turret. After the wrought-iron gate, Kendra had expected a castle or a mansion. Constructed out of dark wood and stone, the house looked old but in good repair. The grounds were more impressive. A bright flower garden bloomed in front of the house. Manicured hedges and a fish pond added character to the yard. Behind the house loomed an immense brown barn, at least five stories tall, topped by a weather vane.

"I love it," Mom said. "I wish we were all staying."

"You've never been here?" Kendra asked.

"No. Your father came here a couple of times before we were married."

"They go the extra mile to discourage visitors," Dad said. "Me, Uncle Carl, Aunt Sophie—none of us have spent much time here. I don't get it. You kids are lucky. You'll have a blast. If nothing else, you can spend your time playing in the pool."

They pulled to a stop outside the garage.

The front door opened and Grandpa Sorenson emerged, followed by a tall, lanky man with large ears and a thin, older woman. Mom, Dad, and Seth got out of the car. Kendra sat and watched.

Grandpa had been clean-shaven at the funeral, but now he wore a stubbly white beard. He was dressed in faded jeans, work boots, and a flannel shirt.

Kendra studied the older woman. She was not Grandma Sorenson. Despite her white hair streaked with a few black strands, her face had an ageless quality. Her almond eyes were black as coffee, and her features suggested a hint of Asian ancestry. Short and slightly stooped, she retained an exotic beauty.

Dad and the lanky man opened the back of the SUV and began removing suitcases and duffel bags. "You coming, Kendra?" Dad asked.

Kendra opened the door and dropped to the gravel.

"Just place the things inside," Grandpa was telling Dad. "Dale will take them up to the bedroom."

"Where's Mom?" Dad asked.

"Visiting your Aunt Edna."

"In Missouri?"

"Edna's dying."

Kendra had barely ever heard of Aunt Edna, so the news did not mean much. She looked up at the house. She noticed that the windows had bubbly glass. Bird nests clung under the eaves.

They all migrated to the front door. Dad and Dale carried the larger bags. Seth held a smaller duffel bag and a cereal box. The cereal box was his emergency kit. It was full of odds and ends he thought would come in handy for an adventure—rubber bands, a compass, granola bars, coins, a squirt gun, a magnifying glass, plastic handcuffs, string, a whistle.

"This is Lena, our housekeeper," Grandpa said. The older woman nodded and gave a little wave. "Dale helps me tend the grounds."

"Aren't you pretty?" Lena said to Kendra. "You must be around fourteen." Lena had a faint accent that Kendra could not place.

"In October."

An iron knocker hung on the front door, a squinting goblin with a ring in its mouth. The thick door had bulky hinges.

Kendra entered the house. Glossy wood floored the entry hall. A wilting arrangement of flowers rested on a low table in a white ceramic vase. A tall, brass coatrack stood off to one side beside a black bench with a high, carved back. On the wall hung a painting of a fox hunt.

Kendra could see into another room where a huge, embroidered throw rug covered most of the wooden floor. Like the house itself, the furnishings were antiquated but in good repair. The couches and chairs were mostly of the sort you would expect to see while visiting a historical site.

Dale was heading up the stairs with some of the bags. Lena excused herself and went to another room.

"Your home is beautiful," Mom gushed. "I wish we had time for a tour."

"Maybe when you get back," Grandpa said.

"Thanks for letting the kids stay with you," Dad said.

"Our pleasure. Don't let me keep you."

"We're on a pretty tight schedule," Dad apologized.

"You kids be good and do whatever Grandpa Sorenson tells you," Mom said. She hugged Kendra and Seth.

Kendra felt tears seeping into her eyes. She fought them back. "Have a fun cruise."

"We'll be back before you know it," Dad said, putting an arm around Kendra and tousling Seth's hair.

Waving, Mom and Dad walked out the door. Kendra went to the doorway and watched them climb into the SUV. Dad honked as they drove off. Kendra fought back tears again as the SUV vanished into the trees.

Mom and Dad were probably laughing, relieved to be off by themselves for the longest vacation of their married lives. She could practically hear their crystal goblets clinking. And here she stood, abandoned. Kendra closed the door. Seth, oblivious as ever, was examining the intricate pieces of a decorative chess set.

Grandpa stood in the entry hall, watching Seth and looking politely uncomfortable.

"Leave the chess pieces alone," Kendra said. "They look expensive."

"Oh, he's all right," Grandpa said. By the way he said it, Kendra could tell he was relieved to see Seth setting the pieces down. "Shall I show you to your room?"

They followed Grandpa up the stairs and down a carpeted hall to the foot of a narrow wooden staircase leading up to a white door. Grandpa continued on up the creaking steps.

"We don't often have guests, especially children," Grandpa said over his shoulder. "I think you'll be most comfortable in the attic."

He opened the door, and they entered after him. Braced for cobwebs and torture devices, Kendra was relieved to find that the attic was a cheerful playroom. Spacious, clean, and bright, the long room had a pair of beds, shelves crowded with children's books, freestanding wardrobes, tidy dressers, a unicorn rocking horse, multiple toy chests, and a hen in a cage.

Seth went straight for the chicken. "Cool!" He poked a finger through the slender bars, trying to touch the orange-gold feathers.

"Careful, Seth," Kendra warned.

"He'll be fine," Grandpa said. "Goldilocks is more a house pet than a barnyard hen. Your grandmother usually takes care of her. I figured you kids wouldn't mind filling in while she's gone. You'll need to feed her, clean her cage, and collect her eggs."

"She lays eggs!" Seth looked astonished and delighted.

"An egg or two a day if you keep her well fed," Grandpa said. He pointed to a white plastic bucket full of kernels near the cage. "A scoop in the morning and another in the evening should take care of her. You'll want to change the lining of her cage every couple days, and make sure she has plenty of water. Every morning, we give her a tiny bowl of milk." Grandpa winked. "That's the secret behind her egg production."

"Can we ever take her out?" The hen had moved close enough for Seth to stroke her feathers with one finger.

"Just put her back afterwards." Grandpa bent down to put a finger in the cage, and Goldilocks instantly pecked at it. Grandpa withdrew his hand. "Never liked me much."

"Some of these toys look expensive," Kendra said, standing beside an ornate Victorian dollhouse.

"Toys are meant to be played with," Grandpa said. "Do your best to keep them in decent shape, and that will be good enough."

Seth moved from the hen cage to a small piano in the corner of the room. He banged on the keys, and the notes that clanged sounded different from what Kendra would have expected. It was a little harpsichord.

"Consider this room your space," Grandpa said. "Within reason, I'll not bother you to pick things up in here, so long as you treat the rest of the house with respect."

"Okay," Kendra said.

"I also have some unfortunate news. We are in the height of tick season. You kids ever hear of Lyme disease?"

Seth shook his head.

"I think so," Kendra said.

"It was originally discovered in the town of Lyme, Connecticut, not too far from here. You catch it from tick bites. The woods are full of ticks this year."

"What does it do?" Seth asked.

Grandpa paused for a solemn moment. "Starts out as a rash. Before long it can lead to arthritis, paralysis, and heart failure. Besides, disease or no, you don't want ticks burrowing into your skin to drink your blood. You try to pull them off and the head detaches. Hard to get out."

"That's disgusting!" Kendra exclaimed.

Grandpa nodded grimly. "They're so small you can hardly see them, at least until they fill up on blood. Then they swell to the size of a grape. Anyhow, point is, you kids are not allowed to enter the woods under any circumstances. Stay on the lawn. Break that rule and your outdoor privileges will be revoked. We understand one another?"

Kendra and Seth nodded.

"You also need to keep out of the barn. Too many ladders and rusty old pieces of farm equipment. Same rules apply to the barn as apply to the woods. Set foot in there, and you will spend the rest of your stay in this room."

"Okay," Seth said, crossing the room to where a little easel stood on a paint-spattered tarp. A blank canvas rested on the easel. Additional blank canvases leaned against the wall nearby, beside shelves stocked with jars of paint. "Can I paint?"

"I'm telling you twice, you have the run of this room," Grandpa said. "Just try not to destroy it. I have many chores to attend to, so I may not be around much. There should be plenty of toys and hobbies here to keep you busy."

"What about a TV?" Seth asked.

"No TV or radio," Grandpa replied. "Rules of the house. If you need anything, Lena will never be far." He indicated a purple cord hanging against the wall near one of the beds. "Tug the cord if you need her. In fact, Lena will be up with your supper in a few minutes."

"Won't we eat together?" Kendra asked.

"Some days. Right now I need to visit the east hayfield. May not be back until late."

"How much land do you own?" asked Seth.

Grandpa smiled. "More than my share. Let's leave it at that. I'll see you kids in the morning." He turned to leave and then paused, reaching into his coat pocket. Turning back, he handed Kendra a tiny key ring holding three miniature keys of varying sizes. "Each of these keys fits something in this room. See if you can figure out what each unlocks."

Grandpa Sorenson walked out of the room, closing the door behind him. Kendra listened as he descended the stairs. She stood at the door, waiting, and then gently tried the handle. It turned slowly. She eased the door open, peered down the empty stairway, and then closed it. At least he had not locked them in.

Seth had opened a toy chest and was examining the contents. The toys were old-fashioned but in excellent condition. Soldiers, dolls, puzzles, stuffed animals, wooden blocks.

Kendra wandered over to a telescope by a window. She peered into the eyepiece, positioned the telescope to look through a windowpane, and began twisting the focus knobs. She could improve the focus but couldn't get it quite right.

She stopped fiddling with the knobs and examined the window. The panes were made of bubbly glass, like those in the front of the house. The images were being distorted before they reached the telescope.

Unfastening a latch, Kendra pushed the window open. She had a good view of the forest east of the house, illuminated by the golden hues of the setting sun. Moving the telescope closer to the window, she spent some time mastering the knobs, bringing the leaves on the trees below into crisp focus.

"Let me see," Seth said. He was standing beside her.

"Pick up those toys first." A mess of toys lay piled near the open chest.

"Grandpa said we can do what we want in here."

"Without making it a disaster. You're already wrecking the place."

"I'm playing. This is a playroom."

"Remember how Mom and Dad said we need to pick up after ourselves?"

"Remember how Mom and Dad aren't here?"

"I'll tell."

"How? Stick a note in a bottle? You won't even remember by the time they get back."

Kendra noticed a calendar on the wall. "I'll write it on the calendar."

"Good. And I'll look through the telescope while you do that."

"This is the one thing in the room I was doing. Why don't you find something else?"

"I didn't notice the telescope. Why don't you share? Don't Mom and Dad also tell us to share?"

"Fine," Kendra said. "It's all yours. But I'm closing the window. Bugs are coming in."

"Whatever."

She shut the window.

Seth looked into the eyepiece and started twisting the focus knobs. Kendra took a closer look at the calendar. It was from 1953. Each month was accompanied by an illustration of a fairyland palace.

She turned the calendar to June. Today was June 11. The days of the week did not match up, but she could still count down to when her parents would return. They would be back June 28.

"This stupid thing won't even focus," Seth complained.

Kendra smiled.

CHAPTER TWO

Collecting Clues

The next morning, Kendra sat at breakfast across from her grandfather. A wooden clock on the wall above him read 8:43. Reflected sunlight flashed in the corner of her eye. Seth was using his butter knife to bounce sun rays. She was not seated close enough to the window to retaliate.

"Nobody likes the sun in their eyes, Seth," Grandpa said.

Seth stopped. "Where's Dale?" he asked.

"Dale and I got up a few hours ago. He's out working. I'm just here to keep you company on your first morning."

Lena set a bowl in front of Seth and another in front of Kendra.

"What's this?" Seth asked.

"Cream of wheat," Lena replied.

"Sticks to your ribs," Grandpa added.

Seth probed the cream of wheat with his spoon. "What's in it? Blood?"

"Berries from the garden and homemade raspberry preserves," Lena said, placing a platter on the table containing toast, butter, a pitcher of milk, a bowl of sugar, and a bowl of jam.

Kendra sampled the cream of wheat. It was delicious. The berries and raspberry preserves sweetened it to perfection.

"This is good!" Seth said. "Just think, Dad is eating snails."

"You kids remember the rules about the woods," Grandpa said.

"And to stay out of the barn," Kendra said.

"Good girl. There's a swimming pool out back that we got ready for you—all the chemicals are balanced and whatnot. There are gardens to explore. You can always play in your room. Just respect the rules and we'll get along fine."

"When is Grandma coming back?" Kendra asked.

Grandpa glanced down at his hands. "That depends on your Aunt Edna. Could be next week. Could be a couple months."

"Good thing Grandma got over her illness," Kendra said.

"Illness?"

"The one that kept her from going to the funeral."

"Right. Yeah, she was still a little under the weather when she left for Missouri."

Grandpa was acting a little peculiar. Kendra wondered if he was uncomfortable around children.

"I'm sad we missed her," Kendra said.

"She's sorry too. Well, I better be off." Grandpa had not eaten anything. He pushed his chair back, stood up, and stepped away from the table, rubbing his palms against his jeans. "If you swim, don't forget to wear sunblock. I'll see you kids later."

"At lunch?" Seth asked.

"Probably not until supper. Lena will help you with anything you need."

He left the room.

✻ ✻ ✻

Dressed in her swimsuit, a towel over one shoulder, Kendra stepped through the door onto the back porch. She carried a handheld mirror she had found in the nightstand by her bed. The handle was mother-of-pearl studded with rhinestones. The day was a bit humid, but the temperature was pleasant.

She walked to the railing of the porch and gazed over the gorgeously manicured backyard. Paths of white stones meandered among flower beds, hedgerows, vegetable gardens, fruit trees, and flowering plants. Tangled grapevines curled along suspended lattices. All the flowers seemed to be in full bloom. Kendra had never seen such brilliant blossoms.

Seth was already swimming. The pool had a black bottom, and it was fringed with rocks to make it seem like a pond. Kendra hurried down the steps and started down a path toward the pool.

The garden teemed with life. Hummingbirds darted among the foliage, wings nearly invisible as they hovered. Huge bumblebees with fuzzy abdomens buzzed from one blossom to another. A stunning variety of butterflies fluttered about on tissue-paper wings.

Kendra passed a small, waterless fountain featuring a statue of a frog. She paused as a large butterfly alighted on the rim of an empty birdbath. It had huge wings—blue, black, and violet. She had never seen a butterfly with such vivid coloring. Of course, she had never visited a world-class garden. The house was not quite a mansion, but the grounds were fit for a king. No wonder Grandpa Sorenson had so many chores.

The path finally deposited Kendra at the pool. Variegated flagstones paved the poolside area. There were a few recliners and a circular table with a big umbrella.

Seth leaped from a stone outcropping into the swimming pool, legs curled up, and hit the water with a big splash. Kendra set her towel and mirror on the table and grabbed a bottle of sunblock. She smeared the white cream over her face, arms, and legs until it disappeared into her skin.

While Seth was swimming underwater, Kendra picked up the mirror. She angled the face so it reflected sunlight onto the water. When Seth surfaced, she made sure the bright splotch of sunlight covered his face.

"Hey!" he shouted, swimming away from her. She kept the glare from the mirror on the back of his head. Gripping the side of the pool, Seth turned to look at her again, throwing up a hand and squinting to ward off the light. He had to look away.

Kendra laughed.

"Cut it out," Seth called.

"You don't like that?"

"Quit it. I won't do it anymore. Grandpa already yelled at me."

Kendra set the mirror on the table. "That mirror is a lot brighter than a butter knife," she said. "I bet it already did permanent damage to your retinas."

"I hope so, then I'll sue you for a billion dollars."

"Good luck. I have about a hundred in the bank. It might be enough for you to buy some eye patches."

He swam toward her angrily, and Kendra walked forward to the edge of the pool. As he started climbing out, she shoved him back in. She was almost a full head taller than Seth and could usually handle him in a fight, although if they ended up wrestling he was pretty squirmy.

Seth changed tactics and started splashing her, making quick scooping motions across the surface of the pool. The water felt cold, and Kendra recoiled at first, then leapt over Seth into the water. After the initial shock, she swiftly grew accustomed to the temperature, stroking over to the shallow end away from her brother.

He chased her, and they ended up in a splash fight. Locking his hands, Seth swung his arms in wide arcs, skimming the top of the water. Kendra pushed at the water with both hands, a churning motion that generated smaller but more focused splashes. Soon they grew tired. It was hard to win a water fight when both participants were already soaked.

"Let's have a race," Kendra suggested as the splashing subsided.

They raced back and forth across the pool. First they raced freestyle, then backstroke, breaststroke, and sidestroke. After that they created handicaps, like racing with no arms or hopping across the width of the shallow end on one foot. Kendra usually won, but Seth was faster at backstroke and some of the handicapped races.

When Kendra grew bored, she got out of the pool. Walking toward the table to retrieve her towel, she stroked her long hair, enjoying the rubbery texture as the wetness made the strands cling together.

Seth climbed on top of a big rock near the deep end. "Watch this can opener!" He jumped with one leg straight and the other bent.

"Good job," Kendra said to placate him when he surfaced. Shifting her gaze to the table, Kendra froze.

Hummingbirds, bumblebees, and butterflies swirled in the air above the handheld mirror. Several other butterflies and a couple of large dragonflies actually rested on the face of the mirror itself.

"Seth, come look at this!" Kendra hissed in a loud whisper.

"What?"

"Just come here."

Seth boosted himself out of the pool and padded over to Kendra, arms folded. He stared at the cloud of life whirling above the mirror. "What's their deal?"

"I don't know," she replied. "Do insects like mirrors?"

"These ones do."

"Look at the red and white butterfly. It's enormous."

"Same with that dragonfly," Seth pointed out.

"I wish I had a camera. I dare you to go get the mirror."

Seth shrugged. "Sure."

He trotted over to the table, grabbed the mirror by the handle, dashed to the pool, and dove in. Some of the insects scattered instantly. The majority drifted in the direction Seth had gone but dispersed before reaching the pool.

Seth surfaced. "Any bees after me?"

"Get the mirror out of the water. You'll ruin it!"

"Settle down, it's fine," he said, stroking over to the side.

"Give it to me." She took the mirror from him and

wiped it dry with her towel. It looked undamaged. "Let's try an experiment."

Kendra placed the mirror face up on a lounge chair and backed away. "Think they'll come back?"

"We'll see."

Kendra and Seth sat down at the table, not far from the lounge chair. After less than a minute, a hummingbird glided over to the mirror and hovered above it. Soon it was joined by a few butterflies. A bumblebee alighted on the face. Before long another swarm of small winged creatures crowded the mirror.

"Go turn the mirror face down," Kendra said. "I want to see whether they like the reflection or the mirror itself."

Seth crept toward the mirror. The little animals took no apparent notice of his approach. He reached forward slowly, flipped the mirror over, and then retreated to the table.

The butterflies and bees that had landed on the mirror took flight when it was overturned, but only a few of the winged creatures flew away. Most of the swarm lingered. A pair of butterflies and a dragonfly landed on the lounge chair at the edge of the mirror. Taking flight, they flipped the mirror over, nearly sliding it off the chair in the process.

With the reflective surface showing again, the swarm pressed close. Several of the creatures landed on the face.

"Did you see that?" Kendra asked.

"That was weird," Seth said.

"How could they be strong enough to lift it?"

"There were a few of them. Want me to flip it again?"

"No, I'm scared the mirror will fall off and break."

"Okay." He draped his towel over his shoulder. "I'm going to go change."

"Would you take the mirror?"

"Fine, but I'm running. I don't want to get stung."

Seth moved toward the mirror slowly, snatched it, and ran off into the garden toward the house. Part of the swarm gave lazy pursuit before scattering.

Kendra wrapped the towel around her waist, picked up the sunblock Seth had left behind, and started toward the house.

When Kendra reached the attic playroom, Seth was dressed in jeans and a long-sleeved camouflage shirt. He picked up the cereal box that served as his emergency survival kit and headed for the door.

"Where are you going?"

"None of your business, unless you want to come."

"How will I know whether I want to come if you don't tell me where you're going?"

Seth gave her a measuring stare. "Promise to keep it a secret?"

"Let me guess. Into the woods."

"Want to come?"

"You'll get Lyme disease," Kendra warned.

"Whatever. Ticks are everywhere. Same with poison

ivy. If people let that stop them, nobody would ever go anywhere."

"But Grandpa Sorenson doesn't want us in the woods," she protested.

"Grandpa isn't going to be around all day. Nobody will know unless you blab."

"Don't do this. Grandpa has been nice to us. We should obey him."

"You're about as brave as a bucket of sand."

"What's so brave about disobeying Grandpa?"

"So you're not coming?"

Kendra hesitated. "No."

"Will you tell on me?"

"If they ask where you are."

"I won't be long."

Seth walked out the door. She heard him tromp down the stairs.

Kendra crossed to the nightstand. The handheld mirror rested on it beside the ring with the three tiny keys. She had spent a long time the night before trying to find what the keys fit. The biggest key opened a jewelry box on the dresser that was full of costume jewelry—fake diamond necklaces, pearl earrings, emerald pendants, sapphire rings, and ruby bracelets. She had not yet discovered what the other two opened.

She picked up the keys. They were all small. The smallest was no longer than a thumbtack. Where could she find such a miniscule keyhole?

The night before, she had spent most of her time on drawers and toy chests. Some of the drawers had keyholes, but they were already unlocked, and the keys did not fit. Same with the toy chests.

The Victorian dollhouse caught her attention. What better place to find tiny keyholes than inside a little house? She unlatched the clasps and opened it, revealing two floors and several rooms full of miniature furniture. Five doll people lived in the house—a father, a mother, a son, a daughter, and a baby.

The detail was extraordinary. The beds had quilts, blankets, sheets, and pillows. The couches had removable cushions. The knobs in the bathtub really turned. Closets had clothes hanging inside.

The armoire in the dollhouse's master bedroom made Kendra suspicious. It had a disproportionately large keyhole in the center. Kendra inserted the tiniest key and turned it. The doors of the armoire sprung open.

Inside was something wrapped in gold foil—opening it, she saw it was a piece of chocolate shaped like a rosebud. Behind the chocolate she found a small golden key. She added it to the key ring. The golden key was larger than the key that opened the armoire, but smaller than the key that opened the jewelry box.

Kendra took a bite of the chocolate rosebud. It was soft and melted in her mouth. It was the richest, creamiest chocolate she had ever tasted. She finished it in three more bites, savoring each mouthful.

Kendra continued scouring the tiny house, investigating every piece of furniture, searching every closet, checking behind every miniature painting on the walls. Finding no more keyholes, she closed the dollhouse and fastened the clasps.

Scanning the room, Kendra tried to decide where to look next. One key left, maybe two if the golden key also opened something. She had been through most of the items in the toy chests, but she could always double-check. She had searched through the drawers in the nightstands, dressers, and wardrobes thoroughly, as well as the knick-knacks on the bookshelves. There could be keyholes in unlikely places, like under the clothes of a doll or behind a bedpost.

Kendra ended up beside the telescope. Improbable as it seemed, she checked it for keyholes. Nothing.

Maybe she could use the telescope to locate Seth. Opening the window, she noticed Dale walking along the lawn at the outskirts of the woods. He was carrying something in both hands, but his back was to her, impeding a view of what he held. He stooped and set it down behind a low hedge, which continued to prevent her from seeing the object. Dale walked off at a brisk pace, glancing around as if to ensure nobody was spying, and soon passed out of view.

Curious, Kendra rushed downstairs and out the back

door. Dale was nowhere in sight. She trotted across the lawn to the low hedge beneath the attic window. Grass continued for about six feet beyond the hedge before stopping abruptly at the perimeter of the forest. On the grass behind the hedge rested a large pie tin full of milk.

An iridescent hummingbird hung suspended over the pie tin, wings a faint blur. Several butterflies flitted around the hummingbird. Occasionally one would descend and splash in the milk. The hummingbird flew away, and a dragonfly approached. It was a smaller crowd than the mirror had attracted, but there was much more activity than Kendra would have expected around a small pool of milk.

She watched as a variety of tiny winged animals came and went, feeding from the pie tin. Did butterflies drink milk? Did dragonflies? Apparently so. It was not long before the level of milk in the pie tin had markedly fallen.

Kendra looked up at the attic. It had only two windows, both facing the same side of the house. She visualized the room behind those gabled windows and suddenly realized that the playroom consumed only half the space the attic should fill.

Abandoning the tin of milk, she walked around to the opposite side of the house. On the far side was a second pair of attic windows. She was right. There was another half to the attic. But she knew of no other stairway granting access to the uppermost story. Which meant there might be some sort of secret passage in the playroom! Maybe the final key unlocked it!

Just as she decided to return to the attic and search for a hidden door, Kendra noticed Dale coming from the direction of the barn with another pie tin. She hurried toward him. When he saw her coming, he looked temporarily uncomfortable, then put on a big smile.

"What are you doing?" Kendra asked.

"Just taking some milk to the house," he replied, changing direction a bit. He had been heading toward the woods.

"Really? Why'd you leave that other milk behind the hedge?"

"Other milk?" He could not have looked more guilty.

"Yeah. The butterflies were drinking it."

Dale was no longer walking. He regarded Kendra shrewdly. "Can you keep a secret?"

"Sure."

Dale looked around as if someone might be watching. "We have a few milking cows. They make plenty of milk, so I put out some of the excess for the insects. Keeps the garden lively."

"Why's that a secret?"

"I'm not sure your grandfather would approve. Never asked permission. He might consider it wasteful."

"Seems like a good idea to me. I noticed all the different kinds of butterflies in your garden. More than I've ever seen. Plus all the hummingbirds."

He nodded. "I like it. Adds to the atmosphere."

"So you weren't taking that milk to the house."

"No, no. This milk hasn't been pasteurized. Full of bacteria. You could catch all sorts of diseases. Not fit for people. Insects, on the other hand, they seem to like it best this way. You won't spoil my secret?"

"I'll keep quiet."

"Good girl," he said with a conspiratorial wink.

"Where are you putting that one?"

"Over there." He jerked his head toward the woods. "I set a few on the border of the yard every day."

"Does it spoil?"

"I don't leave it out long enough. Some days the insects consume all the milk before I collect the pans. Thirsty critters."

"See you later, Dale."

"You seen your brother hereabout?"

"I think he's in the house."

"That so?"

She shrugged. "Maybe."

Kendra turned and started toward the house. She glanced back as she mounted the stairs to the rear porch. Dale was placing the milk behind a small, round bush.

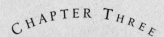

CHAPTER THREE

The Ivy Shack

Seth pressed through dense undergrowth until he reached a faint, crooked path, the kind made by animals. Nearby stood a squat, gnarled tree with thorny leaves and black bark. Seth examined his sleeves for ticks, scrutinizing the camouflage pattern. So far he had not seen a single tick. Of course, it would probably be the ticks he failed to see that would get him. He hoped the insect repellent he had sprayed on was helping.

Stooping, he collected rocks and built a small pyramid to mark the point where he had intersected the path. Finding his way back would probably be no problem, but better safe than sorry. If he took too long, Grandpa might figure out he had disobeyed orders.

Rummaging in his cereal box, Seth withdrew a

compass. The animal track ran northeast. He had set off on an easterly course, but the undergrowth had grown denser as he progressed. A faint trail was a good excuse to veer slightly off course. It would be much easier going than trying to hack his way through shrubbery with a pocketknife. He wished he owned a machete.

Seth followed the trail. The tall trees stood fairly close together, diffusing the sunlight into a greenish glow laced with shadows. Seth imagined that the forest would be black as a cave after nightfall.

Something rustled in the bushes. He paused, removing a small pair of plastic binoculars from his cereal box. Scanning the area, he spotted nothing of interest.

He proceeded along the trail until an animal emerged from the undergrowth onto the path not twenty feet ahead. It was a round, bristly creature no taller than his knees. A porcupine. The animal started down the path in his direction with complete confidence. Seth froze. The porcupine was close enough that he could discern the individual quills, slender and sharp.

As the animal trundled toward him, Seth backed away. Weren't animals supposed to flee from humans? Maybe it had rabies. Or maybe it just hadn't seen him. After all, he was wearing a camouflage shirt.

Seth spread his arms wide, stomped a foot, and growled. The porcupine looked up, twitched its nose, and then turned from the path. Seth listened as it pushed through foliage away from the trail.

He took a deep breath. He had been really scared for a minute there. He could almost feel the quills pricking through his jeans into his leg. It would be pretty hard to conceal his excursion into the woods if he came home looking like a pincushion.

Though he dreaded admitting it, he wished Kendra had come. The porcupine probably would have made her scream, and her fear would have increased his bravery. He could have made fun of her instead of feeling frightened himself. He had never seen a porcupine in the wild before. He was surprised how exposed he felt staring at all those pointy quills. What if he stepped on one in the undergrowth?

He looked around. He had come a long way. Of course, finding his way back would be no trick. He just needed to backtrack along the trail and then head west. But if he turned for home now, he might never make it back this way again.

Seth continued along the trail. Some of the trees had moss and lichen growing on them. A few had ivy twisting around their bases. The path forked. Checking his compass, Seth saw that one path went northwest, the other due east. Staying with his theme, Seth turned east.

There began to be more space between the trees, and the shrubs grew closer to the ground. Soon he could see much farther in all directions, and the forest became a little brighter. To one side of the path, at the limit of his sight, he noticed something abnormal. It looked like a large square of ivy hidden among the trees. The whole point of exploring the woods was to find strange things, so he left the path and walked toward the ivy square.

The dense undergrowth came up to his shins, grasping at his ankles with every step. As he tromped toward the square, he realized it was a structure completely overgrown with ivy. It appeared to be a big shed.

He stopped and looked more closely. The ivy was thick enough that he could not tell what the shed was made of—he could see only leafy vines. He walked around the structure. On the far side a door stood open. Seth almost cried out when he peered inside.

The shed was actually a shack constructed around a large tree stump. Beside the stump, dressed in crude rags, sat a wiry old woman gnawing at a knot in a bristly rope. Shriveled with age, she clutched the rope in bony hands with knobby knuckles. Her long, white hair was matted and had a sickly yellowish tint. One of her filmy eyes was terribly bloodshot. She was missing teeth, and there was blood on the knot she was chewing, apparently from her gums. Her pale arms, bare almost to the shoulder, were thin and wrinkled, with faint blue veins and a few purple scabs.

When the woman saw Seth, she dropped the rope immediately, wiping pink saliva from the corners of her meager lips. Supporting herself against the stump, she stood up. He noticed her long feet, the color of ivory, peppered with insect bites. Her gray toenails looked thick with fungus.

"Hail, young master, what brings you to my home?" Her voice was incongruently melodious and smooth.

For a moment, Seth could only stare. Even as bent and crooked as she was, the woman was tall. She smelled bad. "You live out here?" he finally said.

"I do. Care to come inside?"

"Probably not. I'm just out for a walk."

The woman narrowed her eyes. "Strange place for a boy to walk alone."

"I like exploring. My grandpa owns this land."

"Owns it, you say?"

"Does he know you're here?" asked Seth.

"Depends who he is."

"Stan Sorenson."

She grinned. "He knows."

The rope she had chewed lay on the dirt floor. It had one other knot besides the one she had been gnawing.

"Why were you biting the rope?" Seth asked.

She eyed him suspiciously. "I don't care for knots."

"Are you a hermit?"

"You could say that. Come inside and I will brew some tea."

"I better not."

She looked down at her hands. "I must look frightful. Let me show you something." She turned and crouched behind the stump. A rat ventured a few steps out of a hole in a corner of the shack. When she came back from behind the stump, the rat hid.

The old woman sat with her back to the stump. She held a little wooden puppet about nine inches high. It looked primitive, made entirely of dark wood, with no clothes or painted features. Just a basic human figure with tiny gold hooks serving as joints. The puppet had a stick in its back. The woman set a paddle on her lap. She began making the puppet dance by bobbing the stick and tapping the paddle. There was a musical regularity to the rhythm.

"What is that thing?" Seth asked.

"A limberjack," she replied.

"Where's his ax?"

"Not a *lumberjack*, a *limberjack*. A clog doll. A jigger. Dancing Dan. Shuffling Sam. I call him Mendigo. He keeps me company. Come inside and I'll let you give it a try."

"I better not," he said again. "I don't see how you could live out here like this and not be crazy."

"Sometimes good people grow weary of society." She sounded a little annoyed. "You happened upon me by accident? Out exploring?"

"Actually, I'm selling candy bars for my soccer team. It's a good cause."

She stared at him.

"I have my best luck in the rich neighborhoods."

She kept staring.

"That was a joke. I'm kidding."

Her voice became stern. "You are an impudent young man."

"And you live with a tree stump."

She gave him a measuring glare. "Very well, my arrogant young adventurer. Why not test your courage? Every explorer deserves a chance to prove his mettle." The old woman withdrew into the shack and crouched behind the stump again. She returned to the doorway holding a crude, narrow box made of splintered wood, wire, and long, jutting nails.

"What's that?"

"Place your hand inside the box to prove your valor and earn a reward."

"I'd rather play with the creepy puppet."

"Just reach inside and touch the back of the box." She shook it, and it rattled a bit. The box was long enough that he would have to reach in to his elbow in order to touch the back.

"Are you a witch?"

"A man with a brave tongue should support his words with courageous actions."

"This seems like something a witch would do."

"Stand by your loose words, young man, or you may not have a pleasant journey home."

Seth backed away, watching her closely. "I better get going. Have fun eating your rope."

She clucked her tongue. "Such insolence." Her voice remained soothing and calm, but now held a menacing undertone. "Why not step inside and have some tea?"

"Next time." Seth moved around the shack, not taking

his eyes from the ragged woman in the doorway. She made no move to pursue him. Before he moved out of her sight, the woman raised an arthritic hand with the middle fingers crossed and the others bent awkwardly. Eyes half-shut, she appeared to be murmuring something. Then she was out of view.

On the far side of the shack, Seth plunged through the tangled undergrowth back to the path, glancing over his shoulder all the way. The woman was not chasing him. Just looking back at the ivy-covered shack made him shiver. The old hag looked so wretched and smelled so foul. There was no way he was sticking his hand in her weird box. After she had offered the challenge, all he could think about was learning in school how shark teeth angled inward so fish could swim in but not out. He imagined the homemade box was probably full of nails or broken glass set at cruel angles for a similar purpose.

Even though the woman was not following him, Seth felt unsafe. Compass in hand, he hurried along the path toward home. Without warning, something struck him on the ear, barely hard enough to sting. A pebble the size of a thimble dropped to the path at his feet.

Seth whirled. Somebody had thrown the little stone at him, but he saw nobody. Could the old woman be stealthily following him? She probably knew the woods really well.

Another small object bounced off the back of his neck. It was not as hard or heavy as a stone. Turning, he saw another acorn whistling toward him, and he ducked. The acorns and the pebble had come at him from opposite sides of the path. What was going on?

From above came the sound of wood splitting, and a huge limb fell across the path behind him, a few leaves and twigs swishing against him as it passed. If Seth had been standing two or three yards back along the path, a branch thicker than his leg would have clubbed him on the head.

One look at the heavy limb, and Seth took off down the path at a full sprint. He seemed to hear rustling sounds coming from the shrubbery on either side of the scant trail, but did not slow down to investigate.

Something caught a firm hold on his ankle, sending him tumbling to the ground. Sprawled on his belly, a cut on one hand, dirt in his mouth, he heard something rustling through the foliage behind him, and a strange sound that was either laughter or running water. A dry branch snapped like a gunshot. Not looking back for fear of what he might see, Seth scrambled to his feet and dashed along the path.

Whatever had tripped him had not been a root or a stone. It had felt like a strong cord stretched across the trail. A tripwire. He had noticed no such trap previously on the path. But there was no way the old woman could have done it, even if she had started running the moment he passed out of her view.

Seth raced past the place where the trail forked and sprinted back the way he had come. He scanned the trail ahead for wires or other traps. His breathing became labored, but he did not slow down. The air felt hotter and more humid than it had all day. Sweat began to dampen his forehead and drip down the sides of his face.

Seth remained alert for the little pyramid of rocks that would mark where he should leave the path. When he reached a gnarled little tree with black bark and thorny leaves, he halted. He remembered the tree. He had noticed it when he intersected the path. Using the tree as a reference, he found the spot where he had built the pyramid of rocks, but the rocks were gone.

Leaves crunched behind him off to one side of the trail. Seth glanced at his compass to confirm that he was heading west and ran into the woods. He had walked this way at a leisurely pace, examining toadstools and unusual rocks as he went. Now he tore through the forest at full speed, undergrowth clawing at his legs, branches whipping against his face and chest.

Finally, panting, the energy of his panic wearing thin, he glimpsed the house up ahead through the trees. The sounds of pursuit had dwindled to nothing. As he stepped out into the yard under the sun, Seth wondered how much of what he had heard had actually been something chasing him, and how much had been invented by his flustered imagination.

※ ※ ※

The wall opposite the windows in the playroom held several rows of bookshelves. The door to the stairs was built into that wall. And one of the bulky, freestanding wardrobes was backed up against it.

Kendra held a blue book with golden letters. The title was *Journal of Secrets*. The book was held shut by three sturdy clasps, each with a keyhole. The remaining key Grandpa Sorenson had given her fit none of the keyholes, but the gold key she had found in the dollhouse armoire fit the bottom one. So one of the clasps was unlocked.

She had found the book while searching the bookshelves for a trigger to a secret passage. Using a stool, Kendra had reached even the higher shelves, but so far the search had been in vain. There was no sign of a secret door. When she noticed a locked book with an intriguing title, she had quit the search in order to test her keys.

With the bottom clasp unlocked, Kendra tried to pry up the corner of the book and get a peek. But the cover was solid and the binding firm. She needed to find the other keys.

She heard somebody stampeding up the stairs and knew it could be only one person. Hurriedly she shelved the book and pocketed the keys. She did not want her nosy brother interfering with her puzzle.

Seth charged through the door and slammed it behind him. He was flushed and breathing hard. Dirt smeared the knees of his jeans. His face was smudged with sweat and grime. "You should have come," he sighed, flopping onto his bed.

"You're getting the bedspread filthy."

"It was freaky," he said. "It was so cool."

"What happened?"

"I found this path in the woods and met this weird old lady who lived in a shack. I think she's a witch. A real one."

"Whatever."

He rolled over and looked at her. "I'm serious. You should have seen her. She was a mess."

"So are you."

"No, like all scabby and gross. She was biting an old rope. She tried to make me stick my hand in some box."

"Did you?"

"No way. I took off. But she chased me or something. She threw rocks at me and knocked down this big branch. It could have killed me!"

"You must be pretty bored."

"I'm not lying!"

"I'll ask Grandpa Sorenson if he has homeless people living in his woods," Kendra said.

"No! He'll know I broke the rules."

"Don't you think he would want to know a witch built a shack on his property?"

"She acted like she knew him. I went pretty far. Maybe I was off his property."

"I doubt it. I think he owns everything for a long ways."

Seth leaned back, lacing his fingers behind his head. "You should come visit her with me. I could find my way back."

"Are you nuts? You said she tried to kill you."

"We should spy on her. Find out what she's up to."

"If there really is a weird old lady living in the woods, you should tell Grandpa so he can call the police."

Seth sat up. "Okay. Never mind. I made it up. Feel better?"

Kendra narrowed her eyes.

"I found something else cool," Seth said. "Have you seen the tree house?"

"No."

"Want me to show you?"

"Is it in the yard?"

"Yes, on the edge."

"Okay."

Kendra followed Seth outside and across the lawn. Sure enough, in the corner of the yard opposite the barn, there was a light blue playhouse up in a thick tree. It was situated on the back side of the tree, making it hard to see from most of the yard. The paint was peeling a little, but the little house had shingles on the roof and curtains in the window. Boards had been nailed into the tree to form a ladder.

Seth went up first. The rungs led up to a trapdoor, which he pushed open. Kendra climbed up after him.

Inside, the tree house felt bigger than it looked from the ground. There was a little table with four chairs. The pieces to a jigsaw puzzle were spread out on the table. Only a couple had been fit together.

"See, not bad," Seth said. "I started that puzzle."

"It's beautiful. You must be gifted."

"I didn't work on it long."

"Did you even find the corners?"

"No."

"That's the first thing you do." She sat down and started looking for corner pieces. Seth took a seat and helped. "You never like puzzles," Kendra said.

"It's more fun doing them in a tree house."

"If you say so."

Seth found a corner piece and set it aside. "Think Grandpa would let me move in here?"

"You're a weirdo."

"I'd only need a sleeping bag," he said.

"You'd get freaked out once it was late."

"No way."

"The witch might come get you."

Instead of responding, he started looking more intently for the other corner pieces. Kendra could tell the comment had gotten to him. She decided not to tease him any further. The fact that he seemed scared of the lady he had met in the woods legitimized his story a lot. Seth had never scared easily. This was the kid who had jumped off the roof under the misguided assumption that a garbage bag would work like a parachute. The kid who had put the head of a live snake in his mouth on a dare.

They found the corners and finished most of the perimeter of the puzzle by the time they heard Lena calling them for dinner.

CHAPTER FOUR

The Hidden Pond

Rain pattered endlessly against the roof. Kendra had never heard such a noisy downpour. Then again, she had never been in an attic during a rainstorm. There was something relaxing about the steady drumming, so constant that it almost became inaudible without ever decreasing in volume.

Standing at the window beside the telescope, she watched the deluge. The rain fell straight and hard. There was no wind, just layer upon layer of streaking droplets, blurring into a gray haze in the distance. The gutter below her was about to overflow.

Seth sat on a stool in the corner, painting. Lena had been creating paint-by-numbers canvases for him, sketching them with expert speed, customizing each image to his specifications. The current project was a dragon battling a knight on horseback amid a fuming wasteland. Lena had outlined the images in considerable detail, including subtleties of light and shade, so that the finished products looked quite accomplished. She had taught Seth how to mix paint and given him samples of which hue corresponded to each number. For the current painting, she had incorporated more than ninety different shades.

Kendra had rarely seen Seth demonstrate as much diligence as he did on the paintings. After a few brief lessons on how to apply the paint, including the purposes of different brushes and tools, he had already finished a large canvas of pirates sacking a town and a smaller one of a snake charmer diving away from a striking cobra. Two impressive paintings in three days. He was an addict! And he was almost done with his latest project.

Crossing to the bookshelf, Kendra ran a hand along the spines of the volumes. She had searched the room thoroughly and had yet to find the last keyhole, let alone a secret passage to the other side of the attic. Seth could be a pest, but now that he had become immersed in his painting, she was starting to miss him.

Maybe Lena would outline a painting for her. Kendra had turned down her initial offer, since it sounded childish, like coloring. But the finished products looked much less juvenile than Kendra had anticipated.

Kendra opened the door and descended the stairs. The

house was dim and quiet, the rainfall more distant as she left the attic behind. She walked along the hall and down the stairs to the main floor.

The house seemed too quiet. All the lights were out despite the gloom.

"Lena?"

There was no answer.

Kendra went through the living room, the dining room, and into the kitchen. No sign of the housekeeper. Had she left?

Opening the door to the basement, Kendra peered down the steps into the darkness. The stairs were made of stone, as if leading to a dungeon. "Lena?" she called uncertainly. Surely the woman wasn't down there without any light.

Kendra went back down the hall and slid open the door to the study. Having not yet entered this particular room, she first noticed the huge desk cluttered with books and papers. The massive head of a hairy boar with jutting tusks hung mounted on the wall. A collection of grotesque wooden masks rested on a shelf. Golfing trophies lined another. Plaques decorated the wood-paneled walls, along with a framed display of military medals and ribbons. There was a black-and-white picture of a much younger Grandpa Sorenson showing off an enormous marlin. On the desk, inside a crystal sphere with a flat bottom, was an eerie replica of a human skull no bigger than her thumb. Kendra slid the study door closed.

She tried the garage, the parlor, and the family room. Maybe Lena had run to the store.

Kendra walked out to the back porch, shielded from the rain by the overhang. She loved the fresh, damp scent of rainfall. It continued to come down hard, puddling around the garden. Where did the butterflies hide from such a downpour?

Then she saw Lena. The housekeeper knelt in the mud beside a bush blossoming with large blue and white roses, absolutely soaked, apparently weeding. Her white hair was plastered to her head, and her housecoat was drenched.

"Lena?"

The housekeeper looked up, smiled, and waved.

Kendra retrieved an umbrella from the hall closet and joined Lena in the garden. "You're sopping," Kendra said.

Lena rooted out a weed. "It's a warm rain. I like being out in the weather." She stuffed the weed into a bulging garbage bag.

"You're going to catch a cold."

"I don't often take ill." She paused to stare up at the clouds. "It won't last much longer."

Kendra tilted her umbrella back and gazed heavenward. Leaden skies in all directions. "You think?"

"Wait and see. The rain will pass within the hour."

"Your knees are all muddy."

"You think I've lost my marbles." The diminutive woman stood up and spread her arms wide, tilting her head back. "Do you ever look up at the rain, Kendra? It feels like the sky is falling."

Kendra tilted the umbrella back again. Millions of raindrops rushed toward her, some pelting her face and making her blink. "Or like you're soaring up to the clouds," she said.

"I suppose I should get you inside before my unusual habits rub off."

"No, I didn't mean to disturb you." Back under the protection of the umbrella, Kendra wiped droplets from her forehead. "I guess you don't want the umbrella."

"That would defeat the purpose. I'll be in shortly."

Kendra returned to the house. She stole glances at Lena through a window. It was just so peculiar, she couldn't resist spying. Sometimes Lena was working. Sometimes she was smelling a blossom or stroking its petals. And the rain kept falling.

❧ ❧ ❧

Kendra was sitting on her bed, reading poems by Shel Silverstein, when the room suddenly brightened. The sun was out.

Lena had been right about the rain. It had relented about forty minutes after her prediction. The housekeeper had come inside, changed out of her wet clothes, and made sandwiches.

Across the room, the painting of the knight charging the dragon was complete. Seth had gone outside an hour ago. Kendra was in a lazy mood.

Just as Kendra returned her attention to the latest poem, Seth burst into the room, breathing hard. He wore only socks on his feet. His clothes were streaked with mud. "You *have* to come see what I found in the woods."

"Another witch?"

"No. Way cooler."

"A hobo camp?"

"I'm not going to say; you have to come see."

"Does it involve hermits or lunatics?"

"No people," he said.

"How far from the yard?"

"Not far."

"We could get in trouble. Besides, it's muddy out."

"Grandpa is hiding a beautiful park in the woods," Seth blurted.

"What?" asked Kendra.

"You have to come see it. Put on galoshes or something."

Kendra closed the book.

※　※　※

The sunlight came and went, depending on the shifting clouds. A soft breeze ruffled the foliage. The woods smelled mulchy. Scrambling over a damp, rotting log, Kendra shrieked when she saw a glistening white frog.

Seth turned around. "Awesome."

"Try *disgusting*."

"I've never seen a white frog," said Seth. He tried

to grab it, but the frog took an enormous leap as he approached. "Whoa! That thing flew!"

He checked the underbrush where the frog had landed, but found nothing.

"Hurry up," Kendra said, glancing back the way they had come. The house was no longer in sight. She could not shake the sick, nervous feeling in her stomach.

Unlike her little brother, Kendra was not a natural rule breaker. She was in all the accelerated classes at school, got almost perfect grades, kept her room tidy, and always practiced for her piano lessons. Seth, on the other hand, settled for lousy grades, routinely skipped his homework, and earned frequent detentions. Of course, he was also the one with all the friends, so maybe there was a method to his madness.

"What's the rush?" He took the lead again, blazing a trail through the undergrowth.

"The longer we're gone, the more likely somebody will notice we're missing."

"It isn't much farther. See that hedge?"

It was not exactly a hedge. More like a tall barrier of unkempt bushes. "You call that a hedge?"

"The park is on the far side."

The wall of bushes extended as far as Kendra could see in either direction. "How do we get around it?"

"*Through* it. You'll see."

They reached the bushes and Seth turned left, studying the leafy barricade as he went, occasionally squatting and checking closer. The interlocked bushes ranged from ten to twelve feet tall, and they looked really thick.

"Okay, I think this is where I squirmed through." There was a deep indentation at the base of where two bushes overlapped. Seth dropped to all fours and forced his way in.

"You're going to have a billion ticks," Kendra predicted.

"They're all hiding from the rain," he replied with perfect confidence.

Kendra got down and followed him.

"I don't think this is the same way I got through last time," Seth admitted. "It's a little more cramped. But it should work." He was now slithering on his belly.

"This better be good." Kendra squirmed on her elbows, eyes squinted. The damp ground felt cold, and droplets fell from the bush as she jostled it. Seth reached the far side and stood up. She crawled through as well, her eyes widening as she got to her feet.

Before her lay a pristine pond, a couple of hundred yards across, with a small, verdant island at the center. A series of elaborate gazebos surrounded the pond, interconnected by a whitewashed boardwalk. Flowering vines wound along the latticework of the impressive promenade. Elegant swans glided on the water. Butterflies and hummingbirds wove and darted among the blossoms. On the far side of the pond, peacocks strutted and preened.

"What in the world?" Kendra gasped.

"Come on." Seth started across the lush, neatly mown lawn toward the nearest gazebo. Kendra looked back, understanding why Seth had called the disheveled barrier of bushes a hedge. On this side, the bushes were neatly trimmed. The hedgerow encompassed the entire area, with a single arched entryway off to one side.

"Why didn't we come through the entryway?" Kendra asked, trotting after her brother.

"Shortcut." Seth paused at the white steps leading up to the gazebo to pluck a piece of fruit from an espalier. "Try one."

"You should wash it," Kendra said.

"It just rained." He took a bite. "It's so good."

Kendra tried one. It was the sweetest nectarine she had ever tasted. "Delicious."

Together they mounted the steps of the extravagant pavilion. The wood railing was perfectly smooth. Although unshielded from the elements, all the woodwork appeared to be in flawless condition: no peeling paint, no cracks, no splinters.

The gazebo was furnished with white wicker love seats and chairs. In some places the ubiquitous vines had been woven into living wreaths and other fanciful patterns. A bright parrot sat on a high perch staring down at them.

"Look at the parrot!" Kendra exclaimed.

"Last time I saw some monkeys," Seth said. "Little guys with long arms. They were swinging all over the place. And there was a goat. It ran away as soon as it saw me."

Seth took off, clomping down one of the boardwalks. Kendra followed more slowly, absorbing the scene. It looked like the setting of a fairy-tale wedding. She counted twelve pavilions, each unique. One had a small white quay projecting into the pond. The little pier was connected to a floating shed that had to be a boathouse.

Kendra strolled after Seth, whose ruckus was sending the swans drifting toward the far side of the lake, leaving V-shaped ripples in their wake. The sun broke through the clouds and gleamed upon the water.

Why would Grandpa Sorenson keep a place like this a secret? It was magnificent! Why go through all the trouble of maintaining it if not to enjoy it? Hundreds of people could gather here with room to spare.

Kendra went to the gazebo with the pier and found that the boathouse was locked. It was not large; she guessed it held a few canoes or rowboats. Maybe Grandpa Sorenson would give them permission to paddle around the pond. No, she could not even tell him she knew about this place! Was that why he had told them about the ticks and made rules against venturing into the woods? To keep his little Eden hidden? Could he be so selfish and secretive?

Kendra finished a complete lap around the pond, walking on clean wooden planks the entire way. Across the pond Seth yelled, and a small flock of cockatoos took flight. The sun retreated behind clouds. They needed to get back. Kendra told herself she could return later.

※※※

Kendra was concerned when she cut into her steak. The middle was pink, almost red at the center. Grandpa Sorenson and Dale were already taking bites.

"Is my steak cooked?" Kendra ventured.

"'Course it's cooked," Dale said around a mouthful.

"It's pretty red in the middle."

"Only way to eat a steak," Grandpa said, dabbing his mouth with a linen napkin. "Medium rare. Keeps it juicy and tender. If you cook it all the way through, you might as well eat shoe leather."

Kendra glanced at Lena.

"Go ahead, dear," the woman urged. "You won't get sick; I cooked it plenty."

"I like it," Seth said, chewing on a bite. "We have any ketchup?"

"Why would you go and ruin a perfectly good steak with ketchup?" Dale moaned.

"You put it on your eggs," Lena reminded him, placing a bottle in front of Seth.

"That's different. Ketchup and onions on eggs is a necessity."

"That's sickening," Seth said, upending the bottle over his steak.

Kendra took a bite of the garlic potatoes. They were tasty. Mustering her courage, she sampled the steak. Bursting with flavorful seasoning, it was much easier to chew than other steak she had eaten. "The steak is wonderful," she said.

"Thank you, dear," said Lena.

They ate in silence for a few moments. Grandpa dabbed his mouth with his napkin again and cleared his throat.

"What do you suppose makes people so eager to break rules?"

Kendra felt a jolt of guilt. The question was addressed generally and hung there awaiting a response. When nobody answered, Grandpa continued.

"Is it simply the pleasure of disobedience? The thrill of rebellion?"

Kendra glanced at Seth. He stared at his plate, picking at his potatoes.

"Were the rules unfair, Kendra? Was I being unreasonable?"

"No."

"Did I leave you with nothing to do, Seth? No pool? No tree house? No toys or hobbies?"

"We had things to do."

"Then why did you two go into the woods? I warned you there would be consequences."

"Why are you hiding weird old ladies out in the forest?" Seth blurted.

"Weird old ladies?" Grandpa asked.

"Yeah, what about that?"

Grandpa nodded thoughtfully. "She has a rotten old rope. You didn't blow on it?"

"I didn't go near her. She was freaky."

"She came to me and asked if she could build a shack

on my property. She promised to keep to herself. I saw no harm in it. You shouldn't go bothering her."

"Seth found your private retreat," Kendra said. "He wanted me to see it. My curiosity got the better of me."

"Private retreat?"

"Big pond? Fancy boardwalk? Parrots and swans and peacocks?"

Grandpa looked at Dale, speechless. Dale shrugged.

"I was hoping you'd take us out on a boat," Kendra said.

"Who said anything about a boat?"

Kendra rolled her eyes. "I saw the boathouse, Grandpa."

He tossed his hands up and shook his head.

Kendra set her fork down. "Why would you let such a nice place go to waste?"

"That is my business," Grandpa said. "Yours was to obey my rules, for your own protection."

"We're not afraid of ticks," Seth said.

Grandpa folded his hands and lowered his eyes. "I was not entirely honest about why you needed to stay out of the woods." He lifted his gaze. "On my land, I provide refuge for some dangerous animals, many of them endangered. This includes poisonous snakes, toads, spiders, and scorpions, along with bigger game. Wolves, apes, panthers. I use chemicals and other controls to keep them away from the yard, but the woods are extremely hazardous. Particularly the island in the center of the lake. It is deliberately infested with inland taipans, also called 'fierce snakes,' the deadliest serpent known to man."

"Why didn't you warn us?" Kendra asked.

"My preserve is a secret. I have all the necessary licenses, but if my neighbors complained, those could be revoked. You must not tell a soul, not even your parents."

"We saw a white frog," Seth said breathlessly. "Was that poisonous?"

Grandpa nodded. "Quite lethal. In Central America the indigenous people use them to fashion poisoned darts."

"Seth tried to catch it."

"Had he succeeded," Grandpa said gravely, "he would be dead."

Seth swallowed. "I'll never go into the woods again."

"I trust you won't," Grandpa said. "All the same, a rule is of no value unless the punishment is enforced. You will have to stay in your room for the rest of your stay."

"What?" Seth said. "But you lied to us! Being afraid of ticks is a lame reason to stay out of the woods! I just thought you were treating us like babies."

"You should have brought those concerns to me," Grandpa said. "Was I unclear about the rules or the consequences?"

"You were unclear about the reasons," Seth said.

"That is my right. I am your grandfather. And this is my property."

"I am your grandson. You should tell me the truth. You're not setting a very good example."

Kendra tried not to laugh. Seth was in lawyer mode. He always tried to maneuver out of trouble with their parents. Sometimes he made some pretty good points.

"What do you think, Kendra?" Grandpa asked.

She had not expected him to solicit her opinion. She tried to collect her thoughts. "Well, I agree that you didn't tell us the whole truth. No way would I have gone into the woods if I knew there would be dangerous animals."

"Me neither," Seth said.

"I made two simple rules, you understood them, and you broke them. Just because I chose not to share all my reasons for making the rules, you think you should escape punishment?"

"Yes," Seth said. "Just this once."

"That doesn't sound fair to me," Grandpa said. "Unless the punishments are enforced, rules lose all their power."

"But we won't do it again," Seth said. "We promise. Don't lock us up in the house for two weeks!"

"Don't blame me," Grandpa said. "You locked yourself up by disregarding the rules. Kendra, what do you think would be fair?"

"Maybe you could give us a reduced punishment as a warning. Then the full punishment if we mess up again."

"Reduced punishment," Grandpa mused. "So you still pay a price for your disobedience, but you get one more chance. I might be able to live with that. Seth?"

"Better than the whole punishment."

"That settles it. I will reduce your sentence to a single

day. You will spend tomorrow confined to the attic. You can come down for meals, and you can use the bathroom, but that is all. Break any of my rules again, and you will not leave the attic until your parents come for you. For your own safety. Understood?"

"Yes, sir," Kendra said.

Seth nodded his agreement.

CHAPTER FIVE

Journal of Secrets

"Did you ever notice the keyhole on the belly of the unicorn?" Seth asked. He was lying on the floor beside the fanciful rocking horse, hands laced behind his head.

Kendra looked up from her painting. She had asked Lena to create a paint-by-numbers to help her endure her incarceration. Kendra had wanted to paint the pavilions around the pond, and Lena had quickly sketched a scene with startling accuracy, as if the housekeeper had the place memorized. Seth declined to have another canvas prepped. Stuck in the attic or not, he was sick of painting.

"Keyhole?"

"Weren't you looking for keyholes?"

Kendra got off her stool and crouched beside her

brother. Sure enough, there was a tiny keyhole on the underside of the unicorn. She retrieved her keys from the nightstand drawer. The third key Grandpa Sorenson had given her did the trick. A small hatch swung open. Out fell several rose-shaped chocolates wrapped in gold foil, identical to the one she had found in the miniature armoire.

"What are those?" Seth asked.

"Soap," Kendra said.

Kendra reached up into the hatch and felt around inside the hollow rocking horse. She found a few more rosebud chocolates and a tiny golden key like the one from the armoire. The second key to the locked journal!

"They look like candy," Seth said, snatching one of the ten chocolates.

"Have one. They're perfumed. You'll smell pretty."

He unwrapped it. "Funny color for soap. Smells a lot like chocolate." He popped the whole thing in his mouth. His eyebrows shot up. "Holy cow, this is good!"

"Since you found the keyhole, how about we split them fifty-fifty." She was a little worried he would eat all of them otherwise.

"Sounds fair," he said, grabbing four more.

Kendra placed her five chocolates in the nightstand drawer and retrieved the locked book. As she expected, the second gold key unlocked another clasp. Where could the third one be?

She slapped her forehead. The first two had been hidden

inside things the other keys had opened. The other one must be in the jewelry box!

Opening the jewelry box, she rummaged through the compartments of glittering pendants, brooches, and rings. Sure enough, disguised on a charm bracelet, she found a tiny golden key matching the other two.

Kendra eagerly crossed the room and inserted the key into the final lock on the *Journal of Secrets*. The final clasp unlatched and she opened the book. The first page was blank. So was the second. She thumbed quickly through the pages. The whole book was blank. Just an empty journal. Was Grandpa Sorenson trying to encourage her to keep a diary?

But the whole game with the keys had been so sneaky. Maybe there was a trick to this as well. A hidden message. Disappearing ink or something. What was the trick with disappearing ink? Spray it with lemon juice and hold it up to a light? Something like that. And there was another trick where you rubbed gently with a pencil and a message appeared. Or maybe something even more devious.

Kendra surveyed the journal more carefully, hunting for clues. She held a few pages up against the window to see if the light would betray hidden watermarks or other mysterious evidence.

"What are you doing?" Seth asked. He had only one chocolate rosebud left. She would need to hide her chocolates someplace more secure than the nightstand drawer.

She held up a final page. The light revealed nothing. "Practicing for my audition at the insane asylum."

"I bet you'll win first prize," he teased.

"Unless they see your face," she retorted.

Seth went over and scooped some kernels for Goldilocks. "She laid another egg." He opened the cage to retrieve it and stroked her soft feathers.

Kendra plopped down on the bed, leafing through the last pages. Suddenly she stopped. There was writing on one of the final pages. Not really hidden, just tucked away in an unlikely spot. Three words written near the binding, toward the bottom of an otherwise empty page.

Drink the milk.

Folding the corner, she flipped through the remaining pages. Then she skimmed the rest of the pages from the start to make sure she had missed no similar messages. There were no other cryptic clues.

Drink the milk.

Maybe soaking a page in milk would make words appear. She could soak one in the tins of milk Dale left out.

Or that could be the milk the message was talking about! A challenge to drink unprocessed cow's milk—what purpose could that serve? To give her diarrhea? Dale had made a special point of warning her *not* to drink the milk. Of course, he had acted sort of peculiar about it. He could be hiding something.

Drink the milk.

All the hassle of finding holes for the keys Grandpa Sorenson gave her, in order to uncover extra keys that fit a locked journal, for that odd message? Was she missing something, or overanalyzing? The hunt might have simply been meant to occupy her time.

"Do you think Mom and Dad would let us get a pet chicken?" Seth asked, holding the hen.

"Probably right after they get us a pet buffalo."

"Why don't you ever hold Goldilocks? She's really good."

"Holding a live chicken sounds disgusting."

"Better than holding a dead one."

"I'm fine just petting her."

"You're missing out." Seth held the hen up to his face. "You're a good chicken, aren't you, Goldilocks?" The hen clucked softly.

"She's going to peck your eyes out," Kendra warned.

"No way, she's tame."

Popping one of the rosebud chocolates in her mouth, Kendra replaced the *Journal of Secrets* in the nightstand drawer and returned to her painting. She scowled. Between the gazebos, pond, and swans, the picture required more than thirty shades of white, gray, and silver. Using the sample hues Lena had given her, she prepared her next color.

✼ ✼ ✼

The sun was bright the next day. There was no evidence that it had ever rained or that it would ever rain again. Hummingbirds, butterflies, and bumblebees had returned to the yard. Lena gardened in the back beneath a large sun hat.

Kendra sat in the shade on the back porch. No longer a prisoner in the attic, she felt better able to enjoy the fine weather. She wondered if the diverse butterflies she saw in the yard were among the species Grandpa Sorenson had imported. How did you keep a butterfly from leaving your property? The milk, perhaps?

She passed the time with a game she had found on a shelf in the attic—a triangular board with fifteen holes and fourteen pegs. The object was to jump pegs like checkers until you had only one left, which sounded simple at first. The problem was that in the process of jumping, certain pegs ended up stranded, unable to jump or be jumped. The number of pegs you left stranded on the board determined your score.

Her best effort so far was three, which the directions labeled typical. Leaving two was good. One was genius. Five or more labeled you hopeless.

While resetting the pegs for a fresh attempt, Kendra saw what she had been waiting for. Dale was walking along the perimeter of the yard with a pie tin. Setting the peg game on a table, she hurried to intercept him.

Dale looked mildly distressed at her approach. "I can't let Lena see you talking to me like this," he murmured in low tones. "I'm supposed to put the milk out on the sly."

"I thought nobody knew you put the milk out."

"Right. See, your grandfather doesn't know, but Lena does. We try to keep it our secret."

"I was wondering what the milk tastes like."

He looked nervous. "Didn't you hear me last time? You could get . . . shingles. Scabies. Scurvy."

"Scurvy?"

"This milk is a bacterial stew. That's why the insects like it so well."

"I have friends who have tried milk fresh from the cow. They survived."

"I'm sure those were healthy cows," Dale said. "These cows are . . . never you mind. Idea is, this ain't just any milk. It's highly contaminated. I wash my hands good after even handling the stuff."

"So you don't think I should taste it?"

"Not unless you're aiming for a premature burial."

"Would you at least take me in the barn to see the cows?"

"See the cows? That would be breaking your grandfather's rules!"

"I thought the point was we might get hurt," Kendra said. "I'll be fine if you're with me."

"Your grandfather's rules are your grandfather's rules. He has his reasons. I'm not about to go breaking them. Or bending them either."

"No? Maybe if you let me see the cows, I'll keep your secret about putting out the milk."

"Now see, that's blackmail. I'll not stand for blackmail."

"I wonder what Grandpa will say when I tell him at dinner tonight."

"He'll likely say you ought to mind your own affairs. Now, with your leave, I have chores to do."

She watched him walk away with the tin of milk. He surely had acted defensive and strange. There was definitely some mystery surrounding the milk. But all the talk about bacteria made her reluctant to try it. She needed a guinea pig.

*　*　*

Seth tried a flip off the boulder into the pool, but landed on his back. He never could quite make it all the way around. He surfaced and stroked to the side to try again.

"Nice back-flop," Kendra said, standing beside the pool. "That was one for the blooper reel."

Seth climbed out of the water. "I'd like to see you do a better one. Where have you been?"

"I found out a secret."

"What?"

"I can't explain. But I can show you."

"Good as the lake?"

"Not quite. Hurry up."

Putting a towel over his shoulders, Seth stepped into his sandals. Kendra led him away from the pool through the garden to some flowering shrubs on the outskirts of the yard. Behind the plants lay a large pie tin full of milk where a crowd of hummingbirds were feeding.

"They drink milk?" he asked.

"Yeah, but that isn't the point. Taste it."

"Why?"

"You'll see."

"Have you tried it?"

"Yes."

"What's the big deal?"

"I told you, try it and you'll see."

Kendra watched curiously as he kneeled by the tin. The hummingbirds dispersed. Seth dipped a finger into the milk and put it on his tongue. "Pretty good. Sweet."

"Sweet?"

He lowered his head and puckered his lips against the surface of the milk. Pulling back, he wiped his mouth. "Yeah, sweet and creamy. A little warm, though." Looking beyond Kendra, his eyes bulged. Seth jumped to his feet, screaming and pointing. "What the heck are those?"

Kendra turned. All she saw was a butterfly and a couple of hummingbirds. She looked back at Seth. He was turning in circles, eyes darting around the garden, apparently perplexed and amazed.

"They're everywhere," he said in awe.

"What are?"

"Look around. The fairies."

Kendra stared at her brother. Could the milk have totally fried his brain? Or was he messing around with her? He didn't appear to be faking. He was over by a rosebush gazing at a butterfly in wonder. Tentatively he reached a hand toward it, but it fluttered out of reach.

He turned back to Kendra. "Was it the milk? This is way cooler than the lake!" His excitement seemed genuine.

Kendra eyed the tin of milk. *Drink the milk.* If Seth was playing a prank, his acting skills had suddenly improved tenfold. She dipped a finger and put it in her mouth. Seth was right. It was sweet and warm. For an instant the sun gleamed in her eyes, making her blink.

She glanced back at her brother, who was creeping up on a small group of hovering fairies. Three had wings like butterflies, one like a dragonfly. She could not suppress a shriek at the impossible sight.

Kendra looked back at the milk. A fairy with hummingbird wings was drinking from her cupped hand. Other than the wings, the fairy looked like a slender woman not quite two inches tall. She wore a glittering turquoise slip and had long, dark hair. When Kendra leaned closer, the fairy zipped away.

There was no way she was really seeing this, right? There had to be an explanation. But the fairies were everywhere, near and far, shimmering in vivid colors. How could she deny what was before her eyes?

As Kendra continued to survey the garden, startled disbelief melted into wonder. Fairies of all conceivable varieties flitted about, exploring blossoms, gliding on the breeze, and acrobatically avoiding her brother.

Roaming the pathways of the garden in a daze, Kendra saw that the fairy women appeared to represent all nationalities. Some looked Asian, some Indian, some African, some European. Several were less comparable to mortal women, with blue skin or emerald green hair. A few had antennae. Their wings came in all varieties, mostly patterned after butterflies, but much more elegantly shaped and radiantly colored. All the fairies gleamed brilliantly, outshining the flowers of the garden like the sun outshines the moon.

Rounding a corner on a pathway, Kendra stopped short. There stood Grandpa Sorenson, wearing a flannel shirt and work boots, arms folded across his chest.

"We need to talk," he said.

※ ※ ※

The grandfather clock tolled the hour, chiming three times after the introductory melody. Sitting in a high-backed leather armchair in Grandpa Sorenson's study, Kendra wondered if grandfather clocks got their name because only grandparents owned them.

She looked over at Seth, seated in an identical chair. It looked too big for him. These were chairs for adults.

Why had Grandpa Sorenson left the room? Were they in trouble? After all, he had given her the keys that ended up leading her and the guinea pig to sample the milk.

Even so, she could not quit worrying that she had discovered something that was meant to stay hidden. Not only were fairies real, but Grandpa Sorenson had hundreds in his yard.

"Is that a fairy skull?" Seth asked, pointing to the flat-bottomed globe with the thumb-sized skull on Grandpa's desk.

"Probably," Kendra said.

"Are we busted?"

"We better not be. There were no rules against drinking milk."

The study door slid open. Grandpa entered along with Lena, who carried three mugs on a tray. Lena offered Kendra a mug, then Seth and Grandpa. The mug contained hot chocolate. Lena left the room as Grandpa took a seat behind his desk.

"I am impressed how quickly you solved my puzzle," he said, taking a sip from his mug.

"You *wanted* us to drink the milk?" Kendra said.

"Assuming you were the right kind of people. Frankly, I don't know you that well. I hoped that the kind of person who would take the trouble to solve my little puzzle would be the kind of person who could handle the notion of a preserve full of magical creatures. Fablehaven would be too much to swallow for most people."

"Fablehaven?" Seth repeated.

"The name the founders gave this preserve centuries ago. A refuge for mystical creatures, a stewardship passed down from caretaker to caretaker over the years."

Kendra tried the hot chocolate. It was superb! The flavor made her think of the rosebud chocolates.

"What do you have besides fairies?" Seth asked.

"Many beings, great and small. Which is the true reason the woods are off-limits. There are creatures out there much more perilous than venomous snakes or wild apes. Only certain orders of magical life forms are generally permitted in the yard. Fairies, pixies, and such." Grandpa took another sip from his mug. "You like the hot chocolate?"

"It's wonderful," Kendra said.

"Made from the same milk you sampled in the garden today. Same milk the fairies drink. Just about the only food they'll eat. When mortals drink it, their eyes are opened to an unseen world. But the effects wear off after a day. Lena will prepare you a cup every morning so you can stop stealing from the fairies."

"Where does it come from?" Kendra asked.

"We make it special in the barn. We have some dangerous creatures in there, too, so it's still off-limits."

"Why's everything off-limits?" Seth complained. "I've been a long way into those woods four times and I've always been fine."

"Four times?" Grandpa said.

"All before the warning," Seth amended hastily.

"Yes, well, your eyes were not yet opened to what truly surrounded you. And you were fortunate. Even when you were blind to the enchanted creatures populating the forest, there are many places you could have ventured into from which you would not have returned. Of course, now that you can see them, the creatures here can interact with you much more readily, so the danger is much greater."

"No offense, Grandpa, but is this really the truth?" Kendra asked. "You've told us so many versions of why the woods are forbidden."

"You saw the fairies," he said.

Kendra leaned forward. "Maybe the milk made us hallucinate. Maybe they were holograms. Maybe you just keep telling us whatever you think we'll believe."

"I understand your concern," Grandpa said. "I wanted to protect you from the truth about Fablehaven unless you sought it out for yourselves. It is not the kind of information I wanted to thrust upon you. That is the truth. What I'm telling you now is the truth. You'll have ample opportunity to confirm my words."

"So the animals we saw at the pond were actually other creatures, like how the butterflies were fairies," Kendra clarified.

"Most assuredly. The pond can be a hazardous place. Return there now, and you would find friendly naiads beckoning you near the water in order to pull you under and drown you."

"That's so cruel!" Kendra said.

"Depends on your perspective," Grandpa said, spreading his hands. "To them, your life is so ridiculously short that to kill you is seen as absurd and funny. No more tragic than squashing a moth. Besides, they have a right to punish trespassers. The island at the center of the pond is a shrine to the Fairy Queen. No mortal is permitted to tread there. I know of a groundskeeper who broke that rule. The moment he set foot on the sacred island, he transformed into a cloud of dandelion fluff, clothes and all. He scattered on the breeze and was never seen again."

"Why would he go there?" Kendra asked.

"The Fairy Queen is widely considered the most powerful figure in all fairydom. The groundskeeper had a desperate need and went to plead for her assistance. Apparently she was not impressed."

"In other words, he had no respect for what was off-limits," Kendra said, giving Seth a meaningful look.

"Precisely," Grandpa agreed.

"The queen of the fairies lives on that little island?" Seth asked.

"No. It is merely a shrine meant to honor her. Similar shrines abound on my property, and all can be dangerous."

"If the pond is dangerous, why does it have a boat-house?" Kendra asked.

"A previous caretaker of this preserve had a fascination with naiads."

"The dandelion guy?" Seth asked.

"A different guy," Grandpa said. "It's a long story. Ask Lena about it sometime; I believe she knows the tale."

Kendra shifted in the oversized chair. "Why do you live in such a scary place?"

Grandpa folded his arms on the desk. "It's only frightening if you go where you don't belong. This entire sanctuary is consecrated ground, governed by laws that cannot be broken by the creatures who dwell here. Only on this hallowed soil could mortals interact with these beings with any measure of safety. As long as mortals remain within their boundaries, they are protected by the founding covenants of this preserve."

"Covenants?" Seth asked.

"Agreements. Specifically, a treaty ratified by all the orders of whimsical life forms who dwell here that affords a measure of security for mortal caretakers. In a world where mortal man has become the dominant force, most creatures of enchantment have fled to refuges like this one."

"What are the covenants?" Kendra asked.

"The specific details are complex, with many limitations and exceptions. Speaking broadly, they are based on the law of the harvest, the law of retribution. If you do not bother the creatures, they will not bother you. That is what affords you so much protection when you are unable to see them. You can't interact with them, so they generally behave likewise."

"But now we can see them," Seth said.

"Which is why you must use caution. The fundamental premises of the law are mischief for mischief, magic for magic, violence for violence. They will not initiate trouble unless you break the rules. You have to open the door. If you harass them, you open the door for them to harass you. Hurt them, they can hurt you. Use magic on them, they will use magic on you."

"Use magic?" Seth said eagerly.

"Mortals were never meant to use magic," Grandpa said. "We are nonmagical beings. But I have learned a few practical principles that help me manage things. Nothing you would find very remarkable."

"Can you turn Kendra into a toad?"

"No. But there are beings out there who could. And I would not be able to change her back. Which is why I need to finish this thought: Breaking the rules can include trespassing where you are not allowed. There are geographic boundaries set where certain creatures are allowed and certain creatures, including mortals, are not permitted. The boundaries function as a way to contain the darker creatures without causing an uproar. If you go where you do not belong, you could open the door to vicious retribution from powerful enemies."

"So only good creatures can enter the yard," Kendra said.

Grandpa became very serious. "None of these creatures are good. Not the way we think of good. None are safe. Much of morality is peculiar to mortality. The best creatures here are merely not evil."

"The fairies aren't safe?" Seth asked.

"They aren't out to harm anyone, or I wouldn't allow them in the yard. I suppose they are capable of good deeds, but they would not normally do them for what we would consider the right reasons. Take brownies, for instance.

Brownies don't fix things to help people. They fix things because they enjoy fixing things."

"Do the fairies talk?" Kendra asked.

"Not much to humans. They have a language all their own, although they rarely speak to each other, except to trade insults. Most never condescend to use human speech. They consider everything beneath them. Fairies are vain, selfish creatures. You may have noticed I drained all the fountains and the birdbaths outside. When they are full, the fairies assemble to stare at their reflections all day."

"Is Kendra a fairy?" Seth asked.

Grandpa bit his lip and stared at the floor, obviously trying to choke back a laugh. "We had a mirror outside once and they flocked around it," Kendra said, studiously ignoring both the comment and the reaction. "I wondered what the heck was going on."

Grandpa regained his composure. "Exactly the sort of display I was trying to avoid by draining the birdbaths. Fairies are remarkably conceited. Outside of a sanctuary like this one, they won't even let a mortal glimpse them. Since they consider looking at themselves the ultimate delight, they deny the pleasure to others. Most of the nymphs have the same mentality."

"Why don't they care here?" Kendra asked.

"They still care. But they can't hide when you drink their milk, so they have reluctantly grown accustomed to mortals seeing them. I have to laugh sometimes. The fairies pretend not to care what mortals think about them, but try giving one a compliment. She'll blush, and the others will crowd in for their turn. You would think they'd be embarrassed."

"I think they're pretty," Seth said.

"They're gorgeous!" Grandpa agreed. "And they can be useful. They handle most of my gardening. But good? Safe? Not so much."

Kendra swallowed the last of her hot chocolate. "So if we don't go into the woods or the barn, and don't bother the fairies, we'll be fine?"

"Yes. This house and the yard around it is the most protected location in Fablehaven. Only the gentlest creatures are allowed here. Of course, there are a few nights a year when all the creatures run amuck, and one of those is coming up. But I'll tell you more about it when the time comes."

Seth scooted forward in his chair. "I want to hear about the evil creatures. What's out there?"

"For the sake of your ability to sleep at night, I'm going to keep that to myself."

"I met that weird old lady. Was she really something else?"

Grandpa gripped the edge of the desk. "That encounter is a frightening example of why the woods are forbidden. It could have been disastrous. You ventured toward a very hazardous area."

"Is she a witch?" Seth asked.

"She is. Her name is Muriel Taggert."

"How come I could see her?"

"Witches are mortal."

"Then why don't you get rid of her?" Seth suggested.

"The shack is not her home. It is her prison. She personifies the reasons why exploring the woods is unwise. Her husband was a caretaker here more than a hundred and sixty years ago. She was an intelligent, lovely woman. But she became a frequent visitor to some of the darker portions of the forest, where she consorted with unsavory beings. They tutored her. Before long, she became enamored with the power of witchcraft, and they acquired considerable influence over her. She became unstable. Her husband tried to help her, but she was already too demented.

"When she tried to aid some of the foul denizens of the woods in a treacherous act of rebellion, her husband called in assistance and had her imprisoned. She has been trapped in that shack ever since, held captive by the knots in the rope you saw. Let her story serve as another warning—you have no business in those woods."

"I get it," Seth said. He looked solemn.

"Enough jabbering about rules and monsters," Grandpa said, standing up. "I have chores. And you have a new world to explore. The day is fading, go make the most of it. But stay in the yard."

"What do you do all day?" Kendra inquired, walking out of the study beside Grandpa.

"Oh, I have many chores to keep this place in order. Fablehaven is home to many extraordinary wonders and delights, but it requires a great deal of maintenance. You might be able to accompany me some of the time, now that you know the true nature of the place. Mundane work, mostly. I expect you'd have more fun playing in the garden."

Kendra laid a hand on Grandpa's arm. "I want to see as much as I can."

CHAPTER SIX

Maddox

Kendra snapped awake with her sheets tented over her head. She was supposed to be excited about something. It felt like Christmas morning. Or a day she was going to take off school so her family could visit an amusement park. No, she was at Grandpa Sorenson's. The fairies!

She pushed off the sheets. Seth lay in a contorted position, hair wildly disheveled, mouth open, legs tangled in his covers. Still out cold. They had stayed up late discussing the events of the day, almost like friends rather than siblings.

Kendra rolled out of bed and padded over to the window. The sun was peeking over the eastern horizon, streaming gilded highlights across the treetops. She grabbed some clothes, went down to the bathroom, took off her night-shirt, and got dressed for the day.

Downstairs, the kitchen was empty. Kendra found Lena out on the porch balancing atop a stool. Lena was hanging wind chimes. She had already hung several along the length of the porch. A butterfly flitted around one of the chimes, playing a sweet, simple melody.

"Good morning," Lena said. "You're up early."

"I'm still so excited from yesterday." Kendra looked out at the garden. The butterflies, bumblebees, and hummingbirds were already going about their business. Grandpa was right—many clustered around the newly refilled birdbaths and fountains, admiring their reflections.

"Just a bunch of bugs again," Lena said.

"Can I have some hot chocolate?"

"Let me hang these last chimes," she said, moving the stool and climbing fearlessly on top of it. She was so old! If she fell she would probably die!

"Be careful," Kendra said.

Lena waved a dismissive hand. "The day I'm too old to climb on a stool will be the day I throw myself off the roof." She hung the final chime. "We had to take these down for you kids. Might have made you suspicious to see hummingbirds playing music."

Kendra followed Lena back into the house. "Years ago, there used to be a church within earshot that would play melodies on the bells," Lena said. "It was so funny to watch the fairies imitate the music. They still play those old songs sometimes."

Lena opened the refrigerator, removing an old-fashioned milk bottle. Kendra sat at the table. Lena poured some milk into a pot on the stove and began adding ingredients. Kendra noticed that she was not just scooping in chocolate powder—she was stirring in contents from multiple containers.

"Grandpa said to ask you about the story of the guy who built the boathouse," Kendra said.

Lena paused in her stirring. "Did he? I suppose I am more familiar with that story than most." She resumed stirring. "What did he tell you?"

"He said the guy had an obsession with naiads. What's a naiad, anyhow?"

"A water nymph. What else did he say?"

"Just that you know the story."

"The man was named Patton Burgess," said Lena. "He became caretaker of this property in 1878, inheriting the position from his maternal grandfather. He was a young man at the time, quite good-looking, wore a moustache—there are pictures upstairs. The pond was his favorite place on the property."

"Mine too."

"He would go and gaze at the naiads for hours. They would try to tease him down to the water's edge, as was their custom, in order to drown him. He would draw near, sometimes even pretending he meant to jump in, but always stayed tantalizingly out of reach."

Lena sampled the hot chocolate and stirred some more. "Unlike most of the visitors, who seemed to regard the naiads as interchangeable, he paid special attention to a particular nymph, asking for her by name. He began to pay little heed to the other naiads. On the days when his favorite would not show herself, he left early."

Lena poured the milk from the pot into a pair of mugs. "He became fixated on her. When he built the boathouse, the nymphs wondered what he could be doing. He constructed a broad, sturdy rowboat so he could go out on the water and be closer to the object of his fascination." Lena brought the mugs to the table and sat down. "The naiads tried to upset his craft every time he set forth, but it was too cleverly constructed. They succeeded only in pushing it around the pond."

Kendra took a sip. The hot chocolate was perfection. Barely cool enough to sip comfortably.

"Patton began trying to coax his favorite naiad to leave the water, to come walk with him on the land. She responded by urging him to join her in the pond, for to leave the water would mean to enter mortality. The tug-of-war went on for more than three years. He would serenade her on his violin, and read her poetry, and make her promises about the joys their life together would hold. He showed such sincerity, and such perseverance, that on occasion she would gaze into his kind eyes and falter."

Lena sipped the hot chocolate. "One day in March, Patton got careless. He leaned too close to the gunwale, and a naiad caught hold of his sleeve as he conversed with his favorite. A strong man, he resisted her, but the struggle pulled him to one side of the boat, upsetting his typical equilibrium. A pair of naiads heaved upward on the other side and it capsized."

"He died?" Kendra was horrified.

"He would have died, yes. The naiads had their prize. In their domain he was no match for them. Giddy with the long-awaited victory, they rushed him toward the bottom of the pond to add him to their collection of mortal victims. But it was more than his favorite could bear. She had grown fond of Patton, seduced by his diligent attention, and, unlike the others, she did not consider his death an amusement. She fought off her sisters and returned him to the shore. That was the day I left the pond."

Kendra spewed hot chocolate across the table. "You're the naiad?"

"I was, once."

"You became mortal?"

Lena absently blotted up the hot chocolate Kendra had sprayed, using a small towel. "If I could go back, I would make the same decision every time. We had a joyful life. Patton managed Fablehaven for fifty-one years before passing it off to a nephew. He lived twelve years after that—died at ninety-one. His mind was sharp to the end. Helps to have a young wife."

"How are you still alive?"

"I became subject to the laws of mortality, but they

have taken effect gradually. As I sat by his deathbed, I looked perhaps twenty years older than I had on the day when I carried him from the water. I felt guilty about looking so young as his frail body was shutting down. I wanted to be old like him. Of course, now that my age is finally catching up with me, I don't care for it much."

Kendra sipped more of her hot chocolate. She was so enthralled that she barely tasted it. "What did you do after he passed away?"

"I took advantage of my mortality. I had paid a steep price for it, so I traveled the world to see what it had to offer. Europe, the Middle East, India, Japan, South America, Africa, Australia, the Pacific Islands. I had many adventures. I set some swimming records in Britain, and could have set even more except I was holding back—no sense raising a lot of questions. I worked as a painter, a chef, a geisha, a trapeze artist, a nurse. Many men pursued me, but I never loved again. Eventually, there was a sameness to the traveling, so I returned home, to the place my heart never left."

"Do you ever go back to the pond?"

"Only in memory. It would be unwise. They despise me there, all the more intensely because of their secret envy. How they would laugh at my appearance! They have not aged a day. But I have experienced many things that they will never know. Some painful, some wonderful."

Kendra finished the last of her hot chocolate and wiped her lips. "What was it like being a naiad?"

Lena gazed out the window. "Hard to say. I ask myself the same question. It wasn't just my body that became mortal; my mind transformed as well. I think I prefer this life, but it might be because I have changed fundamentally. Mortality is a totally different state of being. You become more aware of time. I was absolutely content as a naiad. I lived in an unchanging state for what must have been many millennia, never thinking of the future or the past, always looking for amusement, always finding it. Almost no self-awareness. It feels like a blur now. No, like a blink. A single moment that lasted thousands of years."

"You would have lived forever," Kendra exclaimed.

"We weren't quite immortal. We did not age, so I suppose some of our kind could endure forever, if lakes and rivers last forever. Difficult to say. We did not really live, not like mortals. We dreamed."

"Wow."

"At least that was the way of things until Patton," Lena said, more to herself now. "I began looking forward to his visits, and back on them in memory. I suppose that was the beginning of the end."

Kendra shook her head. "And I thought you were just the half-Chinese housekeeper."

She smiled. "Patton always liked my eyes." She batted them. "He said he was of the Asian persuasion."

"What's Dale's story? Is he a pirate king or something?"

"Dale is a regular man. A second cousin of your grandfather. A man he trusts."

Kendra looked into her empty mug. A ring of chocolate sediment circled the bottom. "I have a question," she said, "and I want you to answer honestly."

"If I can."

"Is my Grandma Sorenson dead?"

"What makes you ask that?"

"I think Grandpa makes up phony excuses for her not being around. This is a dangerous place. He has lied about other things. I get the feeling he's trying to protect us from the truth."

"I often wonder if lies are ever a protection."

"She's dead, isn't she."

"No, she's alive."

"Is she the witch?"

"She's not the witch."

"Is she really visiting Aunt Whoever in Missouri?"

"That is for your grandfather to tell."

❧ ❧ ❧

Seth looked over his shoulder. Besides the fairies fluttering about, the garden looked still. Grandpa and Dale were long gone. Lena was in the house dusting. Kendra was off doing whatever boring things kept her occupied. He had his emergency kit in hand, along with a few strategic additions. Operation See Cool Monsters was about to begin.

He hesitantly stepped off the edge of the lawn into the woods, half-expecting werewolves to leap out at him. There were a few fairies up ahead, not as many as in the garden. Otherwise things looked pretty much the same.

He marched forward, setting a brisk pace.

"Where do you think you're going?"

Seth whirled. Kendra was approaching from the garden. He walked back to meet her at the edge of the lawn. "I want to see what's really at the pond. Those nai-thingies and stuff."

"How brain-damaged are you? Didn't you hear a word Grandpa told us yesterday?"

"I'm going to be careful! I won't go near the water."

"You could get killed! I mean really killed, not bitten by a tick. Grandpa made those rules for a reason!"

"Adults always underestimate kids," Seth said. "They get all protective because they think we're babies. Think about it. Mom used to complain all the time about me playing in the street. But I always did it. And what happened? Nothing. I paid attention. I stayed out of the way when a car came."

"This is so different!"

"Grandpa goes all over the place."

Kendra clenched her hands into fists. "Grandpa knows the places to avoid! You don't even know what you're dealing with. Besides, when Grandpa finds out, you'll be stuck in the attic the rest of our stay."

"How's he going to find out?"

"He knew we went into the woods last time! He knew we drank the milk!"

"Because you were there! Your bad luck rubbed off on me. How did you know where I was going?"

"Your secret agent skills need some work," Kendra said. "A good start might be not wearing your camouflage shirt every time you go exploring."

"I need to hide from the dragons!"

"Right. You're practically invisible. Just a floating head."

"I have my emergency kit. If anything attacks, I can scare it away with my gear."

"With rubber bands?"

"I have a whistle. I have a mirror. I have a cigarette lighter. I have firecrackers. They'll think I'm a wizard."

"Do you really believe that?"

"And I have this." He pulled out the little skull in the crystal globe from Grandpa's desk. "That should make them think twice."

"A skull the size of a peanut?"

"There probably aren't even any monsters," Seth said. "What makes you think Grandpa's telling the truth this time?"

"I don't know, maybe the fairies?"

"Well, good job. You blew it. Congratulate yourself. I can't go now."

"I'm going to blow it every time. Not to be a jerk, but because you could really get hurt."

Seth kicked a stone, sending it skidding into the woods. "What am I supposed to do now?"

"How about exploring the enormous garden full of fairies?"

"I already did. I can't catch them."

"Not to catch them. To look at magical creatures that nobody else even knows exist. Come on."

He reluctantly joined her.

"Oh, look, another fairy," he mumbled. "Now I've seen a million."

"Don't forget to put the skull back."

※　※　※

When they responded to the call for dinner, a stranger sat at the table along with Grandpa and Dale. The stranger stood when they entered. He was taller than Grandpa and much broader, with curly brown hair. The layers of furry skins he wore made him look like a mountain man. He was missing the bottom of one earlobe.

"Kids, this is Maddox Fisk," Grandpa said. "Maddox, meet my grandchildren, Kendra and Seth." Kendra shook the man's calloused, thick-fingered hand.

"Do you work here too?" Seth asked.

"Maddox is a fairy broker," Grandpa said.

"Among other things," Maddox added. "Call fairies my specialty."

"You sell fairies?" Kendra asked, taking a seat.

"Trap them, buy them, trade them, sell them. All of the above."

"How do you trap them?" Seth asked.

"A man has to keep his trade secrets private," Maddox said, taking a bite of pork roast. "Let me tell you, apprehending a fairy is no easy task. Slippery critters. The trick usually involves appealing to their vanity. Even then, takes quite a bit of know-how."

"Could you use an apprentice?" Seth inquired.

"Hold that thought about six years." Maddox winked at Kendra.

"Who buys fairies?" Kendra asked.

"Folks who run preserves, like your granddad. A few private collectors. Other brokers."

"Are there lots of preserves?" Seth asked.

"Dozens," Maddox replied. "They're on all seven continents."

"Even Antarctica?" Kendra asked.

"Two in Antarctica, although one is underground. Harsh environment. Perfect for certain species, though."

Kendra swallowed a bite of pork. "What keeps people from discovering the sanctuaries?"

"There has been a worldwide network of dedicated people keeping the preserves secret for thousands of years," Grandpa said. "They are backed by ancient fortunes, held in trust. Bribes get paid. Locations are changed when necessary."

"Helps that most folks are unable to see the little critters," Maddox said. "With the right licenses, you can get butterflies through customs. When you can't, there are other ways to cross borders."

"The preserves are the final refuge for many ancient and wonderful species," Grandpa said. "The goal is to prevent these wondrous beings from passing out of existence."

"Amen," Maddox said.

"You have a good haul this season?" Dale asked.

"Far as trapping goes, pickings are getting slimmer every year. I made a few exciting finds in the wild. One you won't believe. I picked up several rare specimens from preserves in Southeast Asia and Indonesia. I'm sure we can do some trading. I'll tell you more when we adjourn to the study."

"You kids would be welcome to join us," Grandpa said.

"All right!" Seth cheered.

Kendra took another bite of the succulent pork roast. Everything Lena cooked was outstanding. Always perfectly seasoned, typically served with delicious gravies or sauces. Kendra never had any complaints about her mom's cooking, but Lena was in a class all her own.

Grandpa and Maddox discussed people Kendra did not know, other individuals involved in the secretive world of fairy aficionados. She wondered if Maddox would ask about Grandma, but it never came up.

Maddox repeatedly mentioned the evening star. Grandpa seemed to focus on this news with particular interest. Rumors that the evening star was forming again. A woman who claimed the evening star tried to recruit her. Whispers of an attack by the evening star.

Kendra could not resist interjecting. "What's the evening star? It sounds like you're using it as a code word."

Maddox glanced uncertainly at Grandpa. Grandpa gave him a nod.

"The Society of the Evening Star is an arcane organization that we all hoped had gone extinct decades ago," Maddox explained. "Over the centuries, their relevance has waxed and waned. Seems like just when you think you've seen the last of them, you start hearing rumors again."

"They are dedicated to overthrowing preserves in order to use them for their own misguided purposes," Grandpa said. "Members of the Society consort with demons and practitioners of the black arts."

"Are they going to attack us?" Seth asked.

"Not likely," Grandpa said. "The preserves are protected by powerful magic. But I lend an ear to the news all the same. Rarely hurts to be cautious."

"Why the evening star?" Kendra asked. "It's such a pretty name."

"The evening star ushers in the night," Maddox said. They considered the statement in silence. Maddox wiped his lips with a napkin. "Sorry. Not a very cheery topic around the dinner table."

After supper, Lena cleared the table and they all went to the study. On the way there, Maddox collected several cases and crates from the entry hall. Dale, Seth, and Kendra helped. The cases had perforations, evidently to allow the creatures inside to breathe, but Kendra was unable to see into them. All were locked.

Grandpa settled in behind his large desk, Dale and Maddox claimed the oversized armchairs, Lena leaned against the windowsill, and Kendra and Seth found seats on the floor.

"First off," Maddox said, bending over and unlocking a large black crate, "we have some fairies from a preserve on Timor." He opened the hatch, and eight fairies soared out. Two tiny ones, not even an inch tall, darted to the window. They were amber in color, with wings like flies. One banged the windowpane with a miniscule fist. A large fairy, more than four inches tall, hovered in front of Kendra. She looked like a miniature Pacific Islander with dragonfly wings across her back as well as tiny wings on her ankles.

Three of the fairies had elaborate butterfly wings with the appearance of stained glass. Another had oily black wings. The last had furry wings, and her body was coated with pale blue fuzz.

"Whoa!" Seth said. "That one's all hairy."

"A downy fountain sprite, found only on the island of Roti," Maddox said.

"I like the little ones," Kendra said.

"A more common variety—they haunt the Malaysian Peninsula," Maddox said.

"They're so fast," Kendra said. "Why don't they escape?"

"Catching a fairy renders her powerless," Maddox said. "Keep her in a cage, or a sealed room, like this one, and her magic cannot be used to escape. While under confinement they become fairly docile and obedient."

Kendra frowned. "How does Grandpa know they will stay in his garden if he buys them?"

Maddox winked at Grandpa. "Gets right to the point, this one." He turned back to Kendra. "Fairies are highly territorial, nonmigratory creatures. Put them in a livable environment and they stay put. Especially an environment like Fablehaven, with gardens and plentiful food and other enchanted critters."

"I'm sure I can find a trade for the fountain sprite," Grandpa said. "The Banda Sea sunwings are beautiful as well. We can work out the particulars later."

Maddox slapped the side of the crate and the fairies returned. The ones with the stained-glass wings took their time, drifting lazily. The little ones zoomed in. The fountain sprite floated up to a high corner of the room. Maddox patted the side of the crate again and spat a stern command in a language Kendra did not understand. The fuzzy fairy glided into the container.

"Next we have some albino nightgrifters from Borneo." Out of a case flew three milky white fairies, their mothlike wings peppered with flecks of black.

Maddox proceeded to display several other groups of distinctive fairies. Then he began showing fairies one at a time. Kendra found a couple of them disgusting. One had thorny wings and a tail. Another was reptilian, covered in scales. Maddox displayed its chameleonic ability to match different backgrounds.

"Now for my big find," Maddox said, rubbing his hands together. "I captured this little lady in an oasis deep in the Gobi Desert. I've only seen one other of her kind. Could we dim the lights?"

Dale jumped up and shut the lights off.

"What is she?" Grandpa asked.

In answer, Maddox opened the final case. Out soared a dazzling fairy with wings like shimmering veils of gold. Three gleaming feathers streamed beneath her, elegant ribbons of light. She hung gloriously in the center of the room with a regal air.

"A jinn harp?" Grandpa said in astonishment.

"Favor us with a song, I beg you," Maddox said. He repeated the solicitation in another language.

The fairy gleamed even brighter, shedding sparks. The music that followed was mesmerizing. The voice made Kendra imagine a multitude of vibrating crystals. The wordless song had the power of an operatic aria mingled with the sweetness of a lullaby. It was longing, beckoning, hopeful, and heartbreaking.

They all sat transfixed until the song ended. When it was over, Kendra wanted to applaud, but the moment felt too sacred.

"Truly you are magnificent," Maddox said, repeating

the compliment again in a foreign tongue. Chinese? He tapped the side of her case, and with a radiant flourish the fairy was gone.

The room felt dim and bleak in her absence. Kendra tried to blink away the splotchy afterimages.

"How did you make such a find?" Grandpa asked in wonder.

"I caught wind of some local legends near the Mongolian border. Cost me nearly two months of brutal living to track her down."

"The only other known jinn harp has her own shrine in a Tibetan sanctuary," Grandpa explained. "She was thought to be unique. Fairy connoisseurs travel from all corners of the globe to behold her."

"I can see why," Kendra said.

"What a singular treat, Maddox! Thank you for bringing her into our home."

"I'm touring her around the circuit before I take offers," Maddox said.

"I don't mean to pretend I can afford her, but send me word when she becomes available." Standing up, Grandpa looked at the clock and clapped his hands together. "Looks like it's about time for everyone under the age of thirty to head off to bed."

"But it's still early!" Seth said.

"No grousing. I have negotiations to conduct with Maddox tonight. We can't have young people underfoot.

You'll need to stay in your room, no matter what commotion you hear downstairs. Our, ah, negotiations can be a bit spirited. Understood?"

"Yes," Kendra said.

"I want to negotiate," Seth said.

Grandpa shook his head. "It's a dull business. You kids have a good sleep."

"No matter what you might think you hear," Maddox said as Kendra and Seth departed the study, "we aren't having fun."

CHAPTER SEVEN

Prisoner in a Jar

The floorboards creaked gently as Kendra and Seth tiptoed down the stairs. Early morning light filtered through closed blinds and drawn curtains. The house was still. The opposite of last night.

Beneath their covers in the dark attic the night before, Kendra and Seth had found sleeping impossible as they listened to howling laughter, shattering glass, twittering flutes, slamming doors, and the constant din of shouted conversations. When they opened the door to sneak down and spy on the festivities, Lena was always seated at the foot of the attic stairs, reading a book.

"Go back to bed," she said each time they attempted a reconnaissance mission. "Your grandfather is still negotiating."

Eventually Kendra fell asleep. She believed it was the silence that had finally awakened her in the morning. When she rolled out of bed, Seth arose as well. Now they were creeping down the stairs in hopes of glimpsing the aftermath of the night's revelry.

The brass coatrack had toppled in the entry hall, surrounded by hooked triangles of broken glass. A painting lay facedown on the floor, frame cracked. A primitive symbol was scrawled on the wall in orange chalk.

They passed quietly into the living room. Tables and chairs had been overturned. Lampshades hung crooked and torn. Empty glasses, bottles, and plates lay scattered about, several of them cracked or broken. A ceramic pot lay in pieces around a pile of soil and the remnants of a plant. Food stains appeared at every turn—melted cheese caked into the carpeting, tomato sauce drying on the arm of a love seat, a squashed éclair oozing custard all over an ottoman.

Grandpa Sorenson was snoring on the couch, using a curtain for a blanket. The curtain rod was still attached. He clutched a wooden scepter like a teddy bear. The strange staff was carved with vines twisting around the shaft and topped by a large pinecone. Despite all the commotion they had heard the night before, Grandpa was the only sign of life.

Seth roamed off toward the study. Kendra was about to follow when she noticed an envelope on a table near her grandfather. A thick seal of crimson wax had been broken, and part of a folded paper protruded invitingly.

Kendra glanced at Grandpa Sorenson. He was facing away from the letter, and showed no sign of stirring.

If he didn't want a letter read, he shouldn't leave it out in the open, right? It wasn't as if she were stealing it unopened from his mailbox. And she had several unanswered questions about Fablehaven, not the least of which concerned what was actually going on with her grandma.

Kendra eased over to the table, a queasy feeling in her stomach. Maybe she should have Seth read it. Invading privacy wasn't really her forte.

But it would be so simple. The letter was right in front of her, conveniently sticking out of the open envelope. Nobody would know. She tipped the envelope up and found there was no address or return address. The envelope was blank. Hand-delivered. Had Maddox brought it? Probably.

After a final glance to ensure Grandpa still looked comatose, Kendra slid the cream-colored paper out of the envelope and unfolded it. The message was written in bold script.

> *Stanley,*
>
> *I trust this missive finds you in good health.*
>
> *It has come to our attention that the SES has been exhibiting unusual activity in the northeast of the United States. We remain uncertain whether they have pinpointed the location of Fablehaven, but*

one unconfirmed report suggests they are in com-
munication with an individual(s) on your preserve.
Mounting evidence implies the secret is out.

I need not remind you about the attempted infil-
tration of a certain preserve in the interior of Brazil
last year. Nor the significance of that preserve in
connection with the significance of yours.

As you well know, we have not detected such
aggressive activity from the SES in decades. We are
preparing to reassign additional resources to your
vicinity. As always, secrecy and misdirection remain
top priorities. Be vigilant.

I continue to search diligently for a resolution to
the situation with Ruth. Do not lose hope.

With everlasting fidelity,
S

Kendra reread the letter. Ruth was her grandma's name. What situation? SES had to be the Society of the Evening Star. What did the "S" at the end of the letter stand for? The entire message seemed a bit vague, probably deliberately.

"Look at this," Seth whispered from the kitchen.

Kendra jumped, every muscle in her body tensing. Grandpa smacked his lips and shifted on the couch. Kendra stood temporarily immobilized by guilty panic. Seth was not looking at her. He was stooping over something in the kitchen. Grandpa became still again.

Kendra folded the letter and slipped it back into the envelope, trying to situate it as she had found it. Moving stealthily, she joined Seth, who crouched over muddy hoofprints.

"Were they riding horses in here?" he asked.

"It would explain the racket," she murmured, trying to sound casual.

Lena appeared in the doorway, dressed in a bathrobe, hair awry. "Look at you early risers," she said softly. "You caught us before cleanup."

Kendra stared at Lena, trying to keep her expression unreadable. The housekeeper showed no indication of having seen her spying at the letter.

Seth pointed at the hoofprints. "What the heck happened?"

"The negotiations went well."

"Is Maddox still here?" Seth asked hopefully.

Lena shook her head. "He left in a taxi about an hour ago."

Grandpa Sorenson shuffled into the kitchen wearing boxers, socks, and an undershirt stained with brown mustard. He squinted at them. "What are you all doing up at this ungodly hour?"

"It's after seven," Seth said.

Grandpa covered a yawn with his fist. He held the envelope in his other hand. "I'm feeling a little under the weather today—might go lie down for a spell. As you were." He shambled off, scratching his thigh.

"You kids may want to play outside this morning," Lena said. "Your grandfather was up until forty minutes ago. He had a long night."

"I'm going to have a tough time taking Grandpa seriously when he tells us to show respect for the furniture," Kendra said. "It looks like he drove a tractor through here."

"Pulled by horses!" Seth added.

"Maddox enjoys a celebration, and your grandfather is an accommodating host," Lena said. "Without your grandmother here to rein in the merriment, things got a little too festive. Didn't help that they invited the satyrs." She nodded at the muddy hoofprints.

"Satyrs?" Kendra asked. "Like goatmen?"

Lena nodded. "Some would say they liven up a party too much."

"Those are goat prints?" Seth asked.

"Satyr prints, yes."

"I wish I could have seen them," Seth mourned.

"Your parents would be glad you didn't. Satyrs would only teach you bad manners. I think they invented them."

"I'm sad we missed the party," Kendra said.

"Don't be. It was not a party for young people. As caretaker, your grandfather would never drink, but I can't vouch for the satyrs. We'll have a proper party before you leave us."

"Will you invite satyrs?" Seth asked.

"We'll see what your grandfather says," Lena said

doubtfully. "Maybe one." Lena opened the refrigerator and poured two glasses of milk. "Drink your milk and then run along. I have some heavy cleaning ahead of me."

Kendra and Seth took their glasses. Lena opened the pantry, removing a broom and dustpan, and left the room. Kendra drank her milk in several deep swallows and set her empty glass on the counter. "Want to go for a swim?" she asked.

"I'll catch up," Seth said. He still had milk in his glass. Kendra walked away.

After finishing his milk, Seth peeked into the pantry. So many shelves packed with so much food! One shelf featured nothing but large jars of homemade preserves. Closer investigation revealed that the jars were lined up three deep.

Seth backed out of the pantry and looked around. Reentering the pantry, he removed a large jar of boysenberry preserves, pulling another jar forward from the second row to disguise the absence. They might miss a half-empty jar from the fridge. But one of many unopened jars from an overstuffed pantry? Not likely.

He could be sneakier than Kendra knew.

※　※　※

The fairy balanced on a twig protruding from a low hedge beside the pool. Arms extended to either side, she walked along the tiny limb, adjusting as it wobbled. The further out she got, the less stable she became. The miniature beauty queen had platinum hair, a silver dress, and glittering, translucent wings.

Seth sprang forward, slashing downward with the pool skimmer. The blue mesh struck the twig, but the fairy darted away at the last instant. She hovered, shaking a scolding finger at Seth. He swung the skimmer again, and the nimble fairy evaded capture a second time, soaring well out of range.

"You shouldn't do that," Kendra said from the pool.

"Why not? Maddox catches them."

"Out in the wild," Kendra corrected. "These already belong to Grandpa. It's like hunting lions at the zoo."

"Maybe hunting lions at the zoo would be good practice."

"You're going to end up making the fairies mad at you."

"They don't mind," he said, creeping up on a fairy with wide, gauzy wings fluttering inches above a flowerbed. "They just fly away." He slowly moved the pool skimmer into position. The fairy was directly beneath the mesh, less than two feet away from captivity. With a flick of his wrists, he slapped the skimmer down sharply. The fairy dodged around it and glided off.

"What are you going to do if you catch one?"

"Probably let it go."

"So what's the point?"

"To see if I can do it."

Kendra boosted herself out of the water. "Well,

obviously you can't. They're too fast." Dripping, she walked over to her towel. "Oh my gosh, look at that one." She pointed at the base of a blossoming bush.

"Where?"

"Right there. Wait until she moves. She's practically invisible."

He stared at the bush, unsure whether she was teasing him. A bobbing distortion began warping the leaves and blossoms. "Whoa!"

"See! She's clear like glass."

Seth edged forward, clutching the pool skimmer.

"Seth, don't."

Suddenly he charged, opting for a rapid assault this time. The transparent fairy flew away, vanishing against the sky. "Why won't they hold still!"

"They're magic," Kendra said. "The fun is just looking at them, seeing all the variety."

"Real fun. Kind of like when Mom makes us go on drives to look at the leaves changing color."

"I want to grab some breakfast. I'm starving."

"Then go. Maybe I'll have better luck without you squawking."

Kendra walked to the house wrapped in her towel. She entered the back door and found Lena dragging a broken coffee table into the kitchen. Much of the surface of the table had been made of glass. Most of it was broken.

"Need a hand?" Kendra asked.

"Mine are plenty."

Kendra went and grabbed the other end of the table. They set it in a corner of the spacious kitchen. Other broken objects rested there as well, including the jagged fragments of the ceramic pot Kendra had noticed earlier.

"Why pile everything here?"

"This is where the brownies come."

"Brownies?"

"Come look." Lena led Kendra to the basement door, pointing out a second little door at the base, about the size a cat would use. "The brownies have a special hatch that admits them to the basement, and they can use this door to enter the kitchen. They are the only magical creatures with permission to enter the house at will. The brownie portals are guarded by magic against all other creatures of the forest."

"Why let them in?"

"Brownies are useful. They repair things. They make things. They are remarkable craftsmen."

"They'll fix the broken furniture?"

"Improve it if they can."

"Why?"

"It is their nature. They will accept no reward."

"How nice of them," Kendra said.

"In fact, tonight, remind me to leave out some cooking ingredients. By morning, they will have baked us a treat."

"What will they cook?"

"You never know. You don't make requests. You just leave out ingredients and see how they combine them."

"How fun!"

"I'll leave out a bunch. No matter what strange combinations you leave, they always invent something delicious."

"There is so much I don't know about Fablehaven," Kendra declared. "How big is it?"

"The preserve stretches for many miles in some directions. Much bigger than you would suppose."

"And there are creatures throughout?"

"Through most of it," Lena said. "But as your grandfather has warned you, some of those creatures can be deadly. There are many places on the property where even he does not dare venture."

"I want to know more. All the details."

"Be patient. Let it unfold." She turned to the refrigerator and changed the subject. "You must be hungry."

"A little."

"I'll whip up some eggs. Will Seth want some?"

"Probably," Kendra said, leaning against the counter. "I've been wondering: Is everything from mythology true?"

"Explain what you mean."

"I've seen fairies, and evidence of satyrs. Is it all real?"

"No mythology or religion that I know of holds all the answers. Most religions are based on truths, but they are also polluted by the philosophies and imaginations of men. I take it your question refers to Greek mythology. Is there a pantheon of petty gods who constantly bicker and interfere in the lives of mortals? I know of no such beings. Are there some true elements to those ancient stories and beliefs? Obviously. You're talking to a former naiad. Scrambled?"

"What?"

"The eggs."

"Sure."

Lena began cracking eggs into a pan. "Many of the beings who dwell here existed gracefully when primitive man foraged in ragged tribes. We taught man the secrets of bread and clay and fire. But man became blind to us over time. Interaction with mortals became rare. And then mankind began to crowd us. Explosions in population and technology stole many of our ancient homes. Mankind held no particular malice toward us. We had simply faded into colorful caricatures inhabiting myths and fables.

"There are quiet corners of the world where our kind continue to thrive in the wild. And yet the day will inevitably come when the only space remaining to us will be these sanctuaries, a precious gift from enlightened mortals."

"It's so sad," Kendra said.

"Do not frown. My kind do not dwell on these concerns. They forget the fences enclosing these preserves. I should not speak of what used to be. With my fallen mind, I see the changes much more clearly than they do. I feel the loss more keenly."

"Grandpa said a night is coming when all the creatures here will run wild."

"Midsummer Eve. The festival night."

"What's it like?"

"I'd better not say. I don't think your grandfather wants you kids worrying about it until the time comes. He would rather have scheduled your visit to avoid the festival night."

Kendra tried to sound nonchalant. "Will we be in danger?"

"Now I've got you worried. You will be fine if you follow the instructions your grandfather gives you."

"What about the Society of the Evening Star? Maddox sounded worried about them."

"The Society of the Evening Star has always been a threat," Lena admitted. "But these preserves have endured for centuries, some for millennia. Fablehaven is well protected, and your grandfather is no fool. You needn't worry about speculative rumors. I'll not say more on the subject. Cheese in your eggs?"

"Yes, please."

※ ※ ※

With Kendra gone, Seth got out the equipment he had bundled in his towel, including his emergency kit and the jar he had smuggled from the pantry. The jar was now empty, washed clean in the bathroom sink. Taking out his pocket knife, Seth used the awl to punch holes in the lid.

Unscrewing the top, he gathered bits of grass, flower petals, a twig, and a pebble, and placed them in the jar. Then he wandered across the garden from the pool, leaving the skimmer behind. If skill failed, he would resort to cunning.

He found a good spot not far from a fountain, then took the small mirror from his cereal box and placed it in the jar. Setting the jar on a stone bench, he settled in the grass nearby, lid in hand.

It did not take the fairies long. Several flitted around the fountain. A few drifted over, lazily orbiting the jar. After a couple of minutes, a small one with wings like a bee landed on the edge of the jar, staring into it. Apparently satisfied, she dropped inside and began admiring herself in the mirror. Soon she was joined by another. And another.

Seth moved slowly closer until he was within reach of the jar. All the fairies exited it. He waited. Some flew off. New ones came. One entered the jar, followed quickly by two more.

Seth pounced, slapping the lid onto the jar. The fairies were so quick! He expected to catch all three, but two whizzed out just before the lid covered the opening. The remaining fairy pushed against the lid with surprising force. He screwed it shut.

The fairy inside stood no taller than his little finger. She had fiery red hair and iridescent dragonfly wings. The incensed fairy pounded her tiny fists noiselessly against the wall of the jar. All around him, Seth heard the tinkling of miniature bells. The other fairies were pointing and laughing. The fairy in the jar beat against the glass even harder, but to no avail.

Seth had captured his prize.

※　※　※

Grandpa dipped the wand into the bottle and raised it to his lips. As he blew gently, several bubbles streamed from the plastic circle. The bubbles floated across the porch.

"You never know what will fascinate them," he said. "But bubbles usually do the trick."

Grandpa sat in a large wicker rocker. Kendra, Seth, and Dale sat nearby. The setting sun streaked the horizon with red and purple.

"I try not to bring unnecessary technology onto the property," he continued, dipping the wand again. "I just can't resist with bubbles." He blew, and more bubbles took shape.

A fairy, glowing softly in the fading light, approached one of the bubbles. After considering it for a moment, she touched it, and the bubble turned bright green. Another touch and it was an inky blue. Another and it was gold.

Grandpa kept the bubbles coming, and more fairies came to the porch. Soon all the bubbles were changing colors. The hues became more luminous as the fairies competed against one another. Bubbles ruptured with flashes of light.

One fairy gathered bubbles until she had assembled a

bouquet that resembled a bunch of multicolored grapes. Another fairy entered a bubble and inflated it from the inside until it tripled in size and burst with a violet flash. A bubble near Kendra appeared to be full of winking fireflies. One near Grandpa turned to ice, fell to the porch, and shattered.

The fairies flocked near Grandpa, eager for the next bubbles. He kept them coming, and the fairies continued to display their creativity. They filled bubbles with shimmering mist. They linked them in chains. They transformed them into balls of fire. The surface of one reflected like a mirror. Another took on the shape of a pyramid. Another crackled with electricity.

When Grandpa put the bubble solution away, the fairies gradually dispersed. The dwindling sunset was almost gone. A few fairies played among the chimes, making soft music. "Unbeknownst to most of the family," Grandpa said, "a few of your cousins have visited me here. None of them came close to figuring out what is really going on."

"Didn't you give them clues?" Kendra asked.

"No more or less than I gave you. They were not of the proper mind-set."

"Was it Erin?" Seth asked. "She's a goober."

"You be kind," Grandpa scolded. "What I want to say is that I admire how you children have taken all of this in stride. You have adapted impressively to this unusual place."

"Lena said we could have a party with goat people," Seth said.

"I wouldn't hold my breath if I were you. Why was she talking about satyrs?"

"We found hoofprints in the kitchen," Kendra said.

"Things got a bit out of hand last night," Grandpa admitted. "Trust me, Seth, consorting with satyrs is the last thing a boy your age needs."

"Then why did you do it?" Seth asked.

"A visit from a fairy broker is a significant event, and carries certain expectations. I'll concede that the merriment borders on foolishness."

"Can I try blowing bubbles?" Seth asked.

"Another night. I'm planning a special excursion for you tomorrow. In the afternoon I need to visit the granary, and I mean to take you with me, let you see more of the property."

"Will we get to see something besides fairies?" Seth asked.

"Probably."

"I'm glad," Kendra said. "I want to see everything you're willing to show us."

"All in due time, my dear."

※ ※ ※

From her breathing, Seth was pretty sure Kendra was asleep. He sat up slowly. She did not move. He coughed weakly. She did not twitch.

He eased out of bed and crossed the attic floor to his dresser. Quietly he opened the third drawer down. There she was. Twig, grass, pebble, flower petals, mirror, and all. In the dark room, her inherent glimmer illuminated the entire drawer.

Her tiny hands were splayed against the wall of the jar, and she looked up at him desperately. She chirped something in a twittering language, motioning for him to open the lid.

Seth glanced over his shoulder. Kendra had not budged.

"Goodnight, little fairy," he whispered. "Don't worry. I'll feed you some milk in the morning."

He began shutting the drawer. The panicked fairy redoubled her frantic protestations. It looked like she was about to cry, which made Seth pause. Maybe he would let her go tomorrow.

"It's okay, little fairy," he said gently. "Go to sleep. I'll see you in the morning."

She clasped her hands together and shook them in a pleading motion, begging with her eyes. She was so pretty, that fiery red hair against her creamy skin. The perfect pet. Way better than a hen. What chicken could set bubbles on fire?

Closing the drawer, he returned to his bed.

CHAPTER EIGHT

Retaliation

Seth wiped sleep from the corner of his eye and stared at the ceiling for a moment. Rolling over, he saw that Kendra was not in her bed. Daylight streamed through the window. He stretched, arching his back with a groan. The mattress felt inviting. Maybe he could get up later.

No, he wanted to check on the fairy. He hoped some sleep had calmed her. Kicking off the tangled covers, Seth hurried over to the dresser. Pulling it open, he gasped.

The fairy was gone. In her place was a hairy tarantula with striped legs and shiny black eyes. Had it eaten her? He checked the lid. It was still on tight. Then it registered that he had not consumed any milk yet. This could be the other form the fairy appeared in. He would have expected a dragonfly, but supposed a tarantula was possible.

He also noticed that the mirror in the jar was broken. Had she smashed it with the pebble? It seemed like a good way to cut herself. "No roughhousing," he scolded. "I'll be right back."

※　※　※

A round loaf of bread sat on the table, a mottled mixture of white, black, brown, and orange. While Lena sliced it, Kendra took another sip of hot chocolate.

"Considering all the ingredients I left out, I thought they might make a jumble pie," Lena said. "But calico loaves are equally delicious. Try a piece." She handed Kendra a slice.

"They did a great job on the pot," Kendra said. "And the table looks perfect."

"Better than before," Lena agreed. "I like the new beveling. Brownies know their business."

Kendra inspected the slice of bread. The strange coloring continued all the way through, not just on the crust. She took a bite. Cinnamon and sugar dominated the flavoring. Eagerly she took another. It tasted like blackberry jam. The next tasted like chocolate with a hint of peanut butter. The following bite seemed saturated with vanilla pudding. "It has so many flavors!"

"And they never clash like they should," Lena said, taking a bite herself.

Feet bare, hair sticking up, Seth trotted into the room. "Good morning," he said. "Having breakfast?"

"You have to try this calico bread," Kendra said.

"In a minute," he replied. "Can I have a cup of hot chocolate?"

Lena filled a mug.

"Thank you," he said as she handed it to him. "I'll be right back. I forgot something upstairs." He hurried off, drinking from the mug.

"He's so weird," Kendra said, taking a bite of what now tasted like banana nut bread.

"Up to some mischief, if you ask me," Lena replied.

⚔ ⚔ ⚔

Seth set the mug on the dresser. Taking a calming breath, he silently prayed that the tarantula would be gone and the fairy would be there. He slid the drawer open.

A hideous little creature glared up from inside the jar. Baring pointy teeth, it hissed at him. Covered in brown, leathery skin, it stood taller than his middle finger. It was bald, with tattered ears, a narrow chest, a pot belly, and shriveled, spindly limbs. The lips were froglike, the eyes a glossy black, the nose a pair of slits above the mouth.

"What did you do to the fairy?" Seth asked.

The ugly creature hissed again, turning around. It had a pair of nubs above the bony shoulder blades. The nubs wiggled like the remnants of amputated wings.

"Oh, no! What happened to you?"

The creature stuck out a long black tongue and slapped

the glass with calloused hands. It jabbered something in a foul, raspy language.

What had happened? Why had the beautiful fairy mutated into a revolting little devil? Maybe some milk would help.

Seth snatched the jar from the drawer, grabbed the mug from the dresser, and bolted down the stairs from the attic to the hall. He dashed into the bathroom, locking the door behind him.

The mug was still a third full. Holding the jar over the sink, he poured some of the hot chocolate onto the lid. Most ran down the side of the jar, but a little dripped through the holes in the top.

One drop plopped on the creature's shoulder. It angrily motioned for Seth to unscrew the lid, and then pointed at the cup. Apparently it wanted to drink straight from the mug.

Seth examined the room. The window was shut, the door locked. He wadded a towel against the space at the bottom of the door. Inside the jar, the creature made pleading motions and pantomimed drinking from a cup.

Seth unscrewed the lid. With a powerful leap, the creature jumped out, landing on the counter. Crouching, snarling, it glared at Seth.

"I'm sorry your wings fell off," he said. "This might help."

He held the mug out toward the creature, wondering if it would sip the flavored milk or just climb inside the cup. Instead, it snapped at him, barely missing his finger. Seth jerked his hand away, sloshing hot chocolate onto the counter. Hissing, the agile creature dropped to the floor, raced over to the bathtub, and vaulted inside.

Before Seth could react, the creature squirmed down the drain. A final garbled burst of complaints issued from the dark hole, and then the creature was gone. Seth poured the remnants of the hot chocolate into the drain in case it could be of use to the deformed fairy.

He looked back at the jar, empty now except for a few wilting flower petals. He was not sure what he had done wrong, but he doubted Maddox would be very proud.

※　※　※

Later that morning, Seth sat in the tree house trying to find puzzle pieces that fit together. Now that the perimeter was finished, adding pieces was a challenge. They all looked the same.

He had avoided Kendra all morning. He did not feel like talking to anybody. He could not get over how foul the fairy had become. He was not sure what he had done, but he knew it was somehow his fault, some accidental consequence of catching the fairy. That was why she had been so frightened the night before. She knew he had doomed her to change into an ugly little monster.

The puzzle pieces started to vibrate. Soon the whole tree house was trembling. Were they having an earthquake? He had never been in an earthquake before.

Seth ran to the window. Fairies hovered everywhere, gathered in the air all around the tree house. Their arms were raised, and they seemed to be chanting.

One of the fairies pointed at Seth. Several glided closer to the window. One held her palm out in his direction; with a flash of light, the windowpane shattered. Seth jumped away from the window as several fairies flew in.

He ran to the hatch, but the tree house lurched so violently that he fell to the floor. The shaking was becoming intense. The floor was no longer level. A chair tipped over. The door to the hatch had slammed shut. He crawled toward it. Something hot stung the back of his neck. Multicolored lights began flashing.

Seth grabbed the door to the hatch, but it would not open. He tugged hard. Something seared the back of his hand.

Panicked, he returned to the window, struggling to keep his balance as the floor quaked beneath him. The flock of fairies continued to chant. He could hear their little voices. With a loud crack, the tree house suddenly tilted sideways. The view out the window switched from the fairies to the rapidly approaching ground.

Seth experienced a momentary sensation of weightlessness. Every object in the tree house was floating as everything plummeted together. Puzzle pieces filled the air. And then the tree house imploded.

✤ ✤ ✤

Kendra smeared sunblock across her arms, disliking the greasy feel of the lotion against her skin. She was tanner than when she had first arrived, but the sun was hot today, and she did not want to take any chances.

Her shadow was a small puddle at her feet. It was almost noon. Lunch was not far off, and then Grandpa Sorenson would take them to the granary. Kendra quietly hoped she would see a unicorn.

Suddenly she heard a tremendous crash from the corner of the yard. Then she heard Seth screaming.

What could have made such a huge noise? She did not have to run far in order to see the broken pile of rubble at the base of the tree.

Seth was sprinting toward her. His shirt was torn. He had blood on his face. Scores of fairies appeared to be in pursuit. Her initial thought was to make a joke about the fairies wanting revenge for him trying to catch them, until she realized it was probably true. Had the fairies thrown down the tree house?

"They're after me!" he yelled.

"Jump in the pool!" Kendra called.

Seth swerved in the direction of the pool and began pulling off his shirt. The ominous cloud of fairies had no trouble keeping up with him. They hurled sparkling streams of glitter. Casting his shirt aside, Seth sprang into the water.

"The fairies are after Seth!" Kendra cried, watching in horrified dismay.

The fairies hovered over the pool. After a few moments Seth surfaced. In flawless synchronization, the cloud of fairies swooped, diving toward him. He yelled as blazing rays of light began flaring around him, and ducked underwater again. The fairies plunged in after him.

He came to the surface gasping. The water churned. Seth floundered at the center of an underwater pyrotechnics display. Kendra rushed to the edge of the pool.

"Help!" he cried, raising a hand out of the water. The fingers were fused together like a flipper.

Kendra screamed. "They're attacking Seth! Help! Somebody! They're attacking Seth!"

He flailed toward the side of the pool. The roiling mass of fairies converged on Seth again, hauling him to the bottom of the pool amid eerie bursts of light. Kendra ran and seized the pool skimmer, swinging it at the relentless horde of fairies, never touching any of them no matter how dense the swarm appeared.

Seth resurfaced at the edge of the pool and threw his arms up onto the flagstones, trying to drag himself out of the water. Kendra stooped to assist him but shrieked instead. One arm was broad, flat, and rubbery. No elbow, no hand. A flipper coated in human skin. The other was long and boneless, a fleshy tentacle with limp fingers at the end.

She looked at his face. Long tusks curved down from a wide, lipless mouth. Patches of hair were missing. His eyes were glazed with terror.

The frenzied fairies mobbed him again, and he lost his grip on the side, vanishing in another pulsing succession of colored flashes. Steam sizzled up from the seething water.

"What is the meaning of this?" Grandpa Sorenson hollered, hustling to the edge of the pool. Lena followed behind him. The water in the pool flickered a few more times. Many of the fairies whizzed away. A few flew over to Grandpa.

One fairy in particular chirped angrily. She had short blue hair and silvery wings.

"He did what?" Grandpa said.

An unrecognizable monstrosity heaved itself out of the water and lay panting on the flagstones. The deformed creature had no clothes. Lena crouched beside him, placing a hand on his side.

"He had no idea that would happen," Grandpa complained. "It was innocent!"

The fairy twittered her disapproval.

Kendra gaped at the freakish form of her brother. Most of his hair had fallen out, revealing a lumpy scalp stippled with moles. His face was broader and flatter, with sunken eyes and tusks the size of bananas protruding from his mouth. A misshapen hump swelled high above his shoulders. On his back below the hump, four blowholes puckered for air. His legs had united into a single crude tail. He slapped the ground with his flipper arm. The tentacle writhed like a snake.

"An unlucky coincidence," Grandpa said consolingly.

"Most unfortunate. Can't you have mercy on the boy?"

The fairy chirped vehemently.

"I'm sorry you feel that way. I feel terrible about what happened. I assure you the atrocity was unintentional."

After a final outburst of squealing sounds, the fairy zoomed away.

"Are you okay?" Kendra said, squatting beside Seth.

He made a garbled moan, then a second, more distressed complaint that sounded like a donkey gargling mouthwash.

"Hush, Seth," Grandpa said. "You've lost the ability of speech."

"I'll fetch Dale," Lena said, hurrying off.

"What have they done to him?" Kendra asked.

"An act of vengeance," Grandpa said grimly.

"For trying to catch fairies?"

"For succeeding."

"He caught one?"

"He did."

"So they turned him into a deformed walrus? I thought they couldn't use magic against us!"

"He used potent magic to transform the captured fairy into an imp, unwittingly opening the door for magical retribution."

"Seth doesn't know any magic!"

"I'm sure it was accidental," Grandpa said. "Can you understand me, Seth? Slap your flipper three times if you grasp what I am saying."

The flipper flapped against the flagstones three times.

"It was very foolish to catch a fairy, Seth," Grandpa said. "I warned you they were unsafe. But I share some of the blame. I'm sure you were inspired by Maddox and wanted to begin a career as a fairy broker."

Seth nodded awkwardly, his entire bloated torso bobbing up and down.

"I should have specifically forbidden it. I forget how curious and daring children can be. And how resourceful. I would never have supposed you were capable of actually trapping one."

"What magic did he use?" Kendra asked, on the verge of hysterics.

"If a captured fairy is kept indoors from sunset to sunrise, it changes into an imp."

"What's an imp?"

"A fallen fairy. Nasty little creatures. Imps despise themselves as much as fairies adore themselves. Just as fairies are drawn to beauty, imps are drawn to ugliness."

"Their personalities change so quickly?"

"Their personalities remain the same," Grandpa said. "Shallow and self-absorbed. The change in appearance reveals the tragic side of that mind-set. Vanity curdles into misery. They become spiteful and jealous, wallowing in wretchedness."

"What about the fairies Maddox caught? Why don't they change?"

"He avoids leaving the cages indoors overnight. His

captured fairies spend at least part of every night out-doors."

"Just putting the container outside prevents them from becoming imps?"

"Sometimes powerful magic is accomplished by simple means."

"Why did the other fairies attack Seth? Why would they care, if they're so selfish?"

"They care because they are selfish. Each fairy worries she could be next. I am told Seth even left a mirror with the fairy, so she could behold herself after she fell. The fairies considered that act particularly cruel."

Grandpa answered every question with great calm, no matter how accusingly or angrily Kendra asked it. His peaceful demeanor was helping her calm down a bit. "I'm sure it was an accident," she said.

Seth nodded vigorously, blubber jiggling.

"I suspect no malice. It was an unfortunate mishap. But the fairies have little interest in his motives. They were within their rights to exact retribution."

"You can switch him back."

"Restoring Seth to his original form is well beyond my abilities."

Seth let out a long, mournful bellow. Kendra patted his hump. "We have to do something!"

"Yes," Grandpa said. He placed his hands over his eyes and then dragged them down his face. "This would be very complicated to explain to your parents."

"Who can fix him? Maddox?"

"Maddox is no magician. Besides, he is long gone. Though I hesitate, I can think of only one person who might be able to undo the enchantments placed on your brother."

"Who?"

"Seth has met her."

"The witch?"

Grandpa nodded. "Under the circumstances, our only hope is Muriel Taggert."

※　※　※

The wheelbarrow swayed as it bumped over a root. Dale managed to steady it. Seth groaned. He was naked except for a white towel wrapped around his middle.

"Sorry, Seth," Dale said. "This is a tricky path."

"Are we almost there?" Kendra asked.

"Not much farther," Grandpa replied.

They walked single file, Grandpa in the lead, followed by Dale pushing the wheelbarrow, and then Kendra in the rear. What had begun as a nearly indiscernible trail near the barn had broadened into a well-trodden path. Later they branched off onto a smaller track. They had crossed no new paths since then.

"The woods seem so quiet," Kendra said.

"They are quietest when you stay on the paths," Grandpa said.

"It seems too quiet."

"There is a tension in the air. Your brother committed a serious offense. The fall of a fairy is a woeful tragedy. The retribution of the fairies was equally brutal. Eager eyes await to see if the conflict will escalate."

"It won't, right?"

"I hope not. If Muriel cures your brother, the fairies could interpret it as an insult."

"Would they attack him again?"

"Probably not. At least not directly. The punishment has been administered."

"Can we heal the fairy?"

Grandpa shook his head. "No."

"Could the witch?"

"Seth was altered by magic imposed upon him. But the potential to fall and become an imp is a fundamental aspect of being a fairy. She transformed in accordance to a law that has existed as long as fairies have had wings. Muriel might be able to undo the enchantments forced upon Seth. Reversing the fall of a fairy would be far beyond her capacity."

"Poor fairy."

They reached a fork in the path. Grandpa turned left. "Almost there," he said. "Keep silent as we converse with her."

Kendra stared at the bushes and trees, expecting to find spiteful eyes glaring back at her. What creatures would come into view if all the greenery were removed? What would happen if she raced off the path? How long before some gruesome monster devoured her?

Grandpa stopped, pointing away into the trees. "Here we are."

Kendra saw the leafy shack in the distance, off the path through the trees.

"Too much undergrowth for the wheelbarrow," Dale said, scooping Seth into his arms. Although Seth was much more blubbery, he had not increased in size. As they waded through the undergrowth, Dale carried him without much difficulty.

The ivy-shrouded shack drew near. They walked around to the front. The filthy witch sat inside, her back against the tree stump, chewing on a knot in a bristly rope. A pair of imps sat on the tree stump. One was skinny, with prominent ribs and long, flat feet. The other was compact and plump.

"Hello, Muriel," Grandpa said.

The imps sprang from the trunk and scurried out of sight. Muriel looked up, a slow grin revealing decayed teeth. "Could that be Stan Sorenson?" She rubbed her eyes theatrically and squinted at him. "No, I must be dreaming. Stan Sorenson said he would never visit me again!"

"I need your help," Grandpa said.

"And you brought company. I remember Dale. Who is this fine young lady?"

"My granddaughter."

"She got none of your looks, lucky for her. My name is Muriel, dear, pleased to meet you."

"I'm Kendra."

"Yes, of course. You have that lovely pink nightgown with the bow on the bosom."

Kendra shot a look at Grandpa. How could this crazy witch know about her pajamas?

"I know a thing or two," Muriel continued, tapping her temple. "Telescopes are for stars, dear, not for trees."

"Pay her no heed," Grandpa said. "She wants to give you the impression that she has power to spy on you in your bedroom. Witches prey on fear. Her influence does not extend beyond the walls of this shack."

"Won't you step inside for some tea?" she offered.

"What news she has comes from imps," Grandpa continued. "And since imps are banned from the yard, her news came from a particular imp."

Muriel let out a shrieking laugh. The crazed cackle suited her haggard appearance much better than her speaking voice did.

"The imp saw your room, and heard conversations from wherever Seth stashed it," Grandpa concluded. "Nothing to fret about."

Muriel raised a finger in objection. "Nothing to fret about, you say?"

"Nothing the imp saw or heard could be harmful," Grandpa clarified.

"Except, perhaps, her own reflection," Muriel suggested. "Who is our final visitor? This poor, lumpy abomination? Could it be?" She clapped her hands and giggled.

"Did our stalwart adventurer have a mishap? Did his clever tongue finally betray him?"

"You know what happened," Grandpa said.

"I do, I do," she cackled. "I knew he was insolent, but never suspected such cruelty! Lock him in a shed, I say. For the sake of the fairies. Lock him up tight."

"Can you restore him?" Grandpa asked.

"Restore him?" the witch exclaimed. "After what he did?"

"It was an accident, as you are aware."

"Why not ask me to rescue a killer from the noose? To spare a traitor from his shame?"

"Can you do it?"

"Shall I conjure up a medal for him to wear as well? A badge of honor for his crime?"

"Can you?"

Muriel dropped the act. She regarded her visitors with a sly expression. "You know the price."

"I can't loosen a knot," Grandpa said.

Muriel tossed up her gnarled hands. "You know I need the energy from the knot for the spell," she said. "He has more than seventy separate hexes operating on him. You ought to untie seventy knots."

"What about—"

"No dickering. One knot, and your beastly grandson will be restored to his original form. Without the knot, I would never be able to counter the enchantment. This is fairy magic. You knew the price before you came. No dickering."

Grandpa sagged. "Show me the rope."

"Lay the boy at my threshold."

Dale placed Seth in front of the door. Standing in the doorway, Muriel held the rope out to Grandpa. There were two knots. Both had dried blood on them. One was still moist with saliva. "Take your pick," she said.

"Of my own free will, I sever this knot," Grandpa said. Leaning forward, he blew gently on the higher of the two knots. It unraveled.

The air trembled. On hot days, Kendra had seen the air shimmer in the distance. This was similar, but right in front of her. She felt pulsing vibrations, like she was standing in front of a powerful stereo speaker during a song with lots of bass. The ground seemed to be tipping.

Muriel extended a hand over Seth. She mumbled an unintelligible incantation. His blubber rippled as if he were boiling inside. It looked like thousands of worms were under his skin, squirming to find a way out. Putrid vapor fumed up from his flesh. His fat appeared to be evaporating. His misshapen body convulsed.

Kendra extended her arms and swayed as the ground teetered even more. There was a burst of darkness, an anti-flash, and Kendra stumbled, barely catching herself.

The odd sensation ended. The air cleared and balance returned. Seth sat up. He looked exactly like his old self. No tusks. No flippers. No blowholes. Just an eleven-year-old kid with a towel wrapped around his waist. He scrambled away from the shack and got to his feet.

"Satisfied?" Muriel asked.

"How do you feel, Seth?" Grandpa inquired.

Seth patted his bare chest. "I feel better."

Muriel grinned. "Thank you, little adventurer. You did me a great service today. I am indebted."

"You shouldn't have done it, Grandpa," Seth said.

"Had to be done," he said. "We best be going."

"Stay a while," Muriel offered.

"No thanks," Grandpa said.

"Very well. Spurn my hospitality. Kendra, nice to meet you, may you find less happiness than you deserve. Dale, you are as mute as your brother, and nearly as pale. Seth, please have another mishap soon. Stan, you lack the wit of an orangutan, bless your soul. Do not be strangers."

Kendra gave Seth socks, shoes, shorts, and a shirt. Once he put them on, they returned to the path.

"Can I ride in the wheelbarrow on the way back?" Seth asked.

"You ought to push me," Dale grumbled.

"How did it feel being a walrus?" Kendra asked.

"Is that what I was?"

"A mutant humpbacked walrus with a deformed tail," she clarified.

"I wish we had a camera! It was weird breathing through my back. And it was hard to move. Nothing felt right."

"Might be safer not to converse so loudly," Grandpa said.

"I couldn't talk," Seth said more quietly. "I felt like I still knew how, but the words came out all tangled. My mouth and tongue were different."

"What about Muriel?" Kendra asked. "If she unties that last knot, will she be free?"

"She was originally bound by thirteen knots," Grandpa said. "She can loosen none on her own, though it doesn't seem to stop her from trying. But other mortals can undo the knots by asking a favor and blowing on them. Powerful magic holds the knot in place. When released, Muriel can channel that magic into granting the favor."

"So if you ever need her help again . . ."

"I will look elsewhere," Grandpa said. "I never wanted her to get down to a single knot. Freeing her is not an option."

"I'm sorry I ended up helping her," Seth said.

"Did you learn anything from the ordeal?" Grandpa asked.

Seth lowered his head. "I feel really bad about the fairy. She didn't deserve what happened to her." Grandpa made no response, and Seth kept studying his shoes. "I shouldn't have messed around with magical creatures," he finally admitted.

Grandpa placed a hand on his shoulder. "I know you meant no harm. Around here, what you don't know can hurt you. And others. If you have learned to be more careful and compassionate in the future, and to show greater respect for the inhabitants of this preserve, then at least some good came of all this."

"I learned something too," Kendra said. "Humans and walruses should never mix."

CHAPTER NINE

Hugo

The triangular wooden board rested on Kendra's lap. She studied the pegs, planning her next jump. Beside her, Lena gently tilted back and forth on a rocker, watching the moon rise. From the porch, only a few fairies could be seen gliding around the garden. Fireflies twinkled among them in the silver moonlight.

"Not many fairies out tonight," Kendra said.

"It may be some time before the fairies return in force to our gardens," Lena said.

"Can't you explain everything to them?"

Lena chuckled. "They would listen to your grandfather before they would ever heed me."

"Weren't you sort of one of them?"

"That is the problem. Watch." Lena closed her eyes

and began to sing softly. Her high, trilling voice gave life to a wistful melody. Several fairies darted over from the garden, hovering around her in a loose semicircle, interrupting the warbling tune with fervent chirping.

Lena quit singing and said something in an unintelligible language. The fairies chirped back. Lena made a final remark, and the fairies flew away.

"What were they saying?" Kendra asked.

"They told me I should be ashamed to sing a naiadic tune," Lena replied. "They detest reminders that I was once a nymph, especially if those reminders imply that I am at peace with my decision."

"They acted pretty upset."

"Much of their time is spent mocking mortals. Any time one of us crosses over to mortality, it makes the others wonder what they might be missing. Especially if we appear content. They ridicule me mercilessly."

"You don't let it get to you?"

"Not really. They do know how to needle me. They tease me about growing old—my hair, my wrinkles. They ask how I will enjoy being buried in a box." Lena frowned, gazing thoughtfully into the night. "I felt my age today when you called for help."

"What do you mean?" Kendra jumped a peg on the triangular wooden board.

"I tried to rush to your aid, but ended up sprawled on the kitchen floor. Your grandfather reached your side before I did, and he is no athlete."

"It wasn't your fault."

"In my youth I would have been there in a flash. I used to be handy in an emergency. Now I come hobbling to the rescue."

"You still get around great." Kendra was running out of moves. She had already stranded a peg.

Lena shook her head. "I would not last a minute on the trapeze or the tightrope. Once I played on them with facile agility. The curse of mortality. You spend the first portion of your life learning, growing stronger, more capable. And then, through no fault of your own, your body begins to fail. You regress. Strong limbs become feeble, keen senses grow dull, hardy constitutions deteriorate. Beauty withers. Organs quit. You remember yourself in your prime, and wonder where that person went. As your wisdom and experience are peaking, your traitorous body becomes a prison."

Kendra had no moves left on her perforated board. Three pegs remained. "I never thought of it that way."

Lena took the board from Kendra and began setting up the pegs. "In their youth, mortals behave more like nymphs. Adulthood seems impossibly distant, let alone the enfeeblement of old age. But ponderously, inevitably, it overtakes you. I find it a frustrating, humbling, infuriating experience."

"When we talked before, you said you would not change your decision," Kendra reminded her.

"True, given the opportunity, I would choose Patton

every time. And now that I have experienced mortality, I do not imagine I could be content with my former life. But the pleasures of mortality, the thrills of living, come with a price. Pain, illness, the decline of age, the loss of loved ones—those things I could do without."

The pegs were set up. Lena began jumping them. "I am impressed by how glibly most mortals confront the debilitation of the body. Patton. Your grandparents. Many others. They just accept it. I have always feared aging. The inevitability of it haunts me. Ever since I abandoned the pond, the prospect of death has been a menacing shadow in the back of my mind."

She jumped the final peg, leaving only one. Kendra had seen her do it before, but had not yet succeeded in copying her moves.

Lena sighed softly. "Because of my nature, I may have to endure old age for decades longer than regular human beings. The humiliating finale to the mortal condition."

"At least you're a peg-jumping genius," Kendra said.

Lena smiled. "The solace of my winter years."

"You can still paint, and cook, and do all sorts of things."

"I do not mean to complain. These are not problems to share with young minds."

"It's okay. You aren't scaring me. You're right, I can't really picture being grown up. Part of me wonders if high school will ever really happen. Sometimes I think maybe I'll die young."

The door to the house opened, and Grandpa's head poked out. "Kendra, I need to have some words with you and Seth."

"Okay, Grandpa."

"Come to the study."

Lena stood, motioning for Kendra to hurry along. Kendra entered the house and followed Grandpa into the study. Seth was already seated in one of the oversized chairs, drumming his fingers on the armrest. Kendra claimed the other one while Grandpa settled in behind his desk.

"The day after tomorrow is June twenty-first," Grandpa said. "Do either of you know the significance of that date?"

Kendra and Seth shared a glance. "Your birthday?" Seth attempted.

"The summer solstice," Grandpa said. "The longest day of the year. The night before is a holiday of riotous abandon for the whimsical creatures of Fablehaven. Four nights a year, the boundaries that define where different entities can venture dissolve. These nights of revelry are essential to maintaining the segregation that normally prevails here. On Midsummer Eve, the only limits to where any creature can roam and work mischief are the walls of this house. Unless invited, they cannot enter."

"Midsummer Eve is tomorrow night?" Seth said.

"I did not want to leave you time to fret over it. As long as you obey my instructions, the night will pass without incident. It will be loud, but you will be safe."

"What other days do they run wild?" Kendra asked.

"The winter solstice and the two equinoxes. Midsummer Eve tends to be the rowdiest of them all."

"Can we watch out the windows?" Seth asked eagerly.

"No," Grandpa said. "Nor would you enjoy what you saw. On the festival nights, nightmares take shape and prowl the yard. Ancient entities of supreme evil patrol the darkness in search of prey. You will be in bed at sundown. You will wear earplugs. And you will not arise until sunrise dispels the horrors of the night."

"Should we sleep in your room?" Kendra asked.

"The attic playroom is the safest place in the house. Extra protections have been placed on it as a sanctuary for children. Even if, by some misfortune, unsavory creatures entered the house, your room would remain secure."

"Has anything ever gotten into the house?" Kendra asked.

"Nothing unwanted has breached these homestead walls," Grandpa said. "Still, we can never be too careful. Tomorrow you will help prepare some defenses to afford us an extra layer of protection. Because of the recent uproar with the fairies, I fear this could be a particularly chaotic Midsummer Eve."

"Has anyone ever died here?" Seth asked. "On this property, I mean?"

"We should save that topic for another time," Grandpa said, standing up.

"That one guy changed into dandelion seeds," Kendra said.

"Anybody else?" Seth insisted.

Grandpa regarded them soberly for a moment. "As you are learning, these preserves are hazardous places. Accidents have occurred in the past. Those accidents generally happen to people who venture where they do not belong or tamper with matters beyond their understanding. If you adhere to my rules, you should have nothing to worry about."

* * *

The sun had not yet risen far above the horizon as Seth and Dale walked along the rutted lane that ran away from the barn. Seth had never particularly noticed the weedy cart track. The lane began on the far side of the barn and led into the woods. After meandering for some time beneath the trees, the track continued across an expansive meadow.

Overhead, only a few wispy clouds interrupted the bright blue sky. Dale walked briskly, forcing Seth to hustle in order to keep up. Seth was already getting sweaty. The warm day promised to be hot by noon.

Seth kept watch for interesting creatures. He spotted birds, squirrels, and rabbits in the meadow, but saw nothing supernatural.

"Where are all the magical animals?" Seth asked.

"This is the calm before the storm," Dale said. "I expect most of them are resting up for tonight."

"What sort of monsters will be out tonight?"

"Stan warned that you might try to pry information out of me. Best not to be so curious about those kinds of things."

"Not telling me is what makes me curious!"

"It's for your own good," Dale said. "Part of the idea is that telling you might make you scared. The other part is that telling you might make you even more curious."

"If you tell me, I promise I'll stop being curious."

Dale shook his head. "What makes you think you can keep that promise?"

"I can't possibly get more curious than I already am. Not knowing anything is the hardest."

"Well, fact of the matter is, I can't give a very satisfying answer to your question. Have I seen strange things, frightening things, in my time here? You bet. Not just on festival nights. Have I stolen a peek out the window on a festival night? A time or two, sure. But I learned to quit looking. People aren't meant to have things like that in their minds. Makes it hard to sleep. I don't look anymore. Neither does Lena, neither does your grandfather, neither does your grandmother. And we're adults."

"What did you see?"

"How about we change the subject?"

"You're killing me. I have to know!"

Dale stopped and faced him. "Seth, you only think you want to know. It seems harmless to know, walking under a clear blue sky on a fine morning with a friend. But what about tonight, alone in your room, in the dark, when the night outside is full of unnatural sounds? You might regret me putting a face to what is wailing outside the window."

Seth swallowed. He looked up at Dale, eyes wide. "What kind of face?"

"Let's leave it at this. To this day, when I'm out and about after dark, I am sorry I looked. When you're a few years older, a day will come when your grandfather will give you an opportunity to look out the window on a festival night. If you start feeling inquisitive, postpone your curiosity until that moment. If it were me, if I could go back, I'd skip looking altogether."

"Easy to say after you looked."

"Not easy to say. I paid a heavy price to say it. Many sleepless nights."

"What can be so bad? I can imagine some scary things."

"I thought the same thing. I failed to appreciate that imagining and seeing are two very different things."

"If you already looked, why not look again?"

"I don't want to see anything else. I'd rather just guess at the rest." Dale started walking again.

"I still want to know," Seth said.

"Smart people learn from their mistakes. But the real sharp ones learn from the mistakes of others. Don't pout; you're about to see something impressive. And it won't even give you nightmares."

"What?"

"See where the road goes over that rise?"

"Yeah."

"The surprise is on the far side."

"You're sure?"

"Positive."

"It better not be another fairy," Seth said.

"What's the matter with fairies?"

"I've already seen about a billion of them and also they turned me into a walrus."

"It's not a fairy."

"It's not like a waterfall or something?" Seth asked suspiciously.

"No, you'll like it."

"Good, because you're getting my hopes up. Is it dangerous?"

"It could be, but we should be safe."

"Let's hurry." Seth dashed up the rise. He glanced back at Dale, who continued walking. Not a great sign. If the surprise were dangerous, Dale would not want him running ahead.

At the top of the rise Seth halted, staring down the gentle slope on the far side. Not a hundred yards away, a huge creature was wading through a hayfield wielding a pair of gigantic scythes. The hulking figure slashed down wide swaths of alfalfa at a relentless pace, both scythes hissing and chiming without pause.

Dale joined Seth atop the rise. "What is it?" Seth asked.

"Our golem, Hugo. Come see."

Dale left the cart track and started across the field toward the toiling goliath. "What's a golem?" Seth asked, trailing after him.

"Watch." Dale raised his voice. "Hugo, halt!"

The scythes stopped cutting in mid-stroke.

"Hugo, come!"

The herculean mower turned and jogged toward them with long, loping strides. Seth could feel the ground vibrate as Hugo approached. Still clutching the scythes, the massive golem came to a halt in front of Dale, looming over him.

"He's made of dirt?" Seth asked.

"Soil, clay, and stone," Dale said. "Granted the semblance of life by a powerful enchanter. Hugo was donated to the preserve a couple hundred years ago."

"How tall is he?"

"Over nine feet when he stands up straight. Mostly he slouches closer to eight."

Seth gawked at the behemoth. In form he looked more apelike than human. Aside from his impressive height, Hugo was broad, with thick limbs and disproportionately large hands and feet. Tufts of grass and the occasional dandelion sprouted from his earthen body. He had an oblong head with a square jaw. Crude features resembled nose, mouth, and ears. The eyes were a pair of vacant hollows beneath a jutting brow.

"Can he talk?"

"No. He tries to sing. Hugo, sing us a song!"

The wide mouth began to open and close, and out rumbled a series of gravelly roars, some long, some short, none of them bearing much resemblance to music. Hugo cocked his head back and forth, as if swaying to the melody. Seth tried to stifle his laughter.

"Hugo, stop singing."

The golem fell silent.

"He isn't very good," Seth said.

"About as musical as a landslide."

"Does it embarrass him?"

"He doesn't think like we do. Doesn't get happy or sad or angry or bored. He's like a robot. Hugo just obeys commands."

"Can I tell him to do stuff?"

"If I order him to obey you," Dale said. "Otherwise he just listens to me, Lena, and your grandparents."

"What else can he do?"

"He understands a lot. He performs all sorts of manual labor. It would take quite a team to match all the work he does around here. Hugo never sleeps. If you leave him with a list of chores, he'll labor through the night."

"I want to tell him to do something."

"Hugo, put down the scythes," said Dale.

The golem set the scythes on the ground.

"Hugo, this is Seth. Hugo will obey Seth's next command."

"Now?" asked Seth.

"Say his name first, so he knows you're addressing him."

"Hugo, do a cartwheel."

Hugo held out his palms and shrugged.

"He doesn't know what you mean," Dale said. "Can you do a cartwheel?"

"Yeah."

"Hugo, Seth is going to show you a cartwheel."

Seth put up his hands, lunged sideways, and did a cartwheel with sloppy form. "Hugo," Dale said, "obey Seth's next command."

"Hugo, do a cartwheel."

The golem raised his arms, lurched to one side, and completed an awkward cartwheel. The ground trembled.

"Pretty good for a first try," Seth said.

"He duplicated yours. Hugo, when you do a cartwheel, keep your body straighter and aligned on a single plane, like a wheel turning. Hugo, do a cartwheel!"

This time Hugo executed a nearly perfect cartwheel. His hands left prints in the field. "He learns fast," Seth exclaimed.

"Anything physical, leastways." Dale put his hands on his hips. "I'm sick of walking. What do you say we let Hugo take us to our next stop?"

"Really?"

"If you'd rather walk we can always—"

"No way!"

❧ ❧ ❧

Kendra used a hacksaw to separate another pumpkin from the vine. Further down the long trough of soil, Lena was cutting a large red one. Nearly half the greenhouse was devoted to pumpkins, big and small, white, yellow, orange, red, and green.

They had arrived at the greenhouse by a faint trail through the woods. Aside from the pumpkins and plants, the glass structure contained a generator to power the lights and the climate control.

"We really have to cut three hundred?" Kendra asked.

"Just be glad you don't have to load them," Lena said.

"Who does?"

"It's a surprise."

"Are jack-o-lanterns really such a big deal?"

"Do they work? Quite well. Especially if we can convince fairies to fill them."

"With magic?"

"To dwell in them for the night," explained Lena. "Fairy lanterns have long been among the surest protections from creatures with dubious intentions."

"But I thought the house was already safe." Kendra began sawing the stem of a tall orange pumpkin.

"Redundancies in security are wise on festival nights. Particularly on a Midsummer Eve after all the recent commotion."

"How will we ever carve all of them before tonight?"

"Leave that to Dale. He could carve them all himself

with time to spare. Not always the most artful renderings, but the man can mass produce. You carve only for fun; he knows how to carve for need."

"I've never liked pulling out the guts," said Kendra.

"Really?" Lena said. "I love the slimy texture, getting greasy up to my elbows. Like playing in the mud. We'll have delicious pies afterwards."

"Is this white one too small?"

"Maybe save it for autumn."

"Do you think the fairies will come?"

"Hard to say," Lena admitted. "Some, for sure. Normally we have no trouble filling as many lanterns as we care to carve, but tonight might be an exception."

"What if they don't show up?" Kendra asked.

"We'll be fine. Artificial lighting works, just not as well as fairies. With the fairy lanterns, the commotion stays farther from the house. In addition, Stan will be putting out tribal masks, herbs, and other safeguards."

"Is the night really so awful?"

"You'll hear plenty of disturbing sounds."

"Maybe we should have skipped the milk this morning."

Lena shook her head, not lifting her eyes from her work. "Some of the most insidious tricks employed tonight will involve artifice and illusion. Without the milk you could be even more susceptible. It would only broaden their ability to mask their true appearance."

Kendra severed another pumpkin. "Either way, I won't be looking."

"I wish we could transplant some of your common sense to your brother."

"After all that's happened, I'm sure he'll behave tonight."

The door to the greenhouse opened, and Dale poked his head in. "Kendra, come here, I want you to meet somebody."

Kendra walked to the door with Lena behind her. In the doorway, Kendra paused and let out a small shriek. A bulky creature with a simian build was marching toward the greenhouse pulling a rickshaw-type contraption the size of a wagon. "What is it?"

"He's Hugo," Seth crowed from inside the handcart. "He's a robot made of dirt!" He jumped out of the cart and ran over to Kendra.

"I ran ahead so you could see him approach," Dale said.

"Hugo can run really fast when you tell him to," Seth gushed. "Dale let me give him orders and he obeyed everything I said. See? He's waiting for instructions."

Hugo stood motionless beside the greenhouse, still holding the rickshaw. Had she not just seen Hugo moving, Kendra would have assumed he was a crude statue. Seth shouldered past Kendra into the greenhouse.

"What is he?" Kendra asked Lena.

"A golem," she replied. "Animated matter granted rudimentary intelligence. He does most of the heavy labor around here."

"He's loading the pumpkins."

"And rolling them to the house in his cart."

Seth exited the greenhouse toting a fairly large pumpkin. "Can I show her a command?" he asked.

"Sure," Dale said. "Hugo, obey the next command from Seth."

Holding the pumpkin at his waist with both hands, leaning back a bit to stay balanced, Seth approached the golem. "Hugo, take this pumpkin and throw it as far as you can into the woods."

The inert golem sprang to life. Grasping the pumpkin in one massive hand, he twisted and then fiercely uncoiled, hurling the pumpkin into the sky like a discus. Dale whistled softly as the pumpkin shrank into the distance, finally dropping out of sight, an orange speck vanishing behind far-off treetops.

"Did you see that?" Seth cried. "He's better than a water balloon launcher!"

"Regular catapult," Dale murmured.

"Very impressive," Lena agreed dryly. "Forgive me if I hope to put a few of our pumpkins to more practical use. You boys come help us cut the rest of our harvest so we can get them loaded."

"Can't Hugo do a few more tricks?" Seth begged. "He knows cartwheels."

"There will be time for nonsense later," Lena assured him. "We need to finish our preparations for this evening."

CHAPTER TEN

Midsummer Eve

Grandpa prodded the logs in the fireplace with a poker. A shower of sparks swirled up the chimney as one log split open, revealing an interior of glowing embers. Dale poured himself a cup of steaming coffee, adding three spoonfuls of sugar. Lena peered out the window through the blinds.

"The sun will reach the horizon in moments," she announced.

Kendra sat beside Seth on the sofa, watching Grandpa stoke the fire. The preparations were all in place. The entrances to the house were crowded with jack-o'-lanterns. Lena had been right—Dale had carved more than two hundred of them. Not quite thirty fairies had reported for duty, many fewer than Grandpa had expected, even given the recently strained relations.

Eight of the fairy lanterns were placed on the roof outside the attic, four at each window. Glow sticks illuminated most of the pumpkins, two in each. Grandpa Sorenson apparently ordered them in bulk.

"Will it start right when the sun goes down?" Seth asked.

"Things won't really get going until twilight fades," Grandpa said, setting the poker beside the other fire irons. "But the hour has come for you children to retire to your room."

"I want to stay up with you," Seth said.

"The attic bedroom is the safest place in the house," Grandpa said.

"Why don't we all stay in the attic?" Kendra asked.

Grandpa shook his head. "The spells that make the attic impenetrable function only if it is occupied by children. Without children, or with adults in the room, the barriers become ineffectual."

"Isn't the whole house supposed to be safe?" Kendra asked.

"I believe so, but on an enchanted preserve, nothing is ever certain. I am concerned by the scant number of fairies who reported this afternoon. I worry this could be a particularly uproarious Midsummer Eve. Perhaps the worst since I've lived here."

A long, mournful howl underscored his statement. The

disturbing call was answered by a stronger howl, closer, that ended with a cackle. Chills tingled behind Kendra's shoulders.

"The sun is gone," Lena reported from the window. She squinted, then put a hand to her mouth. Closing the slat, she stepped away from the blinds. "They're already entering the yard."

Kendra leaned forward. Lena really looked upset. She had paled visibly. Her dark eyes were unsettled.

Grandpa scowled. "Real trouble?"

She nodded.

Grandpa clapped his hands together. "Up to the attic."

The tension in the room prevented Kendra from uttering any protest. Apparently Seth sensed the same urgency. Grandpa Sorenson followed them up the stairs, down the hall, and up into their bedroom.

"Get under your covers," Grandpa said.

"What's around the beds?" Seth asked, examining the floor.

"Circles of special salt," Grandpa said. "An extra protection."

Kendra stepped carefully over the salt, pulled back the covers, and climbed into bed. The sheets felt cool. Grandpa handed her a pair of small, spongy cylinders.

"Earplugs," he said, passing a pair to Seth as well. "I suggest you wear them. They should help mute the tumult so you can sleep."

"Just cram them in our ears?" Seth said, eyeing one suspiciously.

"That's the idea," Grandpa said.

An eruption of high-pitched laughter blared up from the yard. Kendra and Seth exchanged a concerned glance. Grandpa took a seat at the edge of Kendra's bed.

"I need you kids to be brave and responsible for me tonight," he said.

They nodded silently.

"You should know," he went on, "I didn't let you come here merely as a favor to your parents. Your grandmother and I are getting on in years. The day will come when somebody else will need to care for this preserve. We need to find heirs. Dale is a good man, but he has no interest in running things here. You kids have impressed me so far. You are bright, adventurous, and courageous.

"There are some unpleasant aspects to living here. Festival nights are a good example. Perhaps you wonder why we don't just all go spend the night in a hotel. If we did, we would return to find the house in ruins. Our presence is essential to the magic that protects these walls. If you are ever going to be involved with the work on this preserve, you will need to learn to cope with certain unpleasant realities. Look at tonight as a test. If the chaotic clamor outside is too much for you, then you do not belong here. There is no shame in this. People who belong here are rare."

"We'll be fine," Seth said.

"I believe you will. Listen carefully to my final instructions. Once I leave the room, no matter what you hear, no matter what happens, do not leave your beds. We will not come to check on you until morning. You may think you hear me, or Dale, or Lena, asking to come in. Be forewarned. It will not be us.

"This room is invulnerable unless you open a window or the door. Remain in your beds and that will not happen. With the fairy lanterns at your window, odds are that nothing will come near this part of the house. Try to ignore the tumult of the night, and we'll all share a special breakfast in the morning. Any questions?"

"I'm scared," Kendra said. "Don't go."

"You'll be safer without me. We'll be keeping watch downstairs all night. Everything will be fine. Just go to sleep."

"It's okay, Grandpa," Seth said. "I'll keep an eye on her."

"Keep the other on yourself," Grandpa said sternly. "You mind me tonight. This is no game."

"I will."

Outside the wind began to whistle through the trees. The day had been calm, but now a groaning gust shook the house. Overhead the shingles rattled and the timbers creaked.

Grandpa crossed to the door. "Strange winds are blowing. I better get downstairs. Goodnight, sleep tight, I'll greet you at sunrise." He closed the door. The wind subsided. Goldilocks clucked softly.

"You've got to be kidding," Kendra said.

"I know," Seth said. "I'm practically wetting the bed."

"I don't think I'll sleep all night."

"I know I won't."

"We better try," said Kendra.

"Okay."

Kendra inserted the earplugs. Closing her eyes, she curled up and snuggled into her covers. All she had to do was fall asleep, and she could escape the frightening sounds of the night. She forced herself to relax, letting her body go limp, and tried to clear her mind.

It was hard not to fantasize about inheriting the estate. No way would they give it to Seth! He would blow the whole place up in five minutes! What would it be like to know all the mysterious secrets of Fablehaven? It might be scary if she were alone. She would have to share the secret with her parents so they could live with her.

After a couple of minutes she rolled over to face the other direction. She always had a tough time falling asleep when she was too deliberate about it. She tried to think of nothing, tried to focus on calm, regular breathing. Seth was saying something, but the earplugs muffled it. She pulled them out.

"What?"

"I said, the suspense is killing me. Are you actually using the earplugs?"

"Of course. You're not?"

"I don't want to miss anything."

"Are you crazy?"

"I'm not tired at all," he said. "Are you?"

"Not much."

"Dare me to look out the window?"

"Don't be stupid!"

"It's barely sunset. What better time to look?"

"How about never."

"You're a bigger chicken than Goldilocks."

"You've got less brains than Hugo."

The wind rose again, steadily gaining force. Warbling moans echoed on the breeze, groaning in different pitches, forming eerie, discordant harmonies. A long, birdlike scream overpowered the ghostly chorus of moans, starting at one side of the house, passing overhead, and finally fading. In the distance, a bell began to toll.

Seth no longer looked quite so brave. "Maybe we should try to get some sleep," he said, putting in the earplugs.

Kendra did likewise. The sounds were muffled, but continued: the haunted wind lamenting, the house shuddering, an increasing assortment of shrieks, screams, howls, and wild bursts of gibbering laughter. The pillow grew warm, so Kendra flipped it over to the cold side.

The only light in the room had been filtering through the curtains. As twilight dimmed, the room darkened. Kendra pressed her hands over her ears, trying to augment the dampening power of the earplugs. She told herself the sounds were just a storm.

A deep, throbbing beat joined the cacophony, keeping a steady rhythm. As the pulsing percussion increased in volume and tempo, it was accompanied by chanting in a wailing language. Kendra resisted otherworldly images of vicious demons on the hunt.

A pair of hands closed around her throat. She jumped and flailed, smacking Seth across the cheek with the back of her hand.

"Jeez!" Seth complained, stumbling away.

"You asked for it! What's the matter with you?"

"You should have seen your face," he laughed, recovering from the slap.

"Get back in bed."

He sat on the side of her bed. "You should take out your earplugs. The noise isn't so bad after a while. It reminds me of that CD Dad plays on Halloween."

She removed them. "Except it's shaking the house. And it isn't make-believe."

"Don't you want to look out the window?"

"No! Stop talking about it!"

Seth leaned over and turned on the nightlight—a glowing statuette of Snoopy. "I don't see the big deal. I mean, there are all sorts of cool things out there right now. What's wrong with just taking a little peek?"

"Grandpa said not to get out of your bed!"

"Grandpa lets people look when they get older," Seth said. "Dale told me. So it can't be that dangerous. Grandpa just thinks I'm an idiot."

"Yeah, and he's right!"

"Think about it. You wouldn't want to run across a tiger out in the wilderness. You'd be scared to death. But at a zoo, who cares? It can't get you. This room is safe. Peeking out the window will be like looking at a zoo full of monsters."

"More like looking out of a shark cage."

A sudden, staccato flurry of pounding shook the roof, as if a team of horses were galloping across the shingles. Seth flinched, raising his arms protectively. Kendra heard the creak and rattle of wagon wheels.

"Don't you want to see what that was?" Seth asked.

"Are you trying to tell me that didn't scare you?"

"I expect to be scared. That's the whole point!"

"If you don't get back in bed," warned Kendra, "I'm telling Grandpa in the morning."

"Don't you want to see who's playing the drums?"

"Seth, I'm not kidding. You probably won't even be able to see anything."

"We have a telescope."

Something outside roared, a thunderous bellow of bestial ferocity. It was enough to silence the conversation. The night continued to rage. The roar came again, if anything with greater intensity, momentarily drowning out all the other commotion.

Kendra and Seth eyed one another. "I bet it's a dragon," he said breathlessly, running over to the window.

"Seth, no!"

Seth pulled aside the curtain. The four jack-o'-lanterns shed a mellow illumination across the portion of the roof directly beyond the window. For a moment Seth thought he saw something swirling in the darkness at the edge of the light, a whirling mass of silky black fabric. Then he saw only blackness.

"No stars," he reported.

"Seth, get away from there." Kendra had her sheets pulled up to her eyes.

He squinted through the window a moment longer. "Too dark; I can't see anything." A glimmering fairy floated up from one of the jack-o'-lanterns, peering at Seth through the slightly warped windowpane. "Hey, a fairy came out." The tiny fairy waved an arm and was joined by three others. One made a face at Seth, and then all four streaked away into the night.

Now he could see nothing. Seth closed the curtain and backed away from the window. "You had your look," Kendra said. "Are you satisfied?"

"The fairies in the jack-o'-lanterns flew away," he said.

"Nice work. They probably saw who they were guarding."

"Actually, I think you're right. One made a face at me."

"Get back in bed," Kendra ordered.

The drumming ceased, along with the chanting. The ghostly wind grew quiet. The howls and screams and laughter diminished in volume and frequency. Something pattered across the roof. Then . . . silence.

"Something's wrong," Seth whispered.

"They probably saw you; get back in bed."

"I have a flashlight in my emergency kit." He went to the nightstand by his bed and withdrew a small flashlight from the cereal box.

Kendra kicked off her sheets and lunged at Seth, tackling him onto his bed. She wrenched the flashlight from his grasp and pushed off him to regain her feet. He charged her. Twisting, she used his momentum to shove him onto her bed.

"Quit it, Seth, or I'll go get Grandpa right now!"

"I'm not the one starting a fight!" His expression was a portrait of wounded resentment. She hated when he tried to act like the victim after initiating trouble.

"Neither am I."

"First you hit me, then you jump on me?"

"You stop breaking the rules or I'm going straight downstairs."

"You're worse than the witch. Grandpa should build you a shack."

"Get in your bed."

"Give me my light. I bought it with my own money."

They were interrupted by the sound of a baby crying. There was nothing desperate about it, just the bawling of an upset infant. The crying seemed to emanate from outside the darkened window.

"A little baby," Seth said.

"No, it's some trick."

"Maaamaaaaaaa," the baby whined.

"Sounds pretty real," Seth said. "Let me take a look."

"It's going to be a skeleton or something."

Seth grabbed the flashlight from Kendra. She neither gave it to him nor prevented him from taking it. He jogged over to the window. Holding the front of the flashlight against the windowpane, and cupping a hand around it to minimize reflection, he switched it on.

"Oh my gosh," he said. "It really is a baby!"

"Anything else?"

"Just a crying baby." The crying stopped. "Now he's looking at me."

Kendra could no longer resist. She went and stood behind Seth. There on the roof just beyond the window stood a tear-streaked toddler who looked barely old enough to stand. The baby wore cloth diapers and nothing else. He had wispy blonde curls and a little round tummy with an outie bellybutton. Eyes brimming with tears, the child held out its pudgy arms toward the window.

"It has to be a trick," Kendra said. "An illusion."

Spotlighted by the flashlight, the toddler took a step toward the window and fell to all fours. He pouted, on the verge of crying again. Standing up, the baby tried another wobbly step. Goose bumps stood out on his chest and arms.

"He looks real," said Seth. "What if he's real?"

"Why would a baby be on the roof?"

The baby toddled to the window, pressing a chubby palm against the glass. Something glinted in the light behind him. Seth shifted the beam onto a pair of green-eyed wolves approaching stealthily from the edge of the roof. The animals paused as the light fell on them. Both looked mangy and lean. One of the wolves bared sharp teeth, foam frothing from its mouth. The other was missing an eye.

"They're using him as bait!" Seth yelled.

The baby looked back at the wolves, then turned back toward Seth and Kendra, bawling with renewed vigor, fresh tears streaming, tiny hands slapping the windowpanes. The wolves charged. The toddler wailed.

In her cage, Goldilocks clucked wildly.

Seth threw open the window.

"No!" Kendra shouted, although she reflexively wanted to do the same thing.

The instant the window opened, wind gushed into the room, as if the air itself had been waiting to pounce. The baby dove into the room, transforming grotesquely as it landed on the floor in a deft somersault. The child was replaced by a leering goblin with yellow slits for eyes, a puckered nose, and a face like a dried cantaloupe. Bald and scabrous on top, the head was fringed by long, weblike hair. The sinuous arms were gangly, the hands long and leathery, tipped with hooked claws. Ribs, collarbones, and pelvis jutted hideously. Spidery networks of veins bulged against maroon flesh.

With supernatural haste, the wolves also sailed through the window before Seth could move to close it.

Kendra shoved past Seth and jerked the window shut in time to impede the entrance of a coldly beautiful woman swathed in writhing black garments. The apparition's dark hair undulated like vapor in a breeze. Her pallid face was slightly translucent. Gazing into those empty, searing eyes froze Kendra where she stood. Babbling whispers filled her mind. Her mouth felt dry. She could not swallow.

Seth yanked the curtains shut and tugged Kendra toward the bed. Whatever trance had momentarily gorgonized her dissolved. Disoriented, she ran alongside Seth to the bed, sensing something in pursuit. When they leaped onto the mattress, a brilliant light flared behind them, accompanied by a crisp stutter like firecrackers.

Kendra twisted to get a look. The maroon goblin stood near the bed, coddling its bony shoulder. The scowling creature stood about as tall as Dale. Hesitantly it reached a knobby hand toward her, and another bright flash sent it staggering away.

The circle of salt! At first she had not grasped why Seth was dragging her to the bed. At least one of them was thinking! Glancing down, Kendra saw that the two-inch dune of salt surrounding the bed indeed marked the line the goblin could not cross.

A twelve-foot centipede with three sets of wings and three pairs of taloned feet corkscrewed around the room in a complex aerial display. A brutish monster with a pronounced underbite and plates down its spine hurled a wardrobe across the room. The wolves had shed their disguises as well.

The maroon goblin cavorted around the room in a feral tantrum, tearing down bookshelves, upsetting toy chests, and snapping the horn off the rocking horse. It picked up Goldilocks's cage and flung it against the wall. The slender bars crumpled and the door sprang open. The terrified chicken took to ungainly flight in a flurry of golden feathers.

Goldilocks was coming toward the bed. The winged centipede struck at the flustered hen but missed. The maroon demon made an acrobatic leap and caught the chicken by both legs. Goldilocks clucked and squirmed in mortal panic.

Seth jumped off the bed. Crouching, he scooped up two handfuls from the circle of salt and charged the wiry goblin. Now holding the chicken in one hand, the sneering goblin rushed to meet him. An instant before the outstretched hand of the demon reached him, Seth flung a handful of salt. Releasing Goldilocks, the demon reeled back, scorched by a blinding blaze.

The chicken made straight for the bed, and Seth tossed his other handful of salt in a wide arc to cover their retreat, scalding the flying centipede in the process. The bulky creature with the underbite tried to beat Seth to the bed, arriving too late and receiving a violent shock as it collided with the invisible salt barrier. Back on the bed, Seth clung to Goldilocks, arms quivering convulsively.

The maroon demon growled. His face and chest were charred from the salt. Tendrils of smoke curled up from the burns. Turning, the demon pulled a book from the shelf and tore it in half.

The door flew open, and Dale leveled a shotgun at the monster with the underbite. "You kids stay put no matter what!" he called. All three monsters converged on the doorway. Dale retreated down the stairs, gun silent. The winged centipede spiraled out the door above the other scrambling creatures.

They heard a shotgun blast from down in the hall. "Shut the door and stay put!" Dale hollered.

Kendra ran and slammed the door, then sprinted back to her bed. Seth held Goldilocks, tears streaming down his cheeks. "I didn't mean for this to happen," he whimpered.

"It'll be okay."

From downstairs came repeated gunshots. Growls, roars, shrieks, glass shattering, wood splintering. Outside, the cacophonous uproar resumed louder than ever. Pagan drums, ethereal choirs, tribal chanting, wailing lamentations, guttural snarls, unnatural howls, and piercing screams united in relentless disharmony.

Kendra, Seth, and Goldilocks sat on the bed awaiting dawn. Kendra had to constantly fight images of the woman with the swirling black garments. She could not get the apparition out of her mind. When she had looked into those soulless eyes, even though the lady was outside, Kendra had felt certain there would be no escape.

Late in the night, the furor finally began to relent, replaced by more unnerving sounds. Babies began to cry beyond the window again, calling for mama. When that failed to elicit a response, the voices of young children pleaded for help.

"Kendra, please hurry, they're coming!"

"Seth, Seth, open up, help us! Seth, don't leave us out here!"

After the cries went ignored for a while, snarls and screams would simulate the demise of the young supplicants. Then a new batch of solicitors began begging for admittance.

Perhaps most disconcerting was when Grandpa was inviting them down to breakfast. "We made it, kids, the sun is rising! Come on, Lena cooked hotcakes."

"How do we know you're our grandpa?" Kendra asked, more than a little suspicious.

"Because I love you. Hurry, the food's getting cold."

"I don't think the sun is up yet," Seth replied.

"It's just a little cloudy this morning."

"Go away," Kendra said.

"Just let me in; I want to kiss you good morning."

"Our grandpa never kisses us, you sicko," Seth yelled. "Get out of our house!"

The exchange was followed by vicious banging on the door for a solid five minutes. The hinges shook, but the door held.

The night wore on. Kendra leaned against the headboard

as Seth dozed at her side. Despite the noise, her eyelids began to feel heavy.

Suddenly she jerked awake. Gray light was seeping through the curtains. Goldilocks wandered the floor, pecking at kernels from her spilled bucket of feed.

When the curtains were masking unmistakable sunlight, Kendra nudged Seth. He looked around, blinking, then crept to the window and peeked out.

"The sun is officially up," he announced. "We made it."

"I'm scared to go downstairs," whispered Kendra.

"Everybody's fine," Seth said nonchalantly.

"Then why haven't they come to get us?"

Seth had no response. Kendra had gone easy on him during the night. The consequences for opening the window were brutal enough without placing blame and starting arguments. And Seth had really acted remorseful. But now he was reverting to his idiot self.

Kendra glared at him. "You realize you might have killed them all."

His face fell and he turned away, shoulders shaking with sobs. He buried his face in his hands. "They're probably fine," he squeaked. "Dale had a gun and everything. They know how to handle themselves."

Kendra felt bad, seeing that Seth clearly was worried too. She went to him and tried to give him a hug. He shoved her away. "Leave me alone."

"Seth, whatever happened isn't your fault."

"Of course it's my fault!" His nose was getting congested.

"I mean, they tricked us. I sort of wanted to open the window too, when I saw those wolves charging. You know, in case it wasn't fake."

"I knew it might be a trick," he sobbed. "But that baby looked so real. I thought they might have kidnapped him to use him as bait. I thought I could save him."

"You were trying to do the right thing." She attempted to hug him once more, but he pushed her away again.

"Don't," he snapped.

"I didn't mean to blame you," said Kendra. "You were acting like you didn't even care."

"Of course I care! You don't think I'm terrified to go down there and find out what I did?"

"You didn't do it. They tricked you. I would have opened the window if you hadn't."

"If I would have stayed in bed none of it would have happened," Seth lamented.

"Maybe they're fine."

"Right. And they let a monster come in the house and up to our door pretending to be Grandpa."

"Maybe they had to hide down in the basement or someplace."

Seth was no longer crying. He picked up a doll and used her dress to wipe his nose. "I hope so."

"Just in case something bad did happen, you can't blame yourself. All you did was open a window. If those monsters did something bad, it's their fault."

"Partly."

"Grandpa and Lena and Dale all know that living here is risky. I'm sure they're fine, but if they aren't, you mustn't blame yourself."

"Whatever."

"I'm serious."

"I like it better when you're funny."

"You know what I liked?" Kendra said.

"What?"

"When you saved Goldilocks."

He laughed, snorting a little through his stuffy nostrils. "Did you see how bad the salt burned that guy?" He retrieved the doll and wiped his nose again on the dress.

"It was really brave."

"I'm just glad it worked."

"It was quick thinking."

Seth glanced at the door and then back at Kendra. "We should probably go check out the damage."

"If you say so."

CHAPTER ELEVEN

Aftermath

Kendra knew it would be bad the moment she opened the door. Ragged gouges furrowed the walls of the stairwell. Crude pictograms defaced the far side of the door, along with an abundance of less orderly nicks and scratches. Near the base of the stairs, a crusty brown substance was smeared on the wall.

"I'm grabbing some salt," Seth said. He returned to the ring around the bed and filled his hands and pockets with the salt that had scorched the intruder the night before.

When Seth rejoined her, Kendra started down the stairs. The steps creaked loudly in the quiet house. The hall at the bottom was worse than the stairway. Again the walls had been savagely raked by claws. The bathroom door was off its hinges and had three splintery holes of different sizes. Patches of carpeting were burned and stained.

Kendra moved down the hall, appalled by the aftermath of the violent night. A smashed mirror. A broken light fixture. A table reduced to kindling. And at the end of the hall, a gaping rectangle instead of a window.

"Looks like they let others in," Kendra said, pointing down the hall.

Seth was examining singed hairs in a damp stain on the floor. "Grandpa?" he yelled. "Anybody!"

The silence was an ominous answer.

Kendra descended the stairs to the entry hall. Sections of the banister were gone. The front door hung askew, an arrow protruding from the frame. Primitive drawings marred the walls, some scored, others scrawled.

In a trance, Kendra roamed the lower rooms of the house. The place had been gutted. Almost all the windows were destroyed. Battered doors lay far from their frames. Mutilated furniture bled stuffing onto mangled carpeting. Shredded drapes dangled in tattered ribbons. Chandeliers lay in shattered ruins. Half of one charred sofa was entirely missing.

Kendra wandered to the back porch. Wind chimes lay in tangles. The furniture was scattered around the garden. A broken rocking chair balanced atop a fountain. A wicker love seat protruded from a hedge.

Back in the house, Kendra found Seth in Grandpa's office. It looked as if an anvil had fallen on the desk. Pulverized memorabilia littered the floor.

"Everything's trashed," Seth said.

"It looks like a demolition team came through here with sledgehammers."

"Or hand grenades." Seth indicated where tar appeared to have been slopped against the wall. "Is that blood?"

"It looks too dark to be human."

Seth picked his way around the splintered desk to the empty window. "Maybe they got out."

"I hope so."

"Out on the lawn," Seth said. "Is that a person?"

Kendra approached the window. "Dale?" she shouted.

The prone figure did not move. "Come on," Seth said, hurrying through the wreckage.

Kendra followed him out the front door and around to the side of the house. They dashed over to the figure lying supine near an overturned birdbath.

"Oh, no," Seth said.

It was a painted statue of Dale. A faithful replica, except the paint was more simplified than his actual coloring would have been. His head was turned to one side, eyes squinted shut, arms raised protectively. The proportions were exact. He was wearing the same outfit he had worn the previous night.

Kendra touched the figure. It was made of metal, clothes and all. Bronze, maybe? Lead? Steel? She rapped her knuckles against the forearm. Sounded solid. No hollow ringing.

"They turned him into a statue," Seth said.

"You think it's really him?"

"It has to be!"

"Help me flip him over."

Both of them strained, but Dale did not budge. He was way too heavy.

"I really blew it," Seth said, palms pressed against his temples. "What have I done?"

"Maybe we can change him back."

Seth kneeled down and put his mouth to Dale's ear. "If you can hear me, give us a sign!" he yelled.

The metallic figure made no response.

"Do you think Grandpa and Lena are around here too?" Kendra asked.

"We'll have to look."

Kendra cupped her hands around her mouth. "Grandpa! Grandpa Sorenson! Lena! Can you hear me?"

"Look at this," Seth said, crouching beside the overturned birdbath. The birdbath had tipped over toward a flowerbed. In the flowerbed was a clear footprint—three large toes and a narrow heel. The print was big enough to suggest that it came from a creature at least the size of a grown man.

"Giant bird?"

"Check out the hole behind the heel." He stuck a finger into a nickel-sized hole. "A couple inches deep."

"Weird."

Seth acted excited. "It has a pointy thing on the back of its heel, a spur or something."

"Which means what?"

"We can probably track it."

"Track it?"

Seth moved forward in the direction the toes pointed, scanning the ground. "See!" He crouched, pointing at a hole in the lawn. "That spur digs deep. It should leave a clear trail."

"And what happens if you catch up to whatever made the tracks?"

He patted his pockets. "I throw some salt and rescue Grandpa."

"How do you know it took Grandpa?"

"I don't," he admitted. "But it's a start."

"What if it turns you into a painted statue?"

"I won't look directly at it. Just in mirrors."

"Where'd you get *that* from?"

"History."

"You don't even know what you're talking about," Kendra said.

"We'll see about that. I better get my camo shirt."

"First let's make sure there aren't any other statues in the yard."

"Fine, then I'm out of here. I don't want the trail getting cold."

After scouring the yard for half an hour, Kendra and Seth had come across various articles of furniture from the house or porch in unexpected locations, but they had found no other life-sized painted statues. They ended up by the swimming pool.

"Have you noticed the butterflies?" Kendra asked.

"Yeah."

"Anything special about them?"

Seth slapped his forehead with the heel of his hand. "We haven't had milk today!"

"Yep. No fairies, just bugs."

"If those fairies are smart, they won't show their faces around here," growled Seth.

"Yeah, you'll show them. What do you want to be this time? A giraffe?"

"None of this would have happened if they had kept guarding the window."

"You did torture one of them," Kendra pointed out.

"They tortured me back! We're even."

"Whatever we do, we should drink some milk first."

They went into the house. The refrigerator was lying on its side. Together they pried the door open. Some of the milk bottles had broken, but a few were intact. Kendra grabbed one, uncapped it, and took a sip. Seth drank next.

"I need my stuff," he said, bolting for the stairs.

Kendra started searching for clues. Wouldn't Grandpa have tried to leave them a message? Maybe there hadn't been time. She walked through the rooms, but encountered no hints to explain the fate of either Lena or Grandpa.

Seth showed up in his camouflage shirt, carrying the cereal box. "I was trying to find that shotgun. You haven't seen it?"

"Nope. There's an arrow by the front door. You could toss that at the monster."

"I think I'll stick with the salt."

"We never checked the basement," Kendra said.

"Worth a try."

They opened the door by the kitchen and stared down into the gloom. Kendra realized it was just about the only undamaged door in the house. Stone steps led into the darkness.

"How about that flashlight?" Kendra said.

"No light switch?" he asked. They couldn't find one. He rummaged in the cereal box and withdrew the flashlight.

With some salt from his pocket clutched in one hand and the flashlight in the other, Seth led the way. It was a longer flight than would ordinarily lead to a basement— more than twenty steep stairs. At the bottom the flashlight beam illuminated a short, barren hallway ending at an iron door.

They walked to the door. It had a keyhole below the handle. Seth tugged the handle, but the door was locked. There was a small hatch at the base of the door.

"What's this?" he asked.

"It's for brownies, so they can come in and fix stuff."

He pushed open the hatch. "Grandpa! Lena! Anybody!"

They waited in vain for a reply. He called once more before standing and shining his light into the keyhole.

"None of your keys would fit this?" he asked.

"They're way too small."

"There might be a key stashed in Grandpa's bedroom."

"If they were down here, I think they'd answer."

Kendra and Seth started back up the stairs. At the top, they heard a loud, deep groan that lasted at least ten seconds. The penetrating sound came from outside. It was much too powerful to have been made by a human. They raced to the back porch. The groan had ended. It was difficult to say from which direction it had originated.

They waited, looking around, expecting a recurrence of the unusual sound. After a tense minute or two, Kendra broke the silence. "What was it?"

"I bet it was whatever has Grandpa and Lena," Seth said. "And it didn't sound too far off."

"It sounded big."

"Yeah."

"Like whale big."

"We have the salt," Seth reminded her. "We need to follow that trail."

"Are you sure that's a good idea?"

"You have a better one?"

"I don't know. Wait and see if they show up? Maybe they'll escape."

"If that hasn't happened by now, it isn't going to. We'll be careful, and we'll make sure to get back before dark. We'll be fine. We have the salt. That stuff works like acid."

"If something goes wrong, who saves us?" Kendra asked.

"You don't have to come. But I'm going."

Seth hurried down the porch steps and started across the yard. Kendra reluctantly followed. She wasn't sure how they would pull off a rescue if scalding the monster with salt failed, but Seth was right about one thing—they couldn't just abandon Grandpa.

Kendra caught up with Seth at the flowerbed where they had originally found the prints. Combing through the grass together, they followed a series of nickel-sized holes across the lawn. The holes were spaced roughly five feet apart and followed a generally straight line, passing the barn and eventually leaving the yard along a narrow path into the woods.

No longer obscured by grass, the tracks were even easier to follow. They passed a couple of intersecting paths, but the way was always certain. The prints of whatever creature had left the holes were unmistakable. They made rapid progress. Kendra remained alert, searching the trees for mythical beasts, but spotted nothing more spectacular than a goldfinch and some chipmunks.

"I'm starving," Seth announced.

"I'm okay. I'm getting sleepy, though."

"Just don't think about it."

"My throat is getting sore," Kendra went on. "You know, we've been up almost thirty hours."

"I'm not that tired," Seth said. "Just hungry. We should have foraged for food in the pantry. It can't all be smashed."

"We must not be too hungry if we didn't think about it at the time."

Suddenly Seth stopped short. "Uh-oh."

"What?"

Seth went several paces forward. Leaning close to the ground, he worked his way back past Kendra. He went forward again more slowly, kicking aside any leaves or branches on the trail. Kendra realized the problem before Seth vocalized it. "No more holes."

She helped scan the ground. They both scrutinized the same segment of the path multiple times before Seth began to search off the trail. "This could be bad," he said.

"There's a lot of undergrowth," Kendra agreed.

"If we could even find one hole, we'd know which direction it went."

"If it left the path, we'll never be able to follow it."

Seth crawled on hands and knees along the edge of the path, sifting through the mulch beneath the undergrowth. Kendra picked up a stick and used it to poke around.

"Don't make any holes," Seth cautioned.

"I'm just moving leaves."

"You could do it with your hands."

"If I wanted bug bites and a rash."

"Hey, this is it." He showed Kendra a hole about five feet from the last one on the path. "It turned left."

"Diagonally." She made a line with her hand connecting the two dots and continuing into the woods.

"But it might have turned more," Seth said. "We should find another one."

Finding the next hole took almost fifteen minutes. It proved that the creature had indeed turned almost directly to the left, perpendicular to the path.

"What if it kept turning?" Kendra said.

"It would sort of be backtracking if it turned more."

"Maybe it wanted to throw off pursuit."

Seth went forward five feet and found the next hole almost instantly. It confirmed that the new course was perpendicular to the trail.

"The undergrowth isn't as bad here," Seth said.

"Seth, it would take all day to track it twenty paces."

"I don't mean to track it. Just to walk in this direction for a while. Maybe it will intersect a trail and we can pick up tracks again. Or maybe it lives not much farther ahead."

Kendra put a hand in her pocket, feeling for salt. "I don't like the idea of leaving the trail."

"Me neither. We won't go far. But this thing seems to like trails. It followed one all this way. We may be close to a discovery. It's worth going a little ways just to check."

Kendra stared at her brother. "Okay, and what if we run into a cave?"

"We take a look."

"What if we hear breathing coming from the cave?"

"You don't have to go in. I'll look myself. The point is finding Grandpa."

Kendra bit her tongue. She almost said that if they found him out here, it would probably be in pieces. "Okay, just a little ways."

They walked in a straight line away from the path. They kept scanning the ground, but noticed no more holes. Before long they crossed a dry, rocky streambed. Not far beyond, they wandered into a little meadow. The brush and wildflowers in the meadow grew nearly waist high.

"I don't see any other trails," Kendra said. "Or any monster houses."

"Let's take a good look around the meadow," said Seth. He made a complete search of the perimeter of the meadow, finding neither holes nor trails.

"Let's face it," Kendra said. "If we try to go any farther, we'll be wandering blind."

"What about climbing that hill?" Seth suggested, indicating the highest point visible from the meadow, less than a quarter-mile away. "If I were going to make a home around here, it would be over there. Plus, if we get up there, we'll have a better view of the area. These trees make it hard to see."

Kendra pressed her lips together. The hill was not steep; it would be easy to climb. And it was not too far away. "If we don't find anything there, we go back?"

"Deal."

They marched toward the hill, which was along a

different line from the course they had originally taken from the path. As they picked their way through denser underbrush, a twig snapped off to one side. They paused, listening.

"I'm getting pretty nervous," Kendra said softly.

"We're fine. Probably just a falling pinecone."

Kendra tried to push away images of the pallid woman with the swirling black garments. The thought of her made Kendra freeze. If she saw her out in the woods, Kendra worried she would just curl up in a ball on the ground and let herself be taken.

"I'm losing track of which way we're going," she said. Back under the trees, the line of sight to both hill and meadow was disrupted.

"I have my compass."

"So if all else fails, we can find the North Pole."

"The trail we followed went northwest," Seth assured her. "Then we left it going southwest. The hill is to the west, the meadow is east."

"That's pretty good."

"The only trick is paying attention."

Before long, the trees were thinning and they were walking up the hill. With the trees farther apart, the underbrush grew higher and the bushes bigger. Kendra and Seth wound their way up the moderate slope toward the crest.

"Do you smell that?" Seth asked.

Kendra stopped. "Like somebody cooking."

The smell was faint but, now that she noticed it,

distinct. Kendra studied the area with sudden alarm. "Oh my gosh," she said, crouching down.

"What?"

"Get down."

Seth knelt beside her. Kendra pointed toward the crest of the hill. Off to one side rose a feeble column of smoke—a thin, wavering distortion.

"Yeah," he whispered. "We may have found it."

Again she had to bite her tongue. She hoped someone wasn't cooking Grandpa. "What do we do?"

"Stay here," said Seth. "I'll go check it out."

"I don't want to stay alone."

"Then follow me, but stay back a bit. We don't want to both get caught at the same time. Keep salt ready."

Kendra did not need that reminder. Her only worry about the salt was that her sweaty hands were going to turn it to paste.

Seth crept ahead, staying low, using the bushes for cover, gradually making his way toward the meager line of smoke. Kendra imitated his movements, impressed that his hours of playing army were finally paying off. Even as she followed him, she struggled to come to terms with what they were doing. Sneaking up on a monster cookout was among the activities she could do without. Shouldn't they be sneaking *away*?

The trembling shaft of smoke grew nearer. Seth waved her up to him. She huddled beside him behind a wide bush twice her height, trying to breathe quietly. He put his lips to her ear. "I'll be able to see what's going on when I get around this bush. I'll try to yell if I get captured or anything. Be ready."

She put her mouth to his ear. "If you play a trick on me, I promise I will kill you, I really will."

"I won't. I'm scared too."

He slunk forward. Kendra tried to calm herself. Waiting was torture. She considered moving around the bush to take a peek, but could not muster the courage. The silence was good, right? Unless they had stealthily dropped Seth with a poison dart.

The pause stretched mercilessly. Then she heard Seth coming back less carefully than he had left. When he came around the bush, he was walking upright, saying, "Come here, you have to see this."

"What is it?"

"Nothing scary."

She went around the bush with him, still tense. Up ahead, in a clear area near the summit of the hill, she saw the source of the thin smoke—a waist-high cylinder of stone with a wooden windlass and a dangling bucket. "A well?"

"Yeah. Come smell."

They walked to the well. Even up close, the rising smoke remained vapory and indistinct. Kendra leaned over, staring down into the deep darkness. "Smells good."

"Like soup," Seth said. "Meat, veggies, spices."

"Am I just hungry? It smells delicious."

"I think so too. Should we try some?"

"Lower the bucket?" Kendra asked skeptically.

"Why not?" Seth replied.

"There could be creatures down there."

"I don't think so," he said.

"You think it's just a well full of stew," Kendra scoffed.

"We *are* on a magical preserve."

"As far as we know it could be poisonous."

"It can't hurt to take a look," Seth insisted. "I'm starving. Besides, not everything here is bad. I bet this is where fairy people come for dinner. See, it even has a crank." He began turning the windlass, spooling the bucket down into the darkness.

"I'm staying on lookout," said Kendra.

"Good idea."

Kendra felt exposed. They were far enough from the summit that she could not see anything on the far side of the hill, but they were high enough that she commanded an expansive view of trees and terrain when she looked down the slope. With little cover surrounding the well, she worried that unseen eyes might be spying from the foliage below.

Seth continued unwinding the rope, sending the bucket ever deeper. Eventually he heard it wetly hit bottom. The rope slackened a bit. After a moment he began winding the bucket back up.

"Hurry," Kendra said.

"I am. This thing is deep."

"I'm worried everything in the forest can see us."

"Here it comes." He stopped cranking and pulled the bucket up the last few feet by hand, setting it on the lip of the well.

Kendra joined him. Inside the wooden bucket, bits of meat, cut carrots, potato fragments, and onion floated in a fragrant yellow broth. "Looks like a normal stew," Kendra said.

"Better than normal. I'm trying some."

"Don't!" she warned.

"Lighten up." He tweezed out a piece of dripping meat and tried it. "Good!" he announced. He plucked out a potato and offered a similar report. Tipping the bucket, he slurped some of the broth. "Amazing!" he said. "You have to try it."

From behind the same bush they had used as their final hiding place when approaching the well, a creature emerged. From the waist up, he was a shirtless man with an exceptionally hairy chest and a pair of pointy horns above his forehead. From waist down he had the legs of a shaggy goat. Wielding a knife, the satyr charged straight at them.

Both Kendra and Seth turned in alarm at the sound of his hooves racing up the slope. "Salt," Seth blurted, dipping into his pockets.

As she fumbled for salt, Kendra dashed around the well, placing it between herself and the attacker. Not Seth. He stood his ground, and when the satyr was a couple of steps away, he flung a fistful of salt at the goatman.

The satyr stopped short, obviously surprised by the cloud of salt. Seth threw a second handful, groping in his pockets for more. The salt failed to spark or sizzle. Instead, the satyr appeared bewildered.

"What are you doing?" he asked in a hushed tone.

"I could ask you the same question," Seth replied.

"No you can't. You're spoiling our operation." The satyr lunged past Seth and slashed the rope with his knife. "She's coming."

"Who?"

"I'd save the questions for later," the satyr said. He wound the rope until it was tight around the windlass, seized the bucket, and started down the hill, spilling soup as he went. From the far side of the hill, Kendra heard foliage rustling and branches crunching. She and Seth followed the satyr.

The satyr slid into the bush Kendra had crouched behind earlier. Kendra and Seth dove in alongside him.

An instant after they ducked out of sight, a bulky, hideous woman lumbered into view and approached the well. She had a broad, flat face with saggy earlobes that hung almost to her hefty shoulders. Her misshapen bosom drooped inside a coarse, homespun tunic. Her avocado skin had a ridged texture like corduroy, her graying hair was shaggy and matted, and her build bordered on obese. The well barely came to her knees, making her considerably taller than Hugo. She waddled from side to side as she walked, and she was breathing heavily through her mouth.

Bending over, she pawed at the well, stroking the wooden frame. "The ogress can't see much," the satyr whispered.

When he said it, the ogress jerked her head up. She yammered something in a guttural language. Shambling a couple of steps away from the well, she squatted down and sniffed at the ground where Seth had thrown his salt. "There been peoples here," she accused in a husky, accented voice. "Where you peoples be?"

The satyr placed a finger against his lips. Kendra held perfectly still, trying to breathe softly despite her alarm. She tried to plan which direction she would run.

The ogress lumbered down the slope toward their hiding place, sniffing high and low. "I heared peoples. I smelled peoples. And I smell my stew. Peoples been at my stew again. You come out now to apologize."

The satyr shook his head, slitting his throat with a finger for emphasis. Seth slid a hand into a pocket. The satyr touched his wrist and shook his head with a scowl.

The ogress had already closed half the distance to the bush. "You peoples like my stew so much, maybe you take a bath in it."

Kendra resisted the urge to bolt. The ogress would be on them in moments. But the satyr seemed to know what he was doing. He held up a hand, tacitly signaling for them to keep still.

Without warning, something began crashing through the bushes about twenty yards to their right. The ogress pivoted and stumbled toward the ruckus with a quick, awkward gait.

The satyr nodded. They scrambled out of the bush and started down the hill. Behind them, the ogress skidded to a halt and changed direction, coming after them. The goat-man pitched the bucket of stew into a tangled patch of thorns and bounded over a fallen log. Kendra and Seth sprinted after him.

Propelled by her downward momentum, Kendra found herself taking larger steps than she wanted. Each time her foot touched the ground became a fresh opportunity to lose her balance and tumble forward. Seth stayed a couple of steps ahead of her, and the swift satyr was gradually increasing his lead.

Heedless of obstacles, the ogress pursued them noisily, trampling bushes and tearing through branches. She breathed in damp, wheezing gasps and cursed periodically, reverting to her unintelligible native tongue. Despite her cumbersome size and apparent exhaustion, the misshapen ogress was rapidly gaining.

The slope leveled out. Behind Kendra the ogress fell, branches and deadfalls snapping like fireworks. Kendra glanced back, catching a glimpse of the burly ogress surging to her feet.

The satyr led them into a shallow ravine, where they found the wide entrance to a dark tunnel. "This way," he said, dashing into the tunnel. Although it looked spacious enough for the ogress to enter, Seth and Kendra followed without question. The satyr appeared confident, and he had been right so far.

The tunnel grew darker the deeper they ran. Heavy footsteps followed them. Kendra glanced back. The ogress filled the subterranean passageway, blocking out much of the light filtering in from the opening.

It became hard to see the satyr up ahead. The tunnel was growing narrower. Close behind Kendra, the ogress gasped and coughed. Hopefully she would have a heart attack and collapse.

For a space, the darkness became complete. Then it began to brighten. The tunnel continued to shrink. Soon Kendra had to crouch, and the walls were within reach at either side. The satyr slackened his pace, looking back with a mischievous grin. Kendra checked over her shoulder as well.

The panting ogress crawled and then scooted forward on her belly, wheezing and choking. When she could worm no farther, she roared in frustration, a strained, throaty cry. After that it sounded like she vomited.

Up ahead the satyr was crawling. The passage slanted upward. They emerged through a small gap into a bowl-shaped depression. A second satyr stood waiting for them. The second had redder hair than the first and slightly longer horns. He motioned for them to follow.

The two satyrs and two children charged recklessly through the woods for a few more minutes. When they arrived at a clearing with a tiny pond, the redheaded satyr stopped and faced the others.

"What was the idea, ruining our operation?" he asked.

"Clumsy work," the other satyr agreed.

"We didn't know," Kendra said. "We thought it was a well."

"You thought a chimney was a well?" the redhead complained. "I suppose you sometimes mistake icicles for carrots? Or wagons for outhouses?"

"It had a bucket," Seth said.

"And it was in the ground," Kendra added.

"They have a point," the other satyr said.

"You were on the roof of the ogress's lair," explained the redhead.

"We get it now," Seth said. "We thought it was a hill."

"Nothing wrong with pinching a bit of soup from her cauldron," the redhead continued. "We try to be free with our assets. But you need to use some delicacy. A little finesse. At least wait until the old lady falls asleep. Who are you, anyhow?"

"Seth Sorenson."

"Kendra."

"I am Newel," said the redhead. "This is Doren. You realize we'll probably have to construct a whole new rigging?"

"She'll rip the old one down," Doren explained.

"Almost more work than cooking our own stew," Newel huffed.

"We can't make it come out like she does," Doren mourned.

"She has a gift," Newel agreed.

"We're sorry," Kendra said. "We were a little lost."

Doren waved a hand. "Don't worry. We just like to bluster. If you spoiled our wine, that would be another story."

"Still," Newel said, "a guy has to eat, and free stew is free stew."

"We'll try to find a way to repay you," Kendra said.

"So will we," Newel said.

"You don't happen to have any . . . batteries?" Doren asked.

"Batteries?" Seth asked, wrinkling his nose.

"Size C," Newel clarified.

Kendra folded her arms. "Why do you want batteries?"

"They're shiny," Newel said, nudging Doren with an elbow.

"We worship them," Doren said, nodding sagely. "They seem like little gods to us."

The kids stared at the goatmen in disbelief, unsure how to continue the conversation. They were obviously lying.

"Okay," Newel said. "We have a portable television."

"Don't tell Stan."

"We had a mountain of batteries, but we ran out."

"And our supplier is no longer employed here."

"We could work out an arrangement." Newel spread his hands diplomatically. "Some batteries to repent for disrupting our stew siphoning—"

"Then we can trade for more. Gold, booze, you name

it." Doren lowered his voice slightly. "Of course, we would need to keep our arrangement private."

"Stan doesn't like us watching the tube," said Newel.

"You know our grandpa?" Seth asked.

"Who doesn't?" Newel said.

"You haven't seen him lately?" Kendra asked.

"Sure, just last week," Doren said.

"I mean since last night."

"No, why?" Newel said.

"Haven't you heard?" Seth asked.

The satyrs shrugged at each other. "What's the news?" Newel asked.

"Our grandpa was kidnapped last night," Kendra said.

"Your grandfather is a kid?" Newel said.

"They mean he was abducted," Doren clarified.

Kendra nodded. "Creatures got into the house and took him and our housekeeper."

"Not Dale?" Doren asked.

"We don't think so," Seth said.

Newel shook his head. "Poor Dale. Never been very popular."

"Lousy sense of humor," Doren agreed. "Too quiet."

"You guys don't know who might have taken them?" Kendra asked.

"On Midsummer Eve?" Newel said, tossing up his hands. "Anybody. Your guess would be better than mine."

"Could you help us find him?" Seth asked.

The satyrs shared an uneasy glance. "Yeah, ouch,"

Newel began uncomfortably, "this is a bad week for us."

"Lots of commitments," Doren confirmed, backing away.

"You know, now that I've thought on it," Newel said, "we may have needed a new rigging on the chimney anyhow. How about we go our separate ways and call it even?"

"Don't take anything we said to heart," Doren said. "We were just being satirical."

Seth stepped forward. "Do you know something you aren't telling us?"

"It isn't that," Newel said, continuing his slow retreat. "It's just Midsummer Day. We're booked."

"Thanks for helping us get away from the ogress," Kendra said.

"Our pleasure," Newel replied.

"All part of the package," Doren added.

"Could you guys at least point us toward home?" Seth asked.

The satyrs stopped retreating. Doren extended an arm. "There's a path over there."

"When you reach it, go right," Newel said.

"That will get you started in the right direction."

"Give our best to Stan when he turns up."

The satyrs hastily turned and dashed off into the trees.

CHAPTER TWELVE

Inside the Barn

Kendra and Seth located the path just as the satyrs had instructed, and soon reencountered the nickel-sized holes that served as a perfect trail of breadcrumbs toward home. "Those goat guys were idiots," Seth said.

"They did save us from the ogress," Kendra reminded him.

"They could have helped us rescue Grandpa but they blew us off." He wore a scowl as they continued along the path.

As they neared the yard, they heard the inhuman groan again, the same sound they had heard while exiting the basement, only louder than ever. They halted. The perplexing sound was coming from up ahead. A long, plaintive moan, comparable to a blast from a foghorn.

Seth dug some of the remaining salt out of a pocket and rushed ahead. With their quickened pace, they were soon back at the edge of the yard. Everything appeared normal. They saw no hulking behemoth capable of the enormous sound they had heard.

"You know, that salt didn't do much to the satyr," Kendra whispered.

"It probably only burns the bad creatures," he replied.

"I think the ogre lady picked some up."

"It was all mixed in the dirt by then. You saw it torch those guys last night."

They waited, hesitant to enter the yard. "Now what?" Kendra asked.

The mighty groan resounded across the yard, nearer and louder. The shingles on the barn rattled.

"It's coming from the barn," Seth said.

"We never looked there!" Kendra said.

"I didn't think about it."

The monstrous groan blared a third time. The barn shuddered. Birds flew up from the eaves.

"You think something took Grandpa and Lena to the barn?" Kendra said.

"Sounds like it's still there."

"Grandpa told us never to enter the barn."

"I think I'm already grounded," Seth said.

"No, I mean what if he keeps ferocious creatures in there? It might have nothing to do with his disappearance."

"It's our best chance. Where else are we going to look? We have no other clues. The tracks were a dead end. At least we should try to get a peek inside."

Seth started for the barn, with Kendra following reluctantly behind. The towering structure rose a good five stories tall, topped by a weather vane in the shape of a bull. Kendra had never studied it for entrances until now. She noted the obvious set of large double doors in the front, along with some smaller access doors along the side.

The barn creaked and then started shaking as if there were an earthquake. The sound of timbers splitting filled the air, followed by another mournful moan.

Seth glanced back at Kendra. Something huge was in there. A few moments later the barn grew still.

Chains and a heavy padlock bound the double doors in front, so Seth moved along the side of the building, quietly trying the smaller doors. All were locked. The barn had several windows, but the lowest were three stories off the ground.

They stealthily circled the entire building, finding no doors unlocked. There weren't even any cracks or peepholes. "Grandpa sealed this place up tight," Kendra whispered.

"We may have to make some noise to get inside," Seth said. He started circling the building again.

"I'm not sure that would be smart."

"I'll wait until the barn starts shaking again." Seth sat

down in front of a small door, little more than three feet high. Minutes passed.

"Think it knows we're waiting?" Kendra asked.

"You're just bad luck."

"Stop saying that."

A fairy glided over near them. Seth tried to shoo it away. "Get out of here." The fairy effortlessly dodged his shooing motions. The more vigorously he waved her away, the closer she came.

"Stop it, you're just egging her on," Kendra said.

"I'm sick of fairies."

"Then ignore her and maybe she'll leave."

He stopped paying attention to the fairy. She came up right behind his head. When the proximity earned no reaction, the fairy landed on his head. Seth slapped at her, missing as she wove around his intended blows. Just when he jumped to his feet to chase her, the booming groan came again. The little door trembled.

Seth plopped back down and started ramming the door with both feet. The moaning muffled most of the impact's noise. On the fifth kick, the edge of the little door split and swung open.

Seth rolled away from the opening, and Kendra stepped aside as well. Digging in his pockets, Seth withdrew the remnants of his salt. "Want some?" he mouthed.

Kendra accepted some salt. A second or two later, the deafening moaning ceased. Seth gestured for Kendra to wait. He crept through the small door. Kendra waited, squeezing the salt in her palm.

Seth reappeared in the opening wearing an inscrutable expression. "You have to see this," he said.

"What?"

"Don't worry. Come look."

Kendra ducked through the little doorway. The enormous barn contained just one cavernous room with a few closets around the perimeter. The entire room was dominated by a single gigantic cow.

"Not what I expected," Kendra murmured in disbelief.

She gawked at the colossal bovine in amazement. The huge head was up near the rafters, forty or fifty feet in the air. A hayloft spanning an entire side of the building served as a feedbox. The cow's hooves were the size of hot tubs. The tremendous udder was absolutely bulging. Milk beaded and dripped from teats almost the size of punching bags.

The gargantuan cow cocked its head, staring down at the newcomers to the barn. It let out a long moo, making the barn shake simply by shifting its stance.

"Holy cow," Kendra muttered.

"You can say that again. I doubt Grandpa will be running out of milk anytime soon."

"We're friends," Kendra called up to the cow. The cow tossed its head and began munching from the hayloft.

"Why haven't we heard this thing before?" Seth wondered.

"She probably never moos. I think she's in pain,"

Kendra observed. "See how swollen the udder looks? I bet it could fill a swimming pool."

"Seriously."

"Somebody probably milks her every morning."

"And nobody did today," said Seth.

They stood and stared. The cow continued munching from the hayloft. Seth pointed at the back of the barn. "Look at the manure!"

"Sick!"

"The world's biggest cow pie!"

"You would notice that."

The cow let out another bellowing complaint, the most insistent so far. They clamped their hands over their ears until the lowing stopped.

"We probably should try to milk her," Kendra said.

"How are we supposed to do that!" Seth cried.

"There has to be a way. They must do it all the time."

"We can't even reach her thingies."

"I bet that cow could tear this place apart if she wanted. I mean, look at her! She keeps getting more upset. Her udder looks like it's about to burst. Who knows what kind of powers she has. Her milk lets people see fairies. The last thing we need is a giant magical cow running around loose. It could be total mayhem."

Folding his arms, Seth surveyed the task. "This is impossible."

"We need to search the closets. Maybe they have special tools."

"What about Grandpa?"

"We're out of leads," said Kendra. "If we don't milk this cow, we could end up with a new disaster on our hands."

In the closets they found a variety of tools and equipment, but no obvious gear for milking gargantuan cows. There were empty barrels all around, in and out of closets, which Kendra figured must be used for catching milk. In one closet Kendra found a couple of A-frame ladders. "These might be all we need," she said.

"How do we even get our hands around those things?"

"We don't."

"There has to be a gigantic milking machine," Seth said.

"I'm not seeing anything like that. But it might work if we just hug and drop."

"Are you nuts?"

"Why not?" Kendra said, motioning between the teats and the floor. "It isn't that far from the nipples to the ground."

"We're not trying to use barrels?"

"No, we can waste the milk. Barrels would get in the way. We just need to relieve the pressure."

"What if she steps on us?"

"She hardly has any room to move. If we stay under the udder, we'll be fine."

They dragged the ladders into position, one beside each of two teats on the same side of the mammoth cow. They climbed the ladders. Only by standing one rung from the top were they high enough to grip the teat near the udder.

Seth stood waiting while Kendra tried to get into position. "These feel wobbly," she said.

"Balance."

She hesitantly stood upright. It felt a lot higher than it had looked from the ground. "You ready?"

"No. I bet this barn will hold her."

"We have to at least try."

"Hug the thingy and slide down?" Seth asked.

"We'll trade off, you, then me, then you, then me. Then we'll do the other side."

"How about you start it?"

"You're better at this sort of stuff," Kendra said.

"That's true, I milk a lot of giant cows. I'll show you my trophies sometime."

"Seriously, you start," urged Kendra.

"What if it hurts her?"

"I don't think we're big enough. I'm more worried that we're not going to be able to get any out."

"So I should squeeze as hard as I can," Seth confirmed.

"Sure."

"Once I do it, you'll do it, and we'll just keep going as fast as we can."

"And if I ever find a giant cow milking trophy, I'll buy it for you," Kendra offered.

"I'd rather we kept it our little secret. You ready?"

"Go for it."

Hesitantly Seth placed a hand against the huge teat. The cow mooed, and he recoiled, crouching and grabbing the ladder with both hands to steady himself. Kendra tried to stay balanced as she laughed. Finally the foghorn moo ended.

"I changed my mind," Seth said.

"I'll count to three," said Kendra.

"You go first or I'm not doing it. I almost fell and wet my pants at the same time."

"One . . . two . . . three!"

Seth stepped off the ladder, embracing the teat. He slid down it and fell to the floor along with an impressive jet of milk. Kendra stepped off and hugged the teat as well. Even with her holding tightly, it slid through her embrace faster than she expected. She hit the floor with warm milk already soaking her jeans.

Seth was on his way back up the ladder. "I'm already disgusted," he said, stepping off and sliding down again. This time he kept his feet when he landed. Kendra went up and slid down again. Hugging as hard as she could, she descended a little more slowly, but still fell over when she hit the floor. Already milk was everywhere.

Soon they fell into a rhythm, both of them landing on their feet most of the time. The engorged udder hung low, and they got better at using the teat-hug to control their fall. Milk gushed copiously. While they were sliding, the teats sprayed like fire hoses. It must have been at least seventy jumps each before the output began to slacken.

"Other side," Kendra gasped, breathing hard.

"My arms are dead," Seth complained.

"We have to hurry."

They scooted the ladders over and repeated the process. Kendra tried to pretend she was on a surreal playground, where the kids waded in milk instead of sand and slid down thick, meaty poles.

Kendra focused on climbing the ladder and landing as lightly as possible. She worried that if either action became routine, she could have a bad accident, spraining an ankle, breaking a bone, or worse.

At the first sign that the flow of milk was slackening, they collapsed in exhaustion, not worried about lying in milk because their clothes and hair were already drenched. Both of them gulped air desperately. Kendra put a hand to her neck. "My heart is beating like a jackhammer."

"I thought I was going to puke, that was so foul," complained Seth.

"I'm more tired than sick."

"Think about it. You're dripping with warm, raw milk while your face rubs down a cow nipple about a hundred times."

"More than that."

"We doused the whole barn," Seth said. "I'm never drinking milk again."

"I'm never going to the playground," Kendra vowed.

"What?"

"Hard to explain."

Seth scanned the area under the cow. "The floor has drains, but I don't think much of the milk is going down."

"I saw a hose. I doubt the cow would like milk rotting all over the place." Kendra sat up and squeezed milk out of her hair. "That was the best workout I ever had. I'm dead."

"If I did that every day I'd look like Hercules," said Seth.

"You mind grabbing the ladders?"

"Not if you do the hosing."

The hose was long and had good water pressure, and the drains seemed to have plenty of capacity. Flushing the milk away turned out to be the easiest part of the process. Seth had Kendra hose him off, and then returned the favor.

From the time the milking began in earnest, the cow made no more noise and displayed no more interest in them. They called for Grandpa and Lena in the barn, just to be sure, starting with small voices to avoid startling the cow and gradually building to shouts. As had been their lot all day, their calls went unanswered.

"Should we go back to the house?" Kendra asked.

"I guess. It will be dark before long."

"I'm tired. And hungry. We should look for food."

They left the barn. The day was waning.

"You have a big tear in your shirt," Kendra said.

"I ripped it while we were running from that ogress."

"I have a pink one you can borrow."

"This will work fine," said Seth, "once it dries off."

"The pink one would hide you just as well as the camouflage," Kendra said.

"Are all girls as brainless as you?"

"You're telling me a green shirt will make you invisible to monsters?"

"No. *Less* visible. Less is the point. Less than your blue one."

"I guess I should find a green one too."

An Unexpected Message

Sitting on the floor in the dining room, Kendra took a bite of her second peanut-butter-and-jelly sandwich. Scouring the kitchen, she and Seth had found enough food to last for weeks. The pantry contained canned fruits and vegetables, unbroken jars of preserves, bread, oatmeal, cream of wheat, crackers, tuna, and lots of other stuff.

The fridge still worked, even lying on its side, and they cleaned out the broken glass the best they could. There remained plenty of milk, cheese, and eggs. The freezer held a lot of meat.

Kendra took another bite. Leaning back, she closed her eyes. She had felt hungry enough for a second sandwich, but now she doubted she would finish it. "I'm exhausted," she announced.

"Me too," Seth said. He put a piece of cheese on a cracker and topped it with a sardine bathed in mustard sauce. "My eyes feel itchy."

"My throat feels prickly," Kendra said. "The sun isn't even down."

"What are we going to do about Grandpa?"

"I think the best thing we can do is get some rest. We'll think more clearly in the morning."

"How long did we sleep last night?" Seth asked.

"About half an hour," Kendra guessed.

"We've stayed up for almost two days!"

"Now you'll sleep for two days."

"Whatever," said Seth.

"It's true. Your glands will secrete a cocoon."

"I'm not that gullible."

"That's why you're so hungry. You're storing up fat for hibernation."

Seth finished the cracker. "You should try a sardine."

"I don't eat fish with the heads still attached."

"The heads are the best part! You can feel the eyes pop when you—"

"Enough." Kendra stood up. "I need to get to bed."

Seth rose as well. "Me too."

They climbed the stairs, passed down the cluttered hall, and mounted the steps to the attic. Their room had taken a beating, everything except the beds. Goldilocks strutted over to the corner and started clucking. Her feed was scattered across the floor.

"You're right that the salt didn't seem to be working," Seth said.

"It might only work in here."

"They were jerks, but those goat guys were pretty funny."

"They're called satyrs," Kendra said.

"I need to find some C batteries. They said they'd give us gold."

"They didn't say how much."

"Still, trading batteries for gold! I could become a millionaire."

"I'm not sure I'd trust those guys." Kendra flopped onto her bed, face in her pillow. "What does Goldilocks keep clucking about?"

"I bet she misses her cage." Seth crossed the floor to the flustered hen. "Kendra, you better come see this."

"Can I look in the morning?" she said, her voice muffled by the pillow.

"You need to look now."

Kendra pushed herself off her bed and walked over to Seth. In the corner on the floor, more than a hundred feed kernels had been arranged to form six letters:

I M
GRAM

"You've got to be kidding," Kendra said. She gave Seth a suspicious glance. "Did you write this?"

"No! No way!"

Kendra squatted in front of Goldilocks. "You're my Grandma Sorenson?"

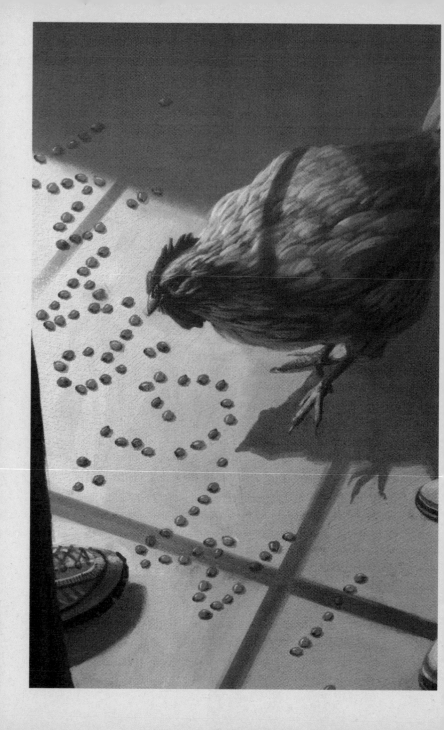

The hen bobbed her head, as if in affirmation.

"Was that a yes?"

The head bobbed again.

"Give me a 'no' so I can be sure," Kendra said.

Goldilocks shook her head.

"How did this happen?" Seth asked. "Somebody transformed you?"

The chicken bobbed her head.

"How do we change you back?" Kendra asked.

Goldilocks held still.

"Why didn't Grandpa change her back?" Seth asked.

"Did Grandpa Sorenson try to restore you?" Kendra inquired.

Goldilocks bobbed her head and then shook it.

"Yes and no?"

The head nodded.

"He tried but failed," Kendra guessed.

The hen gave another affirmative.

"Do you know a way we can change you back?" Kendra asked.

Another head bob.

"Is it something we can do in the house?" Kendra asked.

The head shook.

"Do we need to take you to the witch?" Seth tried.

The head bobbed. And then the hen flapped her wings, moving away.

"Wait, Grandma!" Kendra reached for the hen, but the

flustered bird dodged her grasp. "She's freaking out."

Seth chased her down. "Grandma," he said, "can you still hear us?"

The hen made no acknowledgment of comprehension.

"Grandma," Kendra said, "can you still respond to us?"

The chicken squirmed. Seth kept hold of her. The chicken pecked his hand, and he dropped her. They watched Goldilocks. For several minutes, she did nothing to suggest abnormal intelligence and offered no recognizable reaction to any questions.

"She was answering us before, right?" Kendra asked.

"She wrote us a message!" Seth said, pointing at the I M GRAM in the corner.

"She must have had just a short window to communicate with us," Kendra reasoned. "Once she got the message across, she left it in our hands."

"Why hasn't she spoken up before?"

"I don't know. Maybe she's tried, but we never got the message."

Seth cocked his head thoughtfully and then gave a small shrug. "Do we take her to the witch in the morning?"

"I don't know. Muriel only has one knot left."

"No matter what, we don't undo the last knot. But maybe we could bargain with her."

"Bargain with what?" Kendra asked.

"We could bring food. Or other stuff. Things to make her more comfortable in that shack."

"I don't picture her going for it. She'll know we're desperate to fix Grandma."

"We won't give her another choice."

Kendra bit her lip. "What if she won't budge? She wouldn't for Grandpa. Do we set Muriel free if she will change Grandma back?"

"No way!" said Seth. "As soon as she gets free, what keeps her from turning all of us into chickens?"

"Grandpa said you can't use magic against others here unless they use it on you first. We never caused Muriel any harm, did we?"

"But she's a witch," Seth said. "Why would she be locked up if she wasn't dangerous?"

"I'm not saying I want to let her go. I'm saying, we might be in an emergency situation where we have no other options. It might be worth the risk in order to get Grandma back to help us."

Seth thought about that. "What if we can get her to tell us where Grandpa is?"

"Or both," Kendra said, getting excited. "I bet she would do just about anything to be released. I'm sure she would do those two things at least. Then we might actually get out of this mess."

"You're right that we don't have many options."

"We should sleep on it," Kendra said. "We're both worn out. We can decide what to do in the morning."

"Okay."

Kendra climbed into bed, slid under the covers, let her

head sink into the pillow, and fell asleep before another thought entered her mind.

❊ ❊ ❊

"Maybe we shouldn't have rinsed the milk out of our clothes," Seth said. "Then we could churn butter while we walk."

"Foul!"

"By the end of the day I might have had yogurt in my armpits."

"You're psychotic," said Kendra.

"Then we could add some of Lena's jam and make it fruit-at-the-bottom."

"Quit it!"

Seth seemed pleased with himself. Goldilocks rode in the wheelbarrow inside a burlap sack he had found in the pantry. They had tried to bend the cage back into shape, but could not get the door to stay on. The sack had a drawstring, which they pulled snugly around the hen's neck so her head could stick out.

It was hard to think of the chicken as Grandma Sorenson. The hen had not performed a single grandmotherly action all morning. She showed no reaction to the announcement that they were going to see Muriel, and she had laid an egg on Kendra's bed during the night.

Kendra and Seth had awakened just before sunrise. In the barn they had found the wheelbarrow, which they determined might be easier than carrying Goldilocks the entire way to the ivy shack.

It was Kendra's turn pushing the wheelbarrow. The chicken seemed serene. She was probably enjoying the fresh air. The weather was pleasant—sunny and warm without being hot.

Kendra wondered how the negotiations with Muriel would go. In the end, they had decided it would do no harm to see what terms they could reach with the witch. Then they could base their final decision on the facts of what Muriel would be willing to do, rather than conjecture.

They had loaded food, clothes, tools, and utensils in the wheelbarrow, in case they might be able to barter with comforts instead of freedom. Most of the clothes had been mangled on Midsummer Eve, but they found a few unshredded items for Grandma to wear in case they succeeded in transforming her. They had made sure to feed the chicken some milk in the morning, as well as to drink some themselves.

The trails to the shack were not difficult to remember. Presently they identified the leafy structure where the witch lived. Leaving the wheelbarrow, Seth carried the chicken, while Kendra collected an armful of bartering items. Kendra had already reminded Seth to stay calm and be polite no matter what happened, but she repeated the admonition.

They heard strange music as they drew near the shack, like somebody playing a rubber band while clacking castanets. When they got around to the front door, they found the grimy old hag playing a mouth harp with one hand while making her limberjack dance with the other.

"I did not hope to have visitors again so soon," laughed the witch when her song ended. "Pity about Stanley."

"What do you know about our grandpa?" Seth asked.

"The woods are all abuzz with news of his abduction," Muriel said. "The naiadic housekeeper as well, if one is to lend an ear to the gossip. Quite the scandal."

"Do you know where they are?" Seth tried.

"Look at all the lovely gifts you brought me," the witch gushed, clasping her veiny hands together. "The quilt is gorgeous, but it would be ruined in my humble dwelling. I'll not let you waste your generosity on me; I would not know what to do with such niceties."

"We brought these to trade," Kendra said.

"Trade?" the witch asked theatrically, smacking her lips. "For my tea! Nonsense, child, I would not dream of exacting a toll for my hospitality. Come inside, and the three of us shall drink together."

"Not to trade for tea," Seth said, holding up Goldilocks. "We want you to change our grandma back into herself."

"In exchange for a chicken?"

"She *is* the chicken," Kendra explained.

The witch grinned, stroking her chin. "I thought I recognized her," she mused. "You poor dears, one guardian carried off in the night, the other reduced to poultry."

"We can offer you a quilt, a bathrobe, a toothbrush, and a lot of homemade food," Kendra said.

"Charming as that may be," Muriel said, "I would require the energy of a knot unraveling to work any spell capable of restoring your grandmother to her former state."

"We can't untie your last knot," Seth said. "Grandpa would be furious."

The witch shrugged. "My predicament is simple. Imprisoned in this shack, I am curtailed in my abilities. The problem has nothing to do with my willingness to compromise—the dilemma is that the only way for me to fulfill your request would be to harness the power stored in the final knot. The decision lies in your hands. I have no other options."

"If we untie the last knot, will you also tell us where our grandpa was taken?" Kendra asked.

"Child, I would love nothing more than to reunite you with your lost grandfather. But the truth of the matter is, I haven't the foggiest notion where he was taken. Again, it would require loosing my knot in order for me to marshal sufficient power to discern his whereabouts."

"Could you find Grandpa and change Grandma with the power from one knot?" Kendra asked.

"Lamentably, I would have the opportunity to accomplish only one feat or the other. Both would not be possible."

"Unless you figure out a way, you won't have a chance to do either," Seth said.

"Then we have reached an impasse," the witch apologized. "If you tell me we have no deal unless I am able to accomplish the impossible, then we have no deal. I could fulfill either of your requests, but not both."

"If we have you change Grandma back," Kendra asked, "could you help us find Grandpa once you're free?"

"Perhaps," the witch mused. "Yes, without guarantees, once free I could probably use my abilities to shed light on the location of your grandfather."

"How do we know you won't attack us if we let you go?" Seth asked.

"A fair question," Muriel said. "I might be embittered by long years of imprisonment and eager to work mischief once released. However, I give you my word as a practitioner of the ancient art that I will not inflict any harm upon you or your grandmother upon my deliverance from this confinement. If I held any malice, it would be toward those who initiated my incarceration, enemies who passed from this life decades ago, not those who set me free. If anything, I would consider myself indebted."

"And you would promise to help us find Grandpa Sorenson?" Kendra said.

"Your grandmother might refuse my help. She and your grandfather have never held me in much esteem. But if she will accept my assistance in locating Stan, I will give it."

"We need to talk about this in private," Kendra said.

"Be my guest," Muriel said.

Kendra and Seth returned to the path. Kendra dumped

her bartering items in the wheelbarrow. She spoke in a soft whisper. "I don't think we have any other choice."

"I don't like how nice she's being," said Seth. "It's almost scarier than before. I think she's really anxious to get out."

"I know. But I think we're just as anxious to restore Grandma and maybe find Grandpa."

"She's a liar," Seth cautioned. "I don't think we can count on any of her promises."

"Probably not."

"We should expect her to attack us as soon as she's free. If not, great, but I brought salt, whatever good that will do."

"Don't forget, we'll have Grandma to help us handle her," Kendra said.

"Grandma might not know anything about fighting witches."

"I'm sure she's learned a trick or two. Let's try to ask her."

Seth held up the hen. Kendra stroked her head gently. "Grandma Sorenson," Kendra said. "Ruth. I need you to listen to me. If you can hear me, we need you to answer. This is very important." The hen appeared to be listening. "Should we untie the last knot to have Muriel Taggert restore you?"

The head bobbed.

"Was that a yes?"

The head bobbed again.

"Can you give us a no?"

The hen did not respond.

"Grandma. Ruth. Can you shake your head so we can be sure you hear us?"

Again the chicken made no acknowledgment.

"Maybe it took all she had to answer your first question," Seth speculated.

"It did seem like she nodded," Kendra said. "And I don't know what else we can do. Freeing the witch is a high price to pay, but is it worse than having no hope of finding Grandpa and keeping Grandma trapped forever as a chicken?"

"We should free her."

Kendra paused, scrutinizing her feelings. Was this really their only option? It seemed to be. "Let's go back," she agreed.

They returned to the doorway of the shack. "We want you to restore Grandma," Kendra said.

"You will voluntarily sunder my last knot, the final impediment to my independence, if I restore your grandmother to her human form?"

"Yes. How do we do it?"

"Just say 'of my own free will I sever this knot' and then blow on it. You should probably find something for your grandmother to wear. She will not have any clothes on."

Kendra ran to the wheelbarrow and returned with the bathrobe and a pair of slippers. Muriel stood in the doorway, clutching the rope. "Lay your grandmother at my threshold," she instructed.

"I want to blow on the knot," Seth said.

"Sure," Kendra answered.

"You let Grandma out of the bag."

Kendra squatted and pulled the mouth of the bag wide open. Muriel held the rope out to Seth. The chicken looked up, ruffling her feathers and flapping her wings. Kendra tried to steady her, disgusted by the feel of slender bones moving beneath her hands.

"Of my own free will, I sever this knot," Seth said, as Goldilocks squawked noisily. He blew, and the knot unraveled.

Muriel extended both hands over the flustered hen and began softly chanting indecipherable words. The air wavered. Kendra squeezed the squirming hen. At first it felt like bubbles were shooting through the flesh of the bird; then the delicate bones started to churn. Kendra dropped Goldilocks and stepped back.

Kendra saw everything as if through fun-house lenses. Muriel appeared distorted, first stretching broad, then tall. Seth became an hourglass with a wide head, a tiny waist, and clownish feet. Rubbing her eyes failed to cure her warped vision. When she looked down, the ground curved away in all directions. She leaned and swung her arms to maintain her balance.

The fun-house Muriel began to ripple, as did the startling image of Goldilocks shedding feathers as she expanded into a person. The scene grew dim, as if clouds had blocked the sun, and a dark aura gathered around

Muriel and Grandma. The darkness expanded, momentarily obscuring everything, and then Grandma stood before them, completely naked. Kendra put the bathrobe over her shoulders.

From inside the shack came a sound like the rushing of a terrible wind. The ground rumbled. "Get down," Grandma said, pulling Kendra to the ground. Seth also fell flat.

A furious gale blasted the walls of the shack into shrapnel. The roof rocketed beyond the treetops, a geyser of wooden confetti. The stump split down the center. Fragments of timber and ivy whistled in all directions, clattering against the trunks of trees and slashing through the undergrowth.

Kendra raised her head. Dressed in rags, Muriel gaped in wonder. Chips of wood continued to fall like hail, along with fluttering bits of ivy. Muriel grinned, displaying deformed teeth and inflamed gums. She began to chuckle, tears brimming in her eyes. She flung her wrinkled arms wide. "Emancipation!" she cried. "Justice at last!"

Grandma Sorenson rose to her feet. She was shorter and stouter than Muriel, with hair the color of cinnamon and sugar. "You must vacate this property immediately."

Muriel glowered at Grandma, the joy in her gaze eclipsed by spite. A tear escaped and slid down a crease to her chin. "This is my thanks for unbinding your curse?"

"You have your reward for the services you rendered. You have emerged from confinement. Eviction from this preserve is the consequence of prior indiscretions."

"My debts have been paid. You are not the caretaker."

"My authority is the same as my husband's. In his absence, I am indeed the caretaker. I invite you to leave and never return."

Muriel turned and began tromping away. "Where I go is my business." She did not look back.

"Not on my preserve."

"*Your* preserve, is it? I object to your claims of ownership." Muriel still had not looked back. Grandma started walking after her, an old woman in a bathrobe trailing an old woman dressed in rags.

"New crimes will entail new punishments," Grandma warned.

"You might be surprised who administers the penalties."

"Don't provoke new enmity. Depart in peace." Grandma quickened her pace and caught hold of Muriel by the upper arm.

Muriel twisted free, turning to face Grandma. "Tread lightly, Ruth. If you seek trouble here and now, in front of the little ones, I will oblige you. This is the wrong moment to cling to antiquated protocol. Things have changed more than you realize. I suggest you depart before I regain authority here."

Seth ran toward them. Grandma took a step back. Seth flung a handful of salt at the witch. It had no effect. Muriel pointed at him. "Your recompense is coming, my bold little whelp. I have a long memory."

"Your actions require retribution," Grandma warned.

Muriel was striding away again. "You speak to deaf ears."

"You said you'd tell us how to find our grandpa," Kendra called.

Muriel laughed without looking back.

"Hold your tongues, children," Grandma said. "Muriel, I have commanded you to depart. Your defiance is an act of war."

"You issue evictions in order to build a case for wrongdoing and thereby justify retaliation," Muriel said. "I do not fear a feud with you."

Grandma turned away from Muriel. "Kendra, come here." Grandma pulled Seth to her in a tight hug. When Kendra drew near, she embraced her as well. "I am sorry for misleading you children. I should not have guided you to Muriel. I did not realize this was her final knot."

"What do you mean?" Kendra said. "You heard us talking."

Grandma smiled sadly. "As a chicken, thinking clearly becomes an exhausting challenge. My mind was in a haze. To interact with you like a person, even for a moment, required tremendous concentration."

Seth nodded toward Muriel. "Should we stop her? I bet the three of us could take her."

"If we attack, she will be able to defend herself with magic," Grandma said. "We would forfeit the protection afforded by the foundational covenants of the treaty."

"Have we messed things up?" Seth asked. "Setting her free, I mean."

"Things were already dismal," Grandma said. "Having her on the loose certainly complicates the situation. Whether my assistance can compensate for her interference remains to be seen." Grandma looked flushed. She fanned her face. "Your grandfather left us in quite a predicament."

"It wasn't his fault," Seth said.

Grandma bent over, placing her hands on her knees. Kendra steadied her. "I'm all right, Kendra. Just a little woozy." She stood up experimentally. "Tell me what happened. I know undesirable beings entered the house and took Stan."

"They took Lena, too, and I think they turned Dale into a statue," Kendra reported. "We found him in the yard."

Grandma nodded. "As caretaker, Stan is a valuable trophy. Same with a fallen nymph. By contrast Dale seemed unimpressive and was left behind. Any clue who took them?"

"We found some footprints near Dale," Seth said.

"Did they lead you anywhere?"

"No," Seth said.

"Have you any idea where Grandpa and Lena are being held?"

"No."

"Muriel probably knows," Grandma said. "She has an alliance with the imps."

"Speaking of Muriel," Kendra said, "where did she go?"

They all looked around. Muriel was no longer in sight. Grandma frowned. "She must have special means of hiding or traveling. No matter. We aren't equipped to deal with her now."

"What do we do?" Seth asked.

"Our first order of business is to find your grandpa. Learning his location should dictate how best to proceed."

"How do we do that?"

Grandma sighed. "Our nearest option would be Nero."

"Who?" Kendra said.

"A cliff troll. He has a seeing stone. If we can successfully bargain with him, he should be able to reveal Stan's location."

"Do you know him well?" Seth asked.

"Never met him. Your grandfather had dealings with him once. It will be dangerous, but at present he is probably our best alternative. We should hurry. I'll tell you more on the way."

CHAPTER FOURTEEN

Trolling for Grandpa

H ave you ever heard people conversing while you're falling asleep?" Grandma said. "The words reach you from a distance, and you can barely glimpse the meaning."

"That happened to me in a motel once when we were on a trip," Kendra said. "Mom and Dad were talking. I fell asleep, and their conversation turned into a dream."

"Then to some degree you can grasp my state of mind as a chicken. You say it is June. My last clear memories are from February, when the spell was enacted. For the first couple of days I remained fairly alert. Over time, I lapsed into a twilight consciousness, incapable of rational thought, unable to interpret my surroundings as a human would."

"Weird," Seth said.

"I recognized you kids when you arrived, but it was through a clouded lens. My mind did not reawaken until you let those creatures in through the window. The shock jolted me out of my stupor. It was a struggle to cling to my elevated consciousness. I cannot describe the concentration it required to write that message to you. My mind wanted to slip away, to relax. I wanted to eat the delicious kernels, not arrange them into bizarre patterns."

They traveled along a wide dirt road. Rather than head back toward the house, they had continued on the trail beyond the ivy shack, venturing deeper into the forest. The trail had eventually forked and then intersected the road they were currently following. The sun blazed overhead, the air was heavy and humid, and the forest remained unnaturally silent all around them.

Kendra and Seth had brought a pair of jeans, but they turned out to be from Grandma's skinnier days, and were not even close to fitting. The tennis shoes belonged to Grandpa and were several sizes too big. So Grandma now wore a bathing suit under her robe, and her feet remained in slippers.

Grandma raised her hands, staring as she opened and closed them. "Strange to have proper fingers again," she murmured.

"How did you become a chicken in the first place?" Seth asked.

"Pride made me careless," Grandma said. "A sobering

reminder that none of us are immune to the dangers here, even when we imagine we have the upper hand. Let's save the details for another time."

"Why didn't Grandpa change you back?" Kendra asked.

Grandma's eyebrows shot up. "Probably because I kept laying eggs for his breakfast. I like to think that if he had taken me to Muriel in the first place, I could have prevented all this nonsense from happening. But I suppose he was searching for an alternate cure for my condition."

"Besides asking Muriel," Seth said.

"Exactly."

"Then why did he have Muriel cure me?"

"I'm sure he knew your parents would return soon, leaving insufficient time to discover another remedy."

"You had no idea Seth had become a mutant walrus and been restored by Muriel?" Kendra said.

"I missed all that," Grandma said. "As a hen, most details escaped me. When I urged you to take me to Muriel, I assumed she still had two knots remaining. Only when I looked up and observed the single knot did I begin to fathom the actual predicament. By then it was too late. Incidentally, how did you end up as a walrus?"

Seth and Kendra related the particulars about turning the fairy into an imp and the subsequent retribution. Grandma listened, asking a few clarifying questions.

As the path curved around a tall thicket, a covered bridge came into view up ahead. Spanning a ravine, the bridge was composed of dark wood. Although aged and weathered, it appeared to be in reasonably good repair.

"Our destination draws near," Grandma said.

"Beyond the bridge?" Kendra asked.

"Down in the ravine." Grandma stopped, studying the foliage off to either side of the road. "I am suspicious of the stillness in these woods. A great tension rests upon Fablehaven today." She resumed walking.

"Because of Grandpa?" Seth asked.

"Yes, and your newfound enmity with the fairies. But I worry there may be something more. I am anxious to speak with Nero."

"Will he help us?" Kendra asked.

"He would rather harm us. Trolls can be violent and unpredictable. I would not solicit information from him if our situation were less dire."

"What's the plan?" Seth asked.

"Our only chance is clever bargaining. Cliff trolls are cunning and ruthless, but their avarice can be a weakness."

"Avarice?" Seth asked.

"Greed. Cliff trolls are miserly creatures. Treasure hoarders. Cunning negotiators. They relish the thrill of besting an opponent. Whatever agreement we reach, Nero will have to feel like the undisputed victor. I only hope we can determine something he values that we are willing to part with."

"What if we can't?" Kendra said.

"We must. If we fail to reach an arrangement, Nero will not let us leave unscathed."

They arrived at the brink of the ravine. Kendra placed a hand against the bridge and leaned forward to look down. It was surprisingly deep. Tenacious vegetation clung to the steep walls. A narrow stream trickled along the bottom. "How do we get down there?"

"Carefully," Grandma said, taking a seat at the edge of the precipice. Rolling over onto her stomach, she started backing down the slope feet first, looking ridiculous in her robe and slippers. The incline was not completely vertical, but most of the descent was quite steep.

"If we fall, we'll tumble all the way to the bottom," Kendra observed.

"A sensible reason not to fall," Grandma agreed, moving carefully downward. "Come along, it looks worse than it is. Just find solid handholds and take it one step at a time."

Seth followed Grandma, and then Kendra started down, desperately hugging the side of the ravine, taking tentative steps, hunting blindly for the next place to rest her foot. But Grandma was right. Once she got going, the climb was less difficult than it appeared. There were many handholds, including scrawny bushes with well-anchored stems. After proceeding gingerly at first, she grew in confidence and increased the speed of her descent.

When Kendra reached the bottom, Seth was squatting near a cluster of blossoms at the edge of the stream.

Grandma Sorenson stood nearby. "Took you long enough," Seth said.

"I was being careful."

"I've never seen somebody move an inch per hour before."

"No time for bickering," Grandma said. "Kendra did just fine, Seth. We need to hurry along."

"I like the smell of these flowers," Seth said.

"Come away from those," Grandma insisted.

"Why? They smell great; take a whiff."

"Those flowers are perilous. And we're in a hurry." Grandma waved for him to follow and started walking, picking her way carefully along the rocky floor of the ravine.

"Why are they dangerous?" Seth asked, catching up with her.

"Those are a peculiar class of lotus blossoms. The smell is intoxicating, the taste divine. A tiny nibble of a single petal carries you away into a lethargic trance populated by vivid hallucinations."

"Like drugs?"

"More addictive than most drugs. Sampling a lotus blossom awakens a craving that will never be silenced. Many have wasted their lives pursuing and consuming the petals of those bewitching flowers."

"I wasn't going to eat one."

"No? Sit and smell them for a few minutes, and you'll end up with a petal in your mouth before you know what you're doing."

They proceeded in silence for a few hundred yards. The walls of the ravine grew more sheer and rocky as they progressed. They noticed a few other clusters of lotus blossoms.

"Where is Nero?" Kendra asked.

Grandma scanned the wall of the ravine. "Not much farther. He lives up on a ledge."

"We have to climb up to him?"

"Stan said Nero lowered a rope ladder."

"What's that?" Seth asked, pointing up ahead.

"I'm not sure," Grandma said. A good distance down the ravine, about twenty upright logs of increasing height led from the edge of the stream to the wall of the ravine. The highest log granted access to a rocky ledge. "It might be our destination. This is not what Stan described."

They arrived at the logs. The lowest was three feet tall, the next was six feet, and each subsequent log stood roughly three feet taller than the previous one, until the tallest rose about sixty feet high. The logs were arranged about three feet apart, in a staggered row. None of the logs had any limbs. Short or tall, they were all of a similar circumference, about eighteen inches, and they were all cut flat across the top.

Placing a hand beside her mouth, Grandma called up to the ledge. "Nero! We would like to meet with you!"

"Not a good day," a voice answered, deep and silky. "Try me next week." They could not see the speaker.

"We must meet today or never," Grandma insisted.

"Who has such an urgent need?" the resonant voice inquired.

"Ruth Sorenson and her grandchildren."

"Ruth Sorenson? What is your request?"

"We need to find Stan."

"The caretaker? Yes, I could discern his location. Ascend the stairs and we will discuss terms."

Grandma looked around. "You don't mean these logs," she called.

"I most assuredly do."

"Stan said you had a ladder."

"That was before I set up these logs. No small undertaking."

"Climbing them looks precarious."

"Call it a filter," Nero said. "A means to ensure that those who seek my services are in earnest."

"So we must climb the logs for the privilege of speaking with you? How about we talk from down here?"

"Unacceptable."

"Your stairs are equally unacceptable," Grandma said firmly.

"If your need is dire, you will scale them," observed the troll.

"What have you done with the ladder?"

"I still have it."

"May we please climb it instead? I am not dressed for an obstacle course. We'll make it worth your while."

"How about a compromise? One of you climb the logs.

Then I will lower the ladder for the other two. Final offer. Concede or go acquire your information elsewhere."

"I'll do it," Seth said.

Grandma looked at him. "If anyone is climbing those logs, it will be me. I'm taller and better able to reach from log to log."

"I have smaller feet, so the logs will feel bigger. I'll keep my balance easier."

"Sorry, Seth. This is something I must do."

Seth dashed over to the first log, scrambled onto it without much trouble, and, taking a jump as if he were playing leapfrog, ended up seated atop the second log. Grandma hurried over to the second log. "You get down from there!"

Seth shakily got to his feet. Leaning forward, he placed his hands on the third log. From his position on the second log, the top of the third came almost to the middle of his chest. Another leapfrog jump and he sat atop the nine-foot log. "I can do this," he said.

"It won't be so easy as you get higher," Grandma warned. "You come down and let me do it."

"No way. I already have one dead grandma."

Kendra watched silently. From his seated position, Seth shifted to his knees and rose unsteadily to his feet. He leapt to the next log, now well out of Grandma's reach. Kendra was quietly glad Seth was climbing the logs. She could not picture Grandma doing it successfully, especially dressed in a bathrobe and slippers. At the very least, think of the terrible places she could get splinters! And Kendra could very clearly envision Grandma Sorenson crumpled in a lifeless heap at the base of a log.

"Seth Andrew Sorenson, you mind your grandmother! I want you to come down from there."

"Stop distracting me," he said.

"It may seem like fun on these lower logs, but when you get higher—"

"I climb high stuff all the time," Seth insisted. "My friends and I climb up in the bars under the bleachers at the high school. If we fell there we could die too." He rose to his feet. He seemed to be getting better at it. Seth landed on the next log, straddling it for a moment before getting to his knees.

"Be careful," Grandma said. "Don't think about the height."

"I know you're trying to help," Seth said. "But please stop talking."

Grandma came and stood by Kendra. "Can he do this?" she whispered.

"He has a good chance. He's really brave, and pretty athletic. The height might not get to him. I would freak out."

Kendra wanted to look away. She did not want to see him fall. But she could not take her eyes from her brother as he leapfrogged from log to log, higher and higher. As he jumped to the thirteenth, almost forty feet high now, he leaned precariously to one side. Chills raced through

Kendra as if she were the one losing her balance. Seth gripped with his legs and leaned the other way, regaining his equilibrium. Kendra could breathe again.

Fourteen, fifteen, sixteen. Kendra glanced at Grandma. He was going to make it! Seventeen. He got to his feet, wobbling a bit, hands out to either side. "These tall ones shake a little," he called down.

Seth leapfrogged to the next log and landed awkwardly, teetering too far to one side. For a moment he hovered on the brink of regaining his balance. Every muscle in Kendra's body clenched in horror. Arms pinwheeling, Seth fell. Kendra shrieked. She could not look away.

Something flashed from the ledge—a slender, black chain with a metal weight at the end. The chain coiled around one of Seth's legs. Instead of falling to the ground, he swung into the cliff, colliding roughly with the stone wall.

For the first time Kendra had a view of Nero. Built like a man, the troll had reptilian features. A few bright yellow markings decorated his glossy black body. He held in a webbed hand the chain from which Seth dangled. Muscles bunching powerfully, Nero hauled Seth up to the ledge. They passed out of sight, and then a rope ladder unfurled from the ledge, unwinding all the way to the base of the cliff.

"Are you okay?" Kendra yelled up at Seth.

"I'm fine," he answered. "Just had the wind knocked out of me."

Grandma started up the ladder. Kendra followed, forcing herself to focus on grabbing the next rung, denying the impulse to look down. At length she reached the ledge. She moved to the rear of the ledge, standing beside the low mouth of a dark cave from which wafted a cool draft.

Nero looked even more intimidating up close. Tiny, sleek scales covered his sinuous body. Though he was not much taller than Grandma, the thickness of his brawny physique made him seem massive. He had a snout rather than a nose, and bulging eyes that never blinked. A row of sharp spines ran from the center of his forehead to the small of his back.

"Thank you for rescuing Seth," Grandma said.

"I told myself, if the boy makes it past fifteen logs, I will assist him if he falls. I admit that I am curious to hear what you would exchange to learn the location of your husband." His voice was suave and rich.

"Tell us what you have in mind," Grandma said.

A long, gray tongue popped out of his mouth and licked his right eye. "You would have me speak first? So be it. I do not ask much, an insignificant trifle for the proprietress of this illustrious preserve. Six coffers of gold, twelve puncheons of silver, three casks of uncut gems, and a bucket of opals."

Kendra looked at Grandma. Could she possibly own that much treasure?

"A reasonable sum," Grandma said. "Unfortunately, we have brought no such riches with us."

"I can wait while you retrieve the payment, if you leave the girl as collateral."

"Regrettably we lack the time to shuttle treasure to you, unless you would reveal Stan's location before receiving compensation."

Nero licked his left eye and grinned, a hideous sight that displayed double rows of needle teeth. "I must be paid in full before fulfilling your request."

Grandma folded her arms. "I take it you already possess great caches of treasure. It surprises me that such a meager financial offering as I could supply would entice you to trade."

"Go on," he said.

"You are offering us a service. Perhaps we should repay you with a service as well."

Nero nodded thoughtfully. "Possible. The boy has some spirit. Indenture him to me for fifty years."

Seth looked desperately at Grandma.

Grandma frowned. "I hope to leave the possibility of future business open, therefore I do not wish to leave you feeling slighted. The boy has spirit, but little ability. You would assume the burden of training him as a servant, and find yourself yoked to his incompetence. You would add more value to his life through education than he would to yours through service."

"Your candor is appreciated," Nero said, "although you have much to learn about bargaining. I begin to wonder whether you have anything of value to offer. If not, our discussion will not end well."

"You speak of value," Grandma said. "I ask, what value is treasure to a wealthy troll? The more riches he possesses, the less each new acquisition improves his total worth. A bar of gold means much more to a pauper than to a king. I also question what value a frail human servant would have to a master infinitely more wise and capable? Consider the situation. We want you to render a service of value to us, something we cannot do for ourselves. You should expect no less."

"I agree. Take care. Your words are spreading a net at your feet." A lethal edge was creeping into his voice.

"True, unless I am trained to deliver a service of extraordinary value. Have you ever received a massage?"

"Are you serious? The idea has always struck me as ridiculous."

"The idea seems absurd to all the uninitiated. Beware of rash judgments. We all pursue wealth, and those who gather the most can afford certain comforts unavailable to the masses. Foremost among these luxuries is the inde-scribable release and relaxation of a massage at the hands of one skilled in the art."

"And you claim to be skilled in this so-called art?"

"Trained by a true master. My ability is so great as to be nearly beyond purchase. The only person in the world who has received a full massage at my hands is the caretaker himself, and this because I am his woman. I could give you a full massage, kneading and soothing every muscle in your body. The experience would redefine your understanding of pleasure."

Nero shook his head. "It will take more than florid words and grandiose promises to persuade me."

"Consider my offer in perspective," Grandma said. "People pay exorbitant sums for an expert massage. You will receive yours at no cost, merely in exchange for a service. How long would it take you to ascertain Stan's location?"

"A few moments."

"A massage will take me thirty grueling minutes. And you will be experiencing something new, a delight you have never encountered in all your long years. A similar opportunity may never arise again."

Nero licked an eye. "Granted, I have never received a massage. I could name many things I have never done, mainly because I have no interest in doing them. I have sampled human food and found it wanting. I am not convinced that I will find a massage as satisfying as you describe."

Grandma studied him. "Three minutes. I will give you a sample for three minutes. It will afford you only a narrow glimpse of the unspeakable bliss that awaits, but should place you in a position to make a more educated decision."

"Very well. I see no harm in a demonstration."

"Give me your hand."

"My hand?"

"I will massage a single hand. You will have to use your imagination to envision how this would feel across your entire body."

He held out a hand. Grandma Sorenson took it and began working his palm with her thumbs. At first he tried to keep a straight face, but his mouth began to twitch, and his eyes began to roll. "How is that?" Grandma asked. "Too deep?"

His meager lips quivered. "Just right," he purred.

Grandma continued expertly rubbing his palm and the back of his hand. He started licking his eyes compulsively. She finished with his fingers. "The demonstration is concluded," she announced.

"Thirty minutes of that, you say, across my whole body?"

"The children will assist me," Grandma said. "We will trade a service for a service."

"But I could exchange my service for something more enduring! For treasure! A single massage is too fleeting."

"The law of diminishing returns applies to massages, as it does to most things. The first is the best, and all you really need. Besides, you can always exchange your services for treasure. This may be your only chance to receive an expert massage."

He held out his other hand. "One more example, to help me decide."

"No more samples."

"You offer just one massage? What if you stay on as my personal masseuse for twelve years?"

Grandma grew stern. "I am not petitioning you to look in that stone of yours multiple times for multiple purposes. I am requesting a single piece of information. A service for a service. That is my offer, lopsided in your favor. The massage takes thirty minutes, versus mere moments for you to peer into your stone."

"But you need the information," Nero reminded her. "I do not need a massage."

"Satisfying needs is the burden of the poor. The wealthy and powerful can afford to indulge their wants and whims. If you pass on this opportunity, you will always wonder what you missed."

"Don't do it, Grandma," Kendra said. "Just give him the treasure."

Nero held up a finger. "This proposition is unorthodox, and against my better judgment, but the idea of a massage intrigues me, and I am rarely intrigued. However, thirty minutes is too short. Say . . . two hours."

"Sixty minutes," Grandma said flatly.

"Ninety," Nero countered.

Grandma wrung her hands. She folded and unfolded her arms. She rubbed her brow.

"Ninety minutes is too long," Kendra said. "You've never given Grandpa a massage longer than an hour!"

"Hold your tongue, child," Grandma snapped.

"Ninety or no deal," Nero said.

Grandma sighed in resignation. "All right . . . ninety minutes."

"Very well, I accept. But if I do not approve of the entire massage, the deal is off."

Grandma shook her head. "No caveats. A single ninety-minute massage in exchange for the location of Stan Sorenson. You will treasure the memory until the end of your days."

Nero eyed Kendra and Seth before fixing Grandma with a shrewd gaze. "Agreed. How do we proceed?"

The best table Grandma could find was a fairly narrow stone shelf near the mouth of the cave. Nero stretched out on the shelf, and Grandma showed Kendra and Seth how to massage his legs and feet. She demonstrated how and where to use their knuckles and the heels of their hands.

"He's very strong," she said, grinding her knuckles against the bottom of his foot. "Lean into it as much as you want." She set down his leg and stood beside his head. "The children have their instructions, Nero. The ninety minutes start now."

Kendra hesitantly laid her hands on the troll's bulging calf. Although they were not wet, the scales felt slimy. She had held a snake before, and the texture of Nero's scaly skin was quite similar.

With Nero lying prone, Grandma went to work on the back of his neck and shoulders. She employed a variety of techniques—probing with her thumbs, rubbing with her palms, pressing with her fists, digging with her elbows. She ended up kneeling on the small of his back, careful to avoid the spikes along his spine, squeezing and kneading and applying pressure in diverse ways.

Nero was obviously in ecstasy. He purred and moaned in decadent satisfaction. A constant stream of drowsy compliments flowed from his lips. He languidly encouraged them to rub harder and deeper.

Kendra grew weary, and Grandma periodically demonstrated other techniques for her and Seth to employ. Kendra despised working on Nero's feet the most, from the roughness of his cracked heels, to the smooth pads of his calluses, to the lumpy bunions on his toes. But she tried her best to follow Grandma's tireless example. Besides assisting with his legs and feet, Grandma labored on his head, neck, shoulders, back, arms, hands, chest, and abdomen.

When they finally finished, Nero sat up with a euphoric smile. All the cunning had vanished from his bulbous eyes. He looked ready for the most satisfying nap of his life.

"Closer to a hundred minutes," Grandma said. "But I wanted to do it right."

"Thank you," he said giddily. "I never imagined something like that." He got to his feet, leaning against the wall of the cliff to steady himself. "You have amply earned your reward."

"I've never felt anyone so full of knots and tension," Grandma said.

"I feel loose now," he said, swinging his arms. "I will be right back with the information you seek." Nero ducked into the cave.

"I want to see his magic stone," Seth mumbled.

"Wait patiently," Grandma chided, wiping perspiration from her brow.

"You must be exhausted," Kendra said.

"I'm not in very good condition," Grandma admitted. "That took a lot out of me." She lowered her voice. "But it sure beats barrels of treasure that we don't have."

Seth wandered over to the brink of the ledge and stared down into the ravine. Grandma took a seat on the shelf where they had administered the massage, and Kendra waited beside her.

Before long, Nero emerged. He still looked affable and relaxed, though not quite as loopy as before. "Stan is chained in the basement of the Forgotten Chapel."

Grandma's jaw tightened. "You're sure?"

"It was a little tricky finding him and sneaking a good look, considering who else is confined there, but yes, I am certain."

"He's well?"

"He's alive."

"Lena was with him?"

"The naiad? Sure, I saw her too."

"Was Muriel in the vicinity?"

"Muriel? Why would she . . . oh, that's what that was! Ruth, the agreement was for a single piece of information. But no, I didn't catch sight of her. I believe this concludes our arrangement." He gestured toward the ladder. "If you will excuse me, I need to lie down."

CHAPTER FIFTEEN

The Far Side of the Attic

Grandma refused to talk while they were in the ravine. She wore a dour, thoughtful expression and hushed any attempts at conversation. Kendra waited until they were back on the path beside the covered bridge to try her question again.

"Grandma—" Kendra began.

"Not here," Grandma admonished. "We must not discuss the situation out in the open." She motioned for them to huddle close and continued in a hushed tone. "Let this suffice. We must go after your grandpa today. Tomorrow might be too late. We will return home immediately, get equipped, and go to the place where he is being held. I will reveal his exact whereabouts once we are indoors. Muriel may not yet know his location, and even if she does, I don't want her to learn that we know."

Grandma stopped whispering and hurried them along the path. "Sorry if I have been antisocial since leaving Nero," she said after they had walked in silence for a couple of minutes. "I needed to devise a plan. You kids really did an exceptional job back there. Nobody should have to spend an afternoon rubbing a troll's feet. Seth was heroic on the logs, and Kendra did some well-timed bluffing during the negotiations. You both surpassed my expectations."

"I never knew you were a masseuse," Kendra said.

"I learned from Lena. She has collected expert instruction from around the globe. If you ever get a chance to receive a massage from her, don't turn it down." Grandma tucked some errant strands of hair behind her ear. She became distant again for a moment, pursing her lips and staring remotely as she walked. "I have a few questions for you two, things we can talk about in the open. Have you met a man named Warren?"

"Warren?" Seth repeated.

"Handsome and quiet? White hair and skin? Dale's brother."

"No," Kendra said.

"They might have brought him to the house on Midsummer Eve," Grandma prodded.

"We were with Grandpa, Dale, and Lena until after sundown, but never saw anybody else," Seth said.

"I never even heard him mentioned," Kendra added.

"Me neither," Seth agreed.

Grandma nodded. "He must have stayed at the cabin. Have you met Hugo?"

"Yeah!" Seth said. "He's awesome. I wonder where he went?"

Grandma gave Seth a measuring glance. "I trust he has been attending to his chores in the barn."

"I don't think so," Kendra said. "We had to milk the cow yesterday."

"You milked Viola?" Grandma said, plainly astonished. "How?"

Kendra described how they had set up the ladders and slid down her teats. Seth added details about how milky they had gotten.

"Resourceful children!" Grandma said. "Stan had told you nothing about her?"

"We found her because she was mooing so loud," Seth said. "She was shaking the whole barn."

"It looked like her udder was going to explode," Kendra said.

"Viola is our milch cow," Grandma said. "Every preserve has such an animal, though not all are bovine. She is older than this preserve, which was founded in 1711. At that time, she was brought over from Europe by ship. Born from a milch cow on a preserve in the Pyrenees Mountains, she was about 100 years old when she made the voyage, and was already larger than an elephant.

She has been here ever since, gradually gaining size each year."

"Looks like she's about to outgrow the barn," Seth said.

"Her growth has slowed over the years, but yes, she may one day become too colossal for her current confines."

"She provides the milk the fairies drink," Kendra said.

"More than the fairies drink it. Her ancient breed is nourished and worshipped by all creatures of fairydom. They place daily enchantments on her food and make secret offerings to honor and strengthen her. In return, her milk functions as an ambrosia central to their survival. It is no wonder that cows are still considered sacred in certain parts of the world."

"She must make tons of dung," Seth said.

"Another blessing. Her manure is the finest fertilizer in the world, coaxing plants to mature much more quickly than usual and sometimes to reach incredible proportions. By the power of her dung we can reap multiple harvests from a field in a season, and many tropical plants flourish on this property that would otherwise perish. Did you kids happen to put milk out for the fairies?"

"No," Seth said. "We spilled it all down the drain. We were mainly trying to calm down the cow."

"No matter. The absence of milk might make the fairies a little ornery, but they'll get over it. We'll see they get some tomorrow at the latest."

"So normally Hugo milks Viola," Kendra surmised.

"Correct. It is a standing order, so there must be a reason he has not carried it out during the past couple of days. You have not seen him since Midsummer Eve?"

"No."

"He was probably assigned to watch over Warren and the cabin until summoned. He should come if we call."

"Could something have happened to him?" Seth asked.

"A golem may seem like little more than animated matter granted elementary intelligence, but most creatures on this preserve fear Hugo. Few could harm him if they tried. He will be our chief ally in rescuing your grandfather."

"What about Warren?" Kendra asked. "Will he help too?"

Grandma frowned. "You have not met him because his mind has been ruined. Dale has remained on this preserve mainly in order to care for him. Warren is lost in a catatonic stupor. Fablehaven has many stories. His is another tragic tale of a mortal venturing where he did not belong. Warren will be no help to us."

"Anybody else?" Seth asked. "Like the satyrs?"

"Satyrs?" Grandma exclaimed. "When have you met satyrs? I may have some choice words for your grandfather when we find him."

"We met them by accident in the woods," Kendra assured her. "We were taking stew from what looked like a well, and they warned us that we were actually stealing from an ogress."

"Those rogues were protecting their underhanded operation more than you," Grandma huffed. "They have been pilfering her stew for years. The scoundrels didn't want to have to rebuild their thieving device—probably sounded too much like work. Satyrs live for frivolity. The ultimate fair-weather friends. Your grandfather and I share a mutual respect with various beings on this preserve, but there is not much more loyalty than one would find out in the wild. The herd looks on as the sick or injured are brought down by predators. If your grandfather is to be rescued on such short notice, it will be our doing, with none but Hugo to aid us."

※ ※ ※

It was late afternoon when they reached the yard. Grandma stood with her hands on her hips, taking in the scene. The ruined tree house. The damaged furniture strewn about the garden. The gaping, glassless windows.

"I'm afraid to go inside," she muttered.

"You don't remember how bad it is?" Kendra asked.

"She was a chicken, remember?" Seth said. "We ate her eggs."

Creases appeared on Grandma's brow. "It feels like such a betrayal to have your home violated," she said softly. "I know sinister evils lurk in the woods, but they have never crossed that boundary."

Kendra and Seth followed Grandma across the yard and up the porch steps. Grandma stooped and picked up a copper triangle, attaching it to a hook hanging from a nail. Kendra remembered noticing the triangle dangling among the wind chimes. A short copper rod was linked to the triangle by a chain of beads. Grandma clanged the rod noisily around the inside of the triangle.

"That should bring Hugo," Grandma explained. She crossed the porch and paused in the doorway, staring into her home. "It looks like we were bombed," she murmured. "Such senseless vandalism!"

She roamed the gutted house in a somber daze, occasionally pausing to pick up a damaged frame and examine the torn photograph inside or to run her hand along the remnants of a beloved piece of furniture. Grandma climbed the stairs and went to her room. Kendra and Seth watched her rummage through the closet, finally withdrawing a metal lunch box.

"At least this is intact," Grandma said.

"Hungry?" Seth asked.

Kendra slapped him on the shoulder with the back of her hand. "What is it, Grandma?"

"Follow me."

Downstairs in the kitchen, Grandma opened the lunch box. She removed a handful of photographs. "Help me lay these out."

The photos were of the house. Each room was shown from several angles. The exterior was also displayed from multiple perspectives. In total there were more than a hundred pictures. Grandma and the children began spreading them across the kitchen floor.

"We took these pictures in case the unthinkable ever occurred," Grandma said.

Kendra suddenly made the connection. "For the brownies?"

"Clever girl," said Grandma. "I'm not sure whether they will be up to the challenge, considering the extent of the damage, but they have worked miracles in the past. I'm sorry this calamity befell us during your stay."

"You shouldn't be," Seth said. "It happened because of me."

"You mustn't assume all the blame," Grandma insisted.

"What else can we do?" Kendra said. "We caused it."

"Kendra didn't do anything," Seth said. "She tried to stop me. The whole thing is my fault."

Grandma regarded Seth pensively. "You did not mean to harm Grandpa. Yes, you made him vulnerable through your disobedience. As I understand, you were commanded not to look out the window. Had you heeded the order, you would not have been tempted to open the window, and your grandfather would not have been taken. You must face that fact, and learn from it.

"But the full blame for Stan's predicament is considerably more guilt than you deserve. Your grandfather and I are the caretakers of this estate. We are responsible for the actions of those we bring here, especially children. Stan allowed you to come here to do your parents a favor, but also because we need to start selectively sharing this secret with our posterity. We will not be around forever. The secret was shared with us, and a day came when the responsibility of this enchanted refuge fell on our shoulders. One day we will have to pass the responsibility on to others."

She took Seth and Kendra by the hands and fixed them with a loving gaze. "I know the mistakes you made were not deliberate or malicious. Your grandfather and I have made plenty of mistakes ourselves. So have all the people who ever lived here, no matter how wise or cautious. Your grandfather must share the blame for placing you children in a situation where opening a window with kind intentions could cause such harm and destruction. And clearly the fiends who abducted him are ultimately the most culpable."

Kendra and Seth were silent. Seth scrunched up his face. "If it wasn't for me, Grandpa would be fine right now," he said, fighting hard not to cry.

"And I would still be a chicken in a cage," Grandma said. "Let's worry about fixing the problem instead of the blame. Don't despair. I know we can set things right. Take me to Dale."

Seth nodded, sniffing and rubbing his forearm across his nose. He led the way across the back porch, weaving through the garden toward their destination.

"There really aren't many fairies," Grandma said. "I've never seen the yard so devoid of life."

"There haven't been many around ever since they

attacked Seth," Kendra said. "Since Grandpa vanished there have been even fewer."

When they stood over the painted, life-size metal statue of Dale, Grandma shook her head. "I've never seen this particular enchantment, but that's certainly Dale."

"Can you help him?" Kendra asked.

"Perhaps, given sufficient time. Part of counteracting an enchantment is understanding who placed it, and how."

"We found tracks," Seth said. He showed Grandma the print in the flowerbed. Although the impression had faded a bit, it remained recognizable.

Grandma frowned. "It doesn't look familiar. Many creatures run wild on festival nights that we otherwise never encounter—which is why we take cover indoors. The print may not even be a relevant clue. It could belong to the perpetrator, or to the mount the perpetrator rode, or it could belong to something that just happened to step there sometime during the night."

"So we just ignore Dale for now?" Kendra asked.

"We have no alternative. Time is short. We can only hope that by rescuing your grandfather, we can shed more light on what caused Dale's condition and find a way to reverse the curse. Come."

They returned to the house. Grandma spoke over her shoulder as they mounted the stairs to the second floor. "There are a few special strongholds within the house. One is the room where you have been staying. Another is a second room on the other side of the attic."

"I knew it!" Kendra said. "I could tell from outside there had to be more to the attic. But I could never find a way in."

"You were probably searching in the wrong place," Grandma said, leading them down the hall to her room. "The two sides of the attic are not interconnected. When we get up there, I'll fill you in on my strategy." Grandma crouched and picked through a broken nightstand. She found a few hairpins and used them to pile her hair into a matronly bun. Searching more, she located a key. She led them into the master bathroom, where she used the key to unlock a closet door.

Instead of a closet, the door opened to reveal a second door, this one made of steel with a large combination wheel. A vault door. Grandma began spinning the wheel. "Four turns right to 11, three left to 28, two right to 3, one left to 31, and half a turn right to 18."

She pulled a lever, and the heavy door clacked open. Carpeted stairs led up to another door. Grandma went up first. Seth and Kendra joined her in the attic.

This side of the attic was even larger than the playroom. Grandma flipped a switch, and several lights dispelled the dimness. A long workbench dominated one side of the room, the wall above it covered with tools supported on pegs. Handsome wooden cabinets lined the other walls. Various unusual objects littered the room—a birdcage, a phonograph, a battle-ax, a hanging scale, a mannequin, a globe the size of a beach ball. Trunks and boxes were arranged in rows on the floor, leaving just enough aisle space to access them. Heavy curtains concealed the windows.

Grandma motioned them over to the workbench, where they perched on stools. "What's in all the boxes?" Seth asked.

"Many things, most of them unsafe. This is where we guard our most prized weapons and talismans. Spell books, ingredients for potions, all the good stuff."

"You can tell us more about Grandpa now?" Kendra said.

"Yes. You heard Nero say that Stan and Lena are being held in the Forgotten Chapel. Let me summarize some history to bring the ramifications into view.

"Long ago, this land was possessed by a powerful demon named Bahumat. For centuries, he terrorized the natives who dwelt in the region. They learned to avoid certain areas, yet even with these precautions, nowhere in the vicinity was truly safe. The natives made whatever offerings the demon seemed to require, but still they lived in fear. When a group of Europeans offered to overthrow the demon in exchange for a claim to the lands it haunted, the incredulous local leaders consented.

"Aided by mighty allies and potent magic, the Europeans successfully subdued and imprisoned the demon. Some years later, they founded Fablehaven on the land they wrested from Bahumat.

"Years passed. In the early 1800s, a community comprised chiefly of extended family had developed on this preserve. They built a number of dwellings around the original mansion. This was before the current house and barn were constructed. The old mansion still stands deep within this property, though most of the flimsier structures around it have been swallowed by time and the elements. Although their homes are gone, they did construct one lasting structure—a church.

"In 1826, thanks to human frailty and foolishness, Bahumat nearly escaped. It could have been a serious disaster, because none who remained on the preserve possessed the resources or knowledge to contend successfully with an entity of his power. Although the jailbreak was prevented, the experience proved too unnerving for most who lived here, and the majority departed.

"The prison that held the demon had been damaged. With outside help, Bahumat was moved to a new holding area in the basement of the church. Meetings there ceased a few months after that, and in the intervening years it has become known as the Forgotten Chapel."

"So Bahumat is still there?" Kendra said.

"Believe me, we would know if Bahumat had been loosed. I doubt anyone in the world has the capacity to recapture that fiend if he were to get free. His kind have been absent for too long, imprisoned or destroyed. Those who knew how to defeat such a foe have passed on, with none to replace them. Which brings me to my greatest concern: that Muriel might try to release Bahumat."

"Would she do something that stupid?" Seth cried.

"Muriel is a student of evil. She was originally imprisoned for tampering with such things. If she reaches the Forgotten Chapel first, which she may have already done, assuming her imps have apprised her of the situation, we will have to neutralize her in order to save your grandfather. If we allow her enough time to release Bahumat, we will all need saving. That is why I must try to stop her immediately."

"Not just you," Seth said.

"Hugo and I will handle this. You kids have done enough."

"What?" Seth exclaimed. "No way!"

"Retrieving your grandfather should not be too difficult. But if the worst-case scenario transpires, and I fail, Fablehaven could fall. Bahumat never agreed to the treaty that protects this sanctuary. None of his kind would. He has a claim to this land and is a being of sufficient power to overthrow the treaty, plunging the preserve into endless darkness. Every day would become like those fearful festival nights, and this property would be forever uninhabitable for all but the denizens of shadow. Any mortal trapped here would fall prey to horrors too terrible to contemplate."

"Could that really happen?" Kendra asked quietly.

"It would not be the first time," Grandma said. "Preserves have fallen ever since they were instituted. The causes are myriad, usually stemming from human folly. Some have been reclaimed. Others fell beyond redemption. Currently there are at least thirty fallen preserves in the world. Perhaps most unnerving are the recent whispers about the Society of the Evening Star."

"Maddox told us about them," Seth said.

"Grandpa got a letter warning him to be on the lookout," Kendra added.

"Traditionally, the fall of a preserve was an uncommon occurrence. Maybe one or two a century. About ten years ago, rumors began to circulate that the Society of the Evening Star was working mischief again. Around the same time, preserves began falling at an alarming rate. Four have fallen over the past five years."

"Why would anybody do that?" Kendra asked.

"Many have sought the answer to that question," Grandma said. "To gain riches? Power? We who safeguard the preserves are essentially conservationists. We don't want to see the magnificent magical creatures of the world go extinct. We try not to discriminate against creatures of shadow—we want them to survive as well. But we do compartmentalize them when necessary. Members of the Society of the Evening Star mask their true intentions with rhetoric, alleging that we wrongfully imprison creatures of darkness."

"Do you?" Seth asked.

"The most violent and malevolent demons are imprisoned, yes, but that is for the safety of the world. In pursuit of endless carnage and unlawful dominion, they clashed anciently with good humans and creatures of light, and are paying a heavy price for losing. Many other sinister entities were admitted to preserves only on condition that they would agree to certain limitations—agreements they entered voluntarily. A common restriction is that they are not permitted to leave the preserve, so the Society considers many of these creatures also incarcerated. They argue that the covenants of the preserves create artificial rules that upset the natural order of things. They consider the majority of humanity expendable. Their premise is that chaos and bloodshed are preferable to just regulations. We disagree."

"Do you think the Evening Star people are involved in kidnapping Grandpa?" Kendra asked.

Grandma shrugged. "Possibly. I hope not. If so, it was done with great subtlety. There are powerful limits to how any outsider can intrude on a preserve. And our preserve is more secret than most."

Grandma opened a drawer and pulled out a rolled parchment. Unrolling it, she revealed a map of the world. Large dots and X's were located on diverse portions of the map, aside from the labeling of major cities.

"The X's mark fallen preserves," Grandma said. "The dots mark active ones."

"Fablehaven isn't marked," Kendra noticed.

"Sharp eyes," Grandma said. "There are thirty-seven active preserves noted on the map. And five unmarked preserves, of which Fablehaven is one. Even among those most trusted in our community, very few people know about the unmarked preserves. None know of them all."

"Why?" Seth asked.

"Special artifacts of great power are hidden on those five preserves."

"What artifacts?" Seth asked, excited.

"I cannot say. I don't know most of the details myself. The artifact here at Fablehaven is not in our possession. It is guarded at an undisclosed location on the property. Evildoers, particularly the Society of the Evening Star, would like nothing more than to collect the artifacts from the hidden preserves."

"So there are many reasons Fablehaven must be protected," Kendra said.

Grandma nodded. "Your grandfather and I are prepared to give our lives if necessary."

"Maybe none of us should go after Grandpa," Kendra said. "Can't we get help?"

"There are some who would come to our aid if summoned, but I need to stop Muriel and find your grandfather today. Nobody could reach us that quickly. Fablehaven is protected by secrecy. At times this becomes a hindrance. I do not know what spells bind Bahumat, but I am certain that, given sufficient time, Muriel will find a way to unravel them. I must act now."

Grandma slid off the stool, walked down an aisle, opened a trunk, and withdrew an ornate box embossed with vines and flowers. From the box she removed a small crossbow not much larger than a pistol. She also took out a small arrow with black fletching, an ivory shaft, and a silver head.

"Cool," Seth cried. "I want one!"

"This dart will slay any being that was ever mortal, including the enchanted or undead, if I can lodge it in a lethal place."

"Where is lethal?" Kendra asked.

"The heart and the brain are surest. Witches can be tricky. This is the only talisman I am certain will slay Muriel."

"You're going to kill her?" Kendra whispered.

"Only as a last resort. First I will try to have Hugo capture her. But the stakes are too high for us to sally forth without a failsafe. If the golem should unforeseeably disappoint me, I lack the skills to subdue Muriel myself. Believe me, the last thing I want is her blood on my hands. Killing a mortal is not quite as grievous a crime as killing a mystical being, but it would still dissolve most of the protection afforded me by the treaty. I would probably have to banish myself from the preserve."

"But she's trying to destroy the whole preserve!" Seth complained.

"Not by directly killing anyone," Grandma said. "The chapel is neutral ground. If I go there and kill her, even if I can justify the act, the protection of the treaty will never again be mine."

"I heard Dale shooting guns and stuff the night the creatures came through our window," Kendra said.

"Creatures were invading our territory," Grandma explained. "Regardless of the reason, by coming into this house, they surrender all their protections. Under those circumstances, Dale could slay them with no fear of retribution, meaning his status under the treaty would remain secure. This same principle could work against you if you were to venture into certain forbidden areas of Fablehaven. If you were thus stripped of all protection, it would be open hunting season on Kendra and Seth. Which is precisely why those areas are prohibited."

"I don't get who would punish you for killing Muriel," Seth said.

"The mystical barriers that protect me would be lifted, and the punishment would naturally follow. You see, as mortals, we can choose to break the rules. The mystical creatures that seek asylum here are not afforded that luxury. Many would break the rules if they could, but they are bound. As long as I obey the rules, I am safe. But if I lose the protections afforded by the treaty, the consequences of my vulnerability would inevitably follow."

"So does that mean Grandpa is alive for sure?" Kendra asked in a small voice. "They can't kill him or anything."

"Stan has kept the rules pertaining to bloodshed, and so, even on their night of revelry, the dark creatures of this preserve would not be able to kill him. Nor would they be able to force him to go to a place that would enable them to kill him. Imprisoned, tortured, driven insane, turned to lead—maybe. But he has to be alive. And I have to go after him."

"And I have to come with you," Seth said. "You need backup."

"Hugo is my backup."

Seth scrunched his face, resisting tears. "I'm not going to lose you guys, especially when it's my fault."

Grandma Sorenson embraced Seth. "Sweetheart, I appreciate your courage, but I'm not about to risk losing a grandchild."

"Won't we be in just as much danger here as we would be if we were with you?" Kendra said. "If the demon gets loose, we'll all be fried."

"I mean to send you away, off the preserve," Grandma said.

Kendra folded her arms. "So we can wait outside the gate until our parents get back, tell them you were killed by a demon, and insist that we can't go to the house because it's really a magical preserve that has fallen into darkness?"

"Your parents do not know the true nature of this place," Grandma said. "Nor would they believe without seeing."

"Exactly!" Kendra said. "If you fail, the first thing Dad will do is go straight to your house and investigate. Nothing we could say would keep him away. And he'll probably call the cops, and the whole world will find out about this place."

"They wouldn't see anything," Grandma said. "But many would die inexplicably. And actually, they could see the cow, even without the milk, because Viola remains a mortal being."

"We came in handy with the troll," Seth said. "And no matter what you do or say, I'll follow you anyways."

Grandma tossed up her hands. "Sincerely, children, I think all will be fine. I know I described a dire scenario, but things like this happen on preserves from time to time, and we normally get them resolved. I don't see why this would be any different. Hugo will mend the problem without serious incident, and if it comes to it, I am a crack shot with the crossbow. If you will just wait outside the gates, I'll come for you before it gets too late."

"But I want to see Hugo pound Muriel," Seth insisted.

"If we're supposed to possibly inherit this place someday, you won't always be able to protect us from danger," Kendra said. "Wouldn't it be a good experience for us to watch you and Hugo handle the situation? Maybe we can even help?"

"Field trip!" Seth cried.

Grandma eyed them lovingly. "You kids are growing up so fast," she sighed.

The Forgotten Chapel

As the sun hesitated above the horizon, Kendra stared out the side of the wagon, watching the trees streak past. She remembered staring at trees out the window of the SUV on the way to the preserve with her parents. This ride was much noisier, bumpier, and windier. And the destination was much more intimidating.

Hugo pulled the oversized rickshaw. Kendra doubted that a team of horses could have matched the tireless speed of his loping strides.

They reached an open area, and Kendra saw the tall hedge that surrounded the pond with the gazebo boardwalk. Strange to think that Lena had once lived there as a naiad.

Before they had boarded the wagon, Grandma had

commanded Hugo to obey any instructions from Kendra and Seth. She told Kendra and Seth that if things went wrong, they should make a hasty retreat with Hugo. She also cautioned them to be careful what they told Hugo to do. Since he had no will of his own, the punishments for his actions would fall upon the heads of those issuing the orders.

Grandma had changed out of her bathrobe. She was now dressed in faded jeans, work boots, and a green top—clothing scavenged from the attic. Seth had taken great satisfaction in her choice of a green shirt.

Seth clutched a leather pouch. Grandma had explained it was full of special dust that would keep undesirable creatures away from them. She told Seth he could use it in the same way he had used the salt in the bedroom. She also warned him to use it only as a last resort. Any magic they used would only lead to less tolerable retribution if they failed. She had a pouch of the dust as well.

Kendra was empty-handed. Since she had not yet used magic, Grandma said it would be a mistake for her to start now. Apparently the protections of the treaty were quite strong for those who totally abstained from magic and mischief.

The wagon jolted over a particularly rough spot. Seth caught hold of the side to avoid falling. He looked over his shoulder and smiled. "We're hauling!"

Kendra wished she could be so obliviously calm about the whole thing. She was getting a sick feeling in her stomach. It reminded her of the first time she had to sing a solo in a school play. Fourth grade. She had always done fine in the practices, but when she peeked out past the curtains at the audience, a queasy feeling began brooding in her belly, until she became certain that she would throw up. At her cue, she walked out onto the bright stage, peering into the dim crowd, unable to find her parents in the throng. Her intro was playing, the moment arrived, and, as she started singing, the fear dissipated and the nausea vanished.

Would it be the same today? Was the anticipation worse than the event itself? At least once they got there, reality would replace uncertainty and they would be able to do something, to act. All she could do at present was worry.

How far away was this crazy church? Grandma said it wouldn't take Hugo much more than fifteen minutes, since there was a decent road all the way. Although she kept an eye out for unicorns, Kendra saw no fanciful creatures. Everything was hiding.

The sun dipped below the horizon. Grandma was pointing. Up ahead, in the middle of a clearing, sat an old-fashioned church house. It was a boxy structure with a row of large windows fanged with broken glass and a single cupola that probably contained a bell. The roof sagged. The wooden walls were gray and splintered. There was no guessing what the original color might have been. A short flight of warped steps led up to an empty doorway, where

double doors had once granted access. It looked like a perfect lair for bats and zombies.

Hugo slackened his pace, and they came to a stop in front of the shadowy doorway. The church was completely still. There was no sign anybody had been there in a hundred years.

"I'd rather have the sun, but at least we still have some light," Grandma said, using a tool to set the silver-headed arrow to the string of her undersized crossbow and pull it into position. "Let's get this over with as soon as we can. Evil likes darkness."

"Why is that?" Seth asked.

Grandma thought about the question a moment before answering. "Because evil likes to hide."

Kendra did not appreciate the tingles she got when Grandma said that. "Why don't we talk about happy things?" she suggested as they climbed down from the wagon.

"Because we're hunting witches and monsters," Seth said.

"Kendra's right," Grandma said. "It does us no good to dwell on dark thoughts. But we do want to be on the road and away from here before the twilight is gone."

"I still say we should have brought some shotguns," Seth said.

"Hugo!" Grandma said. "Lead the way quietly into the basement. Protect us from harm, but do not kill."

Kendra felt comforted just looking at the hulking

goliath of earth and stone. With Hugo as their champion, she could not picture anything giving them much trouble.

The steps groaned beneath Hugo as he climbed them. Stepping gingerly, he ducked through the large doorway. The others followed, staying close to their massive bodyguard. Grandma draped a red scarf over the crossbow, apparently to conceal it.

Please let Muriel not be here, Kendra prayed silently. *Please let us just find Grandpa and Lena and nothing else!*

The inside of the church was even gloomier than the exterior. The decaying pews had been smashed and overturned, the pulpit at the front had been thrown down, and the walls were graffitied with maroon scrawlings. Spiderwebs festooned the rafters like gossamer banners. Amber light from the sunset found entry through the windows and some irregular holes in the roof, but not enough to dispel the murkiness. There was no token indicating that this had once been a house of worship. It was just a big, dilapidated, vacant room.

The floorboards creaked as Hugo tiptoed toward a door on the far side of the chapel. Kendra found herself worrying that the floor would give way and Hugo would take an abrupt shortcut to the basement. He had to weigh a thousand pounds.

Hugo eased the corroded door open. Since the doorway was of a normal size, he had to crouch and twist in order to squeeze through.

"Everything will be fine," Grandma said, placing a bracing hand on Kendra's shoulder. "Stay behind me."

The stairs wound down and ended at a doorway without a door. Light poured through into the stairwell. Peering around Hugo as he contorted to pass through the doorway, Kendra glimpsed that they were not alone. As she followed Grandma Sorenson into the spacious basement, the implications of the scene began to register.

The room was cheerfully illuminated by no fewer than two dozen bright lanterns. It had a high ceiling and sparse furnishings. Grandpa Sorenson and Lena were each shackled spread-eagle to the wall.

A peculiar figure stood in front of Grandpa and Lena. Fashioned entirely of smooth, dark wood, it looked like a primitive puppet not much shorter than Grandpa. Instead of proper joints, the wooden parts were connected by golden hooks at the wrists, elbows, shoulders, neck, ankles, knees, hips, waist, and knuckles. The head made Kendra think of a wooden hockey mask, though that was not quite right, because it was cruder and simpler. The unusual mannequin was dancing a little jig, arms swaying, feet tapping and shuffling, gazing toward the far end of the basement.

"Is that her limberjack?" Seth asked quietly.

Of course! It was Muriel's creepy dancing puppet, only much bigger, and no longer guided by a rod in its back!

At the far side of the basement was a large alcove. It looked like someone had torn down some planks to access the niche. A net of knotted ropes crisscrossed the alcove, preventing a view inside the dismal recess. A dark form loomed beyond the ropes. A tall, beautiful woman with a lustrous cascade of honey-blonde hair stood beside the recess blowing on one of the many knots. She wore a spectacular azure gown that emphasized her seductive figure.

The striking woman was surrounded by what looked like human-sized versions of the imps Kendra had seen in Muriel's shack. They were all facing the alcove, staring at the ground. They ranged from five to six feet tall. Some were fat, some were thin, a few were muscular. Some had crooked backs, or humps, or horns, or antlers, or bulging cysts, or tails. A couple were missing a limb or an ear. All had scars. All had weathered, leathery skin and nubs instead of wings. At the feet of the human-sized imps were a multitude of the tiny, fairy-sized versions.

The air shimmered. A pair of black wings made of smoke and shadow unfurled from the alcove. Kendra experienced the sense of vertigo that had overwhelmed her when they were changing Grandma back from being a hen. It seemed like the alcove was growing more distant, like she was looking at it through the wrong end of a telescope. A burst of darkness momentarily eclipsed the steady luminance of the lanterns, and suddenly, in the midst of where all the imps were focusing their attention, a new human-sized imp sprouted up.

Kendra covered her mouth with both hands. The beautiful woman had to be Muriel. Bahumat was imprisoned by a web of knotted ropes, similar to the rope that had trapped her, and she was using wishes to increase the size of her imps, gradually freeing the demon in the process!

"Hugo," Grandma said softly. "Incapacitate the imps and capture Muriel, on the double."

Hugo charged forward.

An imp turned and let out a disgusting yowl, and others spun to face the intruders, revealing cruel, devilish faces. The gorgeous blonde turned, eyes widening in surprise. "Seize them!" she shouted.

There were more than twenty of the big imps, and ten times that many small ones. Led by the biggest and most muscular of the lot, they rushed at Hugo, a motley mob of wiry fiends.

Hugo met them in the center of the room. With fluid precision, he snatched the leader by the waist with one hand, seizing both feet with the other, and twisted briskly in opposite directions. Hugo tossed the howling leader aside as the others descended on him.

Fists flailing like battering rams, Hugo sent imps sailing in wild cartwheels. They swarmed, making agile leaps to land on his shoulders and scratch at his head. But Hugo just kept twirling and twisting and heaving, a violent ballet that sent as many imps as pounced on him careening across the basement.

Some of the imps nimbly dodged around him to sprint toward Grandma and Kendra and Seth. Hugo whirled and charged after them, grabbing a pair of them by the knees and then wielding them like clubs to swat others away.

The resilience of the imps was impressive. Hugo would fling one into the wall, and the tenacious creature would stumble to its feet and wade back in for more. Even the burly leader was still in the fray, staggering awkwardly on mangled legs.

Looking beyond the tumult, Kendra noticed Muriel blowing on a knot. "Grandma, she's up to something."

"Hugo," Grandma cried. "Leave the imps to us and go capture Muriel."

Hugo hurled the imp he was holding. The whining creature skimmed the ceiling the entire distance to the wall, where it impacted with a revolting crunch. Then the golem dashed at Muriel.

"Mendigo, protect me!" Muriel squealed. The wooden man, who still danced near Grandpa and Lena, sprinted to intercept Hugo.

Free from the indomitable onslaught of the golem, the injured imps converged on Grandma, who placed herself in front of Kendra and Seth. Holding a pouch in one hand, Grandma swung it so that it scattered a twinkling cloud of dust. As the imps reached the cloud, electricity crackled, hurling them back. A few lunged into the cloud, trying to force their way through it, but electricity flared brighter and sent them tumbling. Grandma spread more dust in the air.

Great dark wings were spreading out from the alcove. The air undulated. Kendra felt like she was viewing the basement from far away, through a narrow tunnel.

Hugo had almost reached Muriel. The overgrown limberjack dived at the golem's feet, using both arms and legs
to entangle Hugo's ankles. The golem toppled forward.
Hugo kicked free of Mendigo, sending the wooden puppet skidding across the floor, then rose to his knees and
reached for Muriel. His outstretched hands were inches
from taking hold of her when a thunderclap shook the
basement, accompanied by a brief moment of blackness.
The massive golem crumbled into a pile of rubble.

Muriel brayed in triumph, eyes crazed, delirious at having so narrowly avoided Hugo's clutches. Off to one side of
the room, Mendigo sat up. The puppet had lost an arm at
the shoulder. He picked up the limb and reattached it.

Muriel's eyes sharpened as she sensed certain victory.
"Bring them all to me," she trumpeted.

A red scarf fluttered to the floor. Grandma Sorenson
raised the crossbow in one hand while scattering the last
of the contents of her pouch with the other. She discarded
the pouch and stepped forward into the glittering dust
cloud, gripping the crossbow in both hands.

The arrow took flight. Mendigo sprang, desperately
trying to block the dart, but Hugo had knocked the puppet too far away. Muriel shrieked and toppled back against
the net of knotted ropes, a manicured hand covering the
front of her shoulder. She rebounded forward, falling to her
knees, panting, still clutching her shoulder, black feathers
protruding between her slender fingers. "You will pay for
that sting!" she screamed.

"Run!" Grandma Sorenson shouted to the children.

Too late. Eyes closed, lips moving soundlessly, Muriel stretched forth a bloody hand, and a gust of wind stripped away the sparkling dust. The injured imps rushed in, seizing Grandma Sorenson roughly.

Seth sprang forward, throwing a handful of dust over Grandma and the imps. Lightning crackled and the imps stumbled away.

"Mendigo, bring me the boy!" Muriel called.

The wooden servant charged toward Seth, racing on all fours. The imps had fanned out, several clustering near the door to prevent escape. Seth flung dust as Mendigo leaped. The electric cloud repelled the puppet. At the same time, an imp darted in from behind, knocking the pouch from Seth's grasp with a chopping motion.

The tall imp twisted Seth around, grabbed his upper arms, and hoisted him into the air so they were staring eye to eye. The imp hissed, mouth open, black tongue dangling grotesquely.

"Hey," Seth said, recognition dawning. "You're the fairy I caught!"

The imp draped Seth over its shoulder and ran toward Muriel. Another imp seized Grandma to bring her to the witch.

Kendra stood frozen with terror. Imps surrounded her. Escape was impossible. Hugo had been reduced to a pile of debris. Grandma had missed with the arrow, wounding but not killing Muriel. Seth had done his best, but he and

Grandma had been captured. There was no more defense. No more tricks. Nothing between Kendra and whatever horrors Muriel and her imps wished to inflict.

Except that the imps were not taking hold of her. They stood all around her, yet they seemed unable to reach out their hands and grab her. They would lift their arms part of the way and then stop, as if their limbs refused to obey.

"Mendigo, bring me the girl," Muriel commanded.

Mendigo shouldered through the imps. His hand stretched toward her and then stopped, wooden fingers twitching, hooks clinking softly.

"They can't touch you, Kendra," Grandpa called from where he hung shackled to the wall. "You have caused no mischief, worked no magic, inflicted no harm. Run, Kendra, they can't stop you!"

Kendra pushed between a pair of imps, heading for the door. Then she stopped short. "Can't I help you?"

"Muriel is not bound by the laws restraining her minions," Grandpa shouted. "Run all the way home, straight down the road you came by. Do no harm along the way! Don't stray from the path! Then get off the property! Ram the gate with my truck! Fablehaven will fall! One of us has to survive!"

Muriel, clutching her wounded shoulder, was already in pursuit. Kendra raced up the stairs and dashed across the chapel to the front door.

"Child, wait!" called the witch.

Kendra paused at the threshold of the church and

looked back. Muriel leaned in the doorway that led to the basement. She looked pale. Blood drenched the arm of her gown.

"What do you want?" Kendra said, trying to sound brave.

"Why rush off in such a hurry? Stay, we can talk this through."

"You don't look so good."

"This trifle? Loosing a single knot will mend it."

"Then why haven't you done it?"

"I wanted to talk before you hurried away," the witch soothed.

"What is there to talk about? Let my family go!" demanded Kendra.

"I may, in time. Child, you do not want to run off into the woods at this late hour. Who can say what horrors await out there?"

"They can't beat what's going on in here. Why are you releasing that demon?"

"You could never understand," said Muriel.

"Do you think it will be your friend? You're going to end up chained to the wall along with the others."

"Make no speeches about matters far beyond your comprehension," Muriel snapped. "I have made covenants that will place me in a position of unfathomable power. After biding my time for long years, I feel my hour of triumph at hand. The evening star is rising."

"Evening star?" Kendra repeated.

Muriel grinned. "My ambitions extend far beyond hijacking a single preserve. I am part of a movement with much broader objectives."

"The Society of the Evening Star."

"You could never imagine the designs already in motion. I have been locked away for years, yes, but not without means of communicating with the outside world."

"The imps."

"And other collaborators. Bahumat has been orchestrating this day since his capture. Time has been our ally. Watching and waiting, we have quietly leveraged countless opportunities to gradually secure our release. No prison stands forever. At times our efforts have borne little fruit. On gladder occasions, we have toppled many dominoes with a single nudge. When Ephira succeeded in coaxing you to open the window on Midsummer Eve, we were hopeful that events would unfold much as they have."

"Ephira?"

"You looked into her eyes."

Kendra cringed. She did not appreciate a reminder of the translucent woman in the gauzy black garments.

Muriel nodded. "She and others are about to inherit this sanctuary, a vital step toward reaching our ultimate ends. After decades of persistence, nothing can forestall me."

"Then why not just let my family go?" Kendra pleaded.

"They would try to interfere. Not that they could at this point—they had their chance and failed—but I will take no risks. Come, face the end with your loved ones, instead of alone in the night."

Kendra shook her head.

Muriel extended her uninjured arm. The fingers, red with her own blood, contorted into an unnatural shape. She spoke in a garbled language that made Kendra think of angry men whispering. Kendra ran out of the church, down the steps, and over to the wagon. She paused to look back. Muriel did not appear in the doorway. Whatever spell the witch had tried to cast apparently had no effect.

Kendra raced down the road. The sunset was still fairly bright. They had been inside the church for only a few minutes. Tears began to blind her, but she kept running, unsure whether she was being pursued.

Her whole family was lost! Everything had happened so fast! One moment Grandma was confidently offering assurance; the next, Hugo was destroyed and Seth and Grandma were captured. Kendra should have been captured as well, except she had been so overcautious since arriving at Fablehaven that she was still apparently shielded by the full power of the treaty. The imps had not been able to lay a finger on her, and Muriel had been too injured to give proper chase.

Kendra looked back along the empty road. The witch would have cured the injury by now, but would probably not come after her until freeing Bahumat, since Kendra had such a big head start.

Then again, Muriel could possibly use magic to catch

up with her. But Kendra suspected that the urgency of unleashing the demon would prevent Muriel from giving chase for now.

Should she turn around and head back? Try to rescue her family? How? Throw rocks? Kendra could envision nothing but certain capture if she were to return.

But she had to do something! When the demon was released, it would destroy the treaty, and Seth would die, along with Grandpa, Grandma, and Lena!

The only possibility she could think of was returning to the house and trying to find a weapon in the attic. Could she remember the combination to the vault door? She had watched Grandma open it an hour ago, heard her speak the numbers aloud. She could not recall them, but felt she might once she saw it.

Kendra knew she was without hope. The house was miles away. How many? Eight? Ten? Twelve? She would be lucky to make it there, let alone back, before Bahumat was free.

There were many knots, and it looked like Muriel could undo only one at a time. Each knot seemed to take at least a few minutes. But still, at that rate, it would be a matter of hours, not days, before the demon was free.

At least finding a weapon at the house was a goal. No matter how desperate the odds, it gave her a direction to head and a reason for going there. Who knew what the weapon would be, or how she would use it, or whether she could even get into the attic? But at least it was a plan. At least she could tell herself there was a brave reason for running away.

CHAPTER SEVENTEEN

A Desperate Gamble

Dreading nightfall did nothing to prevent it. The sunset diminished and disappeared, until Kendra had only the light reflected from half a moon to guide her. The night grew cooler, but not cold. The forest was swathed in gloomy shadow. Occasionally she heard unsettling sounds, but she never caught sight of what made them. Although she glanced back frequently, the road behind remained as empty as the road ahead.

Kendra alternated between jogging and walking. Without landmarks, it was difficult to discern how much ground she was covering. The dirt road seemed to stretch on forever.

She worried about Grandma Sorenson. Since she had shot Muriel and used Hugo to cripple the imps, there would probably be no protection for Grandma from similar torture. Kendra began to wish she had accepted Muriel's invitation to stay at the church with her family. The guilt of being the only escapee was almost too much to bear.

It was hard to calculate the passage of time. The night wore on, as endless as the road. The moon gradually migrated across the sky. Or was it the road changing direction?

Kendra felt certain she had been on the road for hours when she reached an open area. The moonlight showed a scant trail branching away from the road. It ran toward a tall, shadowy hedge.

The pond with the gazebos! Finally, a landmark. She could not be more than half an hour from the house, and there was still no hint of dawn.

How long before Bahumat would be set free? Maybe the demon was already loose. Would she know when it happened, or would she not find out until she was mobbed by monsters?

Kendra rubbed her eyes. She felt weary. Her legs did not want to walk any farther. She noticed that she was very hungry. She stopped and stretched for a minute. Then she started jogging. She could run the rest of the way, right? It wasn't too far.

As she passed the meager trail branching from the road, Kendra skidded to a halt. A new thought had occurred to her, inspired by the irregular hedge looming off to the side of the road.

The Fairy Queen had a shrine on the island in the middle of the pond. Wasn't she supposed to be the most powerful person in all the fairy world? Maybe Kendra could try asking her for help.

Kendra folded her arms. She knew so little about the Fairy Queen. Apart from hearing that the queen was powerful, she had heard only that to set foot on her island meant certain death. Some guy had tried it and turned into dandelion seeds.

But why was he trying it? Kendra did not think she had been given a specific reason, just that he had a desperate need. But the fact that he had tried meant he thought he might succeed. Maybe he just didn't have a good enough reason.

Kendra considered her need. Her grandparents and brother were about to be killed. And Fablehaven was about to be destroyed. That would be bad for the fairies too, wouldn't it? Or would the fairies not care? Maybe they would just go elsewhere.

Indecisive, Kendra stared at the faint trail. What weapon did she expect to find at the house? Probably nothing. So she would most likely end up crashing through the gate or climbing it to get away before Bahumat and Muriel caught up and finished her off. And her family would perish.

But this Fairy Queen idea might work. If the queen was so powerful, she would be able to stop Muriel and maybe even Bahumat. Kendra needed an ally. Despite her noble intentions, she could not see any way she could succeed on her own.

Kendra had felt a new sensation inside ever since the idea had popped into her head. The feeling was so unexpected that it took a moment to recognize it as hope. There were no combination locks in the way. She just had to throw herself at the mercy of an all-powerful being and plead for her family.

What was the worst that could happen? Death, but on her terms. No bloodthirsty imps. No witches. No demons. Just a big poof of dandelion fluff.

What was the best possibility? The Fairy Queen could turn Muriel into dandelion seeds and rescue Kendra's family.

Kendra started down the trail. She felt butterflies in her stomach. It was an encouraging kind of nervousness, much preferable to the dread of certain failure. She started running.

No crawling under the hedge this time. The path led to an archway. Kendra ran under the archway and onto the manicured lawn beyond.

By moonlight the whitewashed pavilions and boardwalk were even more picturesque than during the day. Kendra really could envision a Fairy Queen living on the island at the center of the tranquil pond. Of course, the queen didn't actually live there. It was just a shrine. Kendra would have to go petition her and hope the queen would respond.

Getting to the island would be the first challenge. The pond was full of naiads who liked to drown people, which meant she needed a sturdy boat.

Kendra hurried across the lawn toward the nearest gazebo. She tried to ignore the shifting shadows she saw ahead—various creatures ducking out of sight. Anticipating what she was about to attempt, Kendra felt like her intestines were caught in an eggbeater. She forced away all fear. Would Grandpa turn and flee? Would Grandma? Would Seth? Or would they try their best to save her?

She charged up the steps of the nearest pavilion and started running along the boardwalk. Her shoes pounded noisily against the boards, defying the silence. She saw her destination—the boathouse, three gazebos away.

The surface of the lake was a black mirror reflecting the moonlight. A few twinkling fairies hovered just above the water. Otherwise there was no sign of life.

Kendra reached the pavilion attached to a small pier. She dashed down the steps and out onto the quay. She reached the boathouse and tried the door. Just like before, it was locked. The door was not big, but it looked sturdy.

Kendra kicked it hard. The impact jolted up the length of her leg, making her wince. She rammed the door with her shoulder, again hurting herself instead of the door.

Kendra stepped back. The boathouse was basically a large shed floating on the water. It had no windows. She hoped it still had boats inside. If it did, they would be sitting in the water, protected by walls and a roof but no floor. If she jumped into the lake, she could surface inside the boathouse and climb into a boat.

She studied the water. The black, reflective surface was impenetrable. There could be a hundred naiads waiting in ambush, or none—it was impossible to tell.

The whole plan would be pointless if she drowned before reaching the island. Based on what she had heard from Lena, there would be naiads eagerly waiting for her to get near the water. Jumping in would be suicide.

She sat down and started bucking the door with both feet, the same method Seth had used to break into the barn. She made a lot of noise, but did not seem to be harming the door at all. Kicking harder only made her legs hurt more.

She needed a tool. Or a key. Or some dynamite.

Kendra ran back up to the pavilion, searching for something she could use to pry the door open. She saw nothing. If only there were a sledgehammer lying around.

She tried to calm herself. She had to think! Maybe if she just kept pounding, the door would eventually give. Sort of like erosion. But it hadn't budged yet, and she didn't have all night. There had to be a smarter solution. What did she have to work with? Nothing! Nothing but a few shadowy creatures who ducked out of sight at her approach.

"Okay, listen up!" she shouted. "I know you can hear me. I have to get inside the boathouse. A witch is setting Bahumat free, and all of Fablehaven is going to be destroyed. I'm not asking for anybody to stick their necks out. I just need somebody to beat down the boathouse door. My grandfather is the caretaker here, and I give you full permission. I am going to turn my back and close my eyes. When I hear the door break, I'll wait ten seconds before turning back around."

Kendra turned around and closed her eyes. She heard nothing. "Anytime, just smash down the door. I promise I won't look."

She heard a gentle splash and a tinkling sound.

"Okay! Sounds like we have a taker! Just break down the door."

She heard nothing. She suddenly realized that something could have emerged from the water and be sneaking up behind her. Unable to resist, she turned and peeked.

No dripping creatures were in sight. All was quiet. There were ripples on the previously glassy pond. And lying on the dock near the boathouse was a key.

Kendra rushed down the stairs and picked up the key. It was wet, corroded, and a little slimy. Longer than a regular key, it looked old-fashioned.

Wiping it against her shirt, she carried the key to the boathouse and inserted it in the keyhole. It fit perfectly. She turned it, and the door swung inward.

Kendra shivered. The implications were disturbing. Apparently a naiad had tossed her the key. They wanted her out on the water.

With only the moonlight seeping through the door

to provide illumination, the boathouse was very dim. Squinting, Kendra could see three boats tied to the narrow pier: two large rowboats, one slightly broader than the other, and a smaller paddleboat. The paddleboat was the kind with bicycle pedals. Kendra had once ridden in one at a park with a lake.

On one wall hung several oars of varying length. Near the door were a crank and a lever. Kendra tried to turn the crank, but it would not move. She pulled the lever. Nothing happened. She tried the crank again, and this time it turned. A sliding door on the opposite side of the boathouse from the dock began to open, letting in more light. Kendra kept cranking, relieved that she would be able to paddle a boat directly out of the boathouse onto the pond.

Standing in the gloom of the boathouse, staring out the open door at the pond, Kendra began to doubt. She felt nauseated with fear. Was she really prepared to go to her death? To have naiads drown her, or to fall victim to a spell protecting a forbidden island?

Grandpa and Grandma Sorenson were resourceful. They might have already escaped. Was she doing this for nothing?

Kendra remembered an occasion three years ago at a community pool. She had desperately wanted to jump off the high dive. Her mom had warned her that it was higher than it looked, but nothing could dissuade her. Many kids were jumping off it, several her age or younger.

She stood in line at the base of the ladder. When her turn came, she started climbing, amazed at how much higher she seemed with each step. When she arrived at the top, she felt like she was standing on a skyscraper. She wanted to turn back, but all the kids in line would know she was scared. Plus her parents were watching.

She walked forward along the diving board. There was a slight breeze. She wondered if the people on the ground could feel it. When she approached the end of the board, she stared down at the rippling water. She could see all the way to the bottom of the pool. Jumping no longer seemed like a fun thing to do.

Realizing that the longer she hesitated, the more attention she would draw, she turned around quickly and descended the ladder, trying to avoid eye contact with the people waiting in line at the bottom. She had not been up a high dive since. In fact, she rarely took any sort of risk.

Once again she was standing on the brink of something frightening. But this was different. Jumping off a high dive, or riding a roller coaster with multiple loops, or passing a note to Scott Thomas—those were all voluntary thrills. There was no real consequence to avoiding the risk. In her current situation, her family would probably die if she failed to act. She had to stand by her previous decision and carry out her plan, regardless of the consequences.

Kendra considered the oars. She had never rowed a boat and could easily picture herself floundering, especially if nasty naiads were giving her a hard time. She examined the paddleboat. Designed for a single passenger, it was wider than it needed to be, presumably for additional stability. The childish craft was not nearly as big as the rowboats, and she would be close to the water, but at least Kendra thought she could maneuver it.

Kendra sighed. Kneeling, she untied the little boat, tossing the slender rope onto the seat. The paddleboat wobbled when she stepped aboard, and she had to crouch and use her hands to avoid falling into the water. The bottom of the novelty craft was completely closed, which meant nothing could grab at her feet.

After getting situated, Kendra sat facing the dock. There was a steering wheel to control lateral movement. Turning the wheel all the way to one side, she pedaled backwards and slid away from the dock. Cranking the wheel the other way, she started pedaling forward, and the boat quietly slid out of the boathouse.

Ripples radiated out from the front of the paddleboat as she steered it toward the island, pedaling briskly. The island was not far—maybe eighty yards. The paddleboat moved steadily closer to her destination. Until it started moving *away* from the island.

She pedaled harder, but the boat kept sliding diagonally backward. Something was towing her. The boat began to spin. Turning the wheel and paddling did nothing. Then the boat suddenly tilted precariously to one side. Something was trying to tip her!

Kendra leaned to prevent the boat from capsizing, and

the boat abruptly rocked the other way. Kendra changed position, counterbalancing desperately. She saw wet fingers holding the side of the boat and slapped at them. The action was rewarded by giggling.

The boat began to rotate quickly. "Leave me alone!" Kendra demanded. "I have to get to the island." This earned a longer titter from multiple voices.

Kendra paddled furiously, but it did no good. She kept spinning and getting hauled in the wrong direction. The naiads started rocking the boat again. Thanks to the low center of gravity, Kendra found that leaning was enough to prevent the boat from capsizing, but the naiads were relentless. They tried to distract her by banging the bottom of the vessel and by waving at her. The boat pitched and rocked and spun, and then suddenly the naiads would heave in earnest, trying to catch her off balance. Time after time, Kendra reacted quickly, shifting her weight to spoil their attempts to flip her. It was a stalemate.

The naiads did not show themselves. She heard their laughter and glimpsed their hands, but never saw a face.

Kendra decided to quit paddling. It was getting her nowhere, and wasting energy. She resolved to exert herself only to keep the boat from tipping.

The attempts grew less frequent. She said nothing, made no response to the taunting giggles, ignored the hands on the side of the boat. She simply leaned as needed when they tried to tip the boat. She was getting better at it. They were not able to tilt it as much.

The attempts stopped. After about a minute of no activity, Kendra started paddling toward the island. Her progress was soon halted. She quit paddling immediately. The naiads spun her and rocked her some more.

She waited. After another minute of tranquility she paddled again. Again they pulled her away. But less eagerly. She sensed them giving up, getting bored.

On her eighth try using this technique, the naiads apparently lost interest. The island grew closer. Twenty yards. Ten yards. She expected them to stop her at the last moment. They didn't. The front of her paddleboat scraped against the shore. Everything remained still.

The moment of truth had arrived. When she set foot on the island, either she would transform into a cloud of dandelion fluff and drift away, or she wouldn't.

Almost indifferent at this point, Kendra leaped out of the boat and landed on the shore. There did not seem to be anything magical or even special about it, and she did not turn into a cloud of seeds.

There was, however, a barrage of laughter from behind her. Kendra whirled in time to see her paddleboat drifting away from the island. It was already too late to do anything without jumping into the water. She slapped herself on the forehead with the heel of her hand. The naiads had not given up—they were trying a different strategy! She had been so distracted by the prospect of becoming dandelion fluff that she had not hauled the boat out of the water as she should have. She could have at least kept hold of the rope!

Well, one more favor to ask the Fairy Queen.

The island was not large. It took only about seventy paces for Kendra to walk around the edge of it. Her tour of the perimeter revealed nothing interesting. The shrine was probably near the center.

Although the island had no trees, it had many shrubs, many of them taller than Kendra. There were no trails, and pressing through them was irritating. What would the shrine look like? She pictured a little building, but after crisscrossing the island a few times, she realized there was no such structure.

Maybe she had not turned to dandelion seeds because the island was a hoax. Or maybe the shrine was no longer here. Either way, she was stranded on a tiny island in the middle of a pond full of creatures who wanted to drown her. What would drowning feel like? Would she actually inhale water, or just pass out? Or would the demon get her first?

No! She had come this far. She would look again, more carefully. Maybe the shrine was something natural, like a special bush or stump.

She walked around the perimeter of the island again, more slowly this time. She noticed a thin trickle of water. It was strange to find a stream, no matter how small, on such a tiny island. She followed the stream toward the center of the island until she found the place where it came bubbling out of the ground.

There, at the source of the spring, was a two-inch-tall

statue of a fairy, finely carved. It rested on a white pedestal that added a few more inches to the height. A small silver bowl sat in front of it.

Of course! Fairies were so tiny, it made sense that the shrine would be miniature as well!

Kendra fell to her knees beside the spring, directly in front of the small figurine. The night was very still. Looking to the sky, Kendra noticed that the eastern horizon was turning purple. Night was coming to an end.

All Kendra could think to do was pour her heart out in complete sincerity. "Hello, Fairy Queen. Thank you for letting me visit you without changing me into dandelion seeds."

Kendra swallowed. This felt weird, talking to a diminutive statue. There was nothing regal about it. "If you can help me, I really need it. A witch named Muriel is about to set free a demon named Bahumat. The witch has my Grandpa and Grandma Sorenson prisoner, along with my brother, Seth, and my friend Lena. If that demon gets out, it will wreck this whole preserve, and there is no way I can stop it from happening without your help. Please, I really love my family, and if I don't do something, that demon is going to, he's going to—"

The reality of what she was saying hit her like a great weight and spilled out as tears. For the first time, the fact that Seth was going to die fully entered her mind. She thought of moments with him, both endearing and annoying, and realized that there would be no more of either.

She shook with sobs. Hot tears streamed down her

cheeks. She let them come. She needed the release, to stop trying to suppress the horror of it all. The tears she had shed while fleeing the Forgotten Chapel had been of shock and terror. These were tears of realization.

Tears slid down her chin and plopped into the silver bowl. Her breathing came in ragged gasps between sobs. "Please help me," she finally managed.

An aromatic breeze drifted over the island. It smelled of rich soil and new blossoms, with just a hint of the sea.

Her crying began to subside. Kendra brushed the tears from her cheeks and wiped her nose on her sleeve. She sniffed, amazed at how swiftly congestion could appear.

The miniature statue was wet. Had she cried on it? No! Water was seeping from its eyes, trickling down into the silver bowl.

The air stirred again, still redolent with potent aromas. Kendra inexplicably sensed a presence. She was no longer alone.

I accept your offering, and join you in weeping.

The words were not audible, but they struck her mind with such a forceful impression that Kendra gasped. She had never experienced anything similar. Clear fluid continued to leak from the statue into the bowl.

From tears, milk, and blood, devise an elixir, and my hand-maidens will attend you.

The tears were obvious. All Kendra could picture was Viola for the milk. Whose blood? Her own? The cow's? The handmaidens had to be the fairies.

"Wait, what do I do?" Kendra asked. "How do I get off the island?"

In reply, the wind swirled for a moment, and then gusted. The pleasant aromas vanished. The little statue no longer wept. The indefinable presence had departed.

Kendra picked up the bowl. About the size of her palm, it was nearly a third of the way full. She had hoped the Fairy Queen would resolve the situation for her. Instead she had apparently shown her a way to resolve the problem herself. The telepathic message felt as precise as spoken words. Her family was still in danger, but the spark of hope was now a flame.

How would she get off the island? Rising, Kendra walked to the shore. Unbelievably, the paddleboat was drifting in her direction. It steadily approached until reaching the island.

Kendra stepped inside the boat. It pulled away from the shore spontaneously, turned around, and started toward the little white pier.

Kendra said nothing. She did not paddle. She was afraid to do anything that might disrupt the effortless progress to the pier. She held the bowl in her lap, careful not to spill a drop.

Then she saw it, a dark figure standing on the pier, awaiting her return. A puppet the size of a man. Mendigo.

Her throat constricted with fear. She had worked magic on the island! Getting the tears from the statue—that was magic, right? Her protected status was finished. And Mendigo had come to apprehend her.

"Can you drop me off someplace else?" she asked.

The boat moved steadily forward. What could she do? Even if they dropped her off elsewhere, Mendigo would just follow.

The boat was twenty yards from the pier, then ten. She had to protect the contents of her bowl. And she could not let Mendigo haul her away. But how could she stop him?

The paddleboat brushed up against the pier, coming to a stop alongside it. Mendigo made no move to grab her. He seemed to be waiting for her to disembark. Kendra set the bowl on the pier and stood up, noticing that the boat was being held steady.

When she stepped onto the pier, Mendigo moved forward, but as before, he could not seem to grab her. He stood with both arms half-raised, fingers fluttering. Kendra picked up the bowl and walked around the limberjack. Mendigo followed her along the length of the pier.

Why would Muriel have sent Mendigo after her if he could not seize her? Did Muriel know she had communed with the Fairy Queen? If so, the puppet sure moved quickly. His being there was probably precautionary.

The problem it posed was severe. Evidently Kendra had not actually worked magic on the island; she had merely collected an ingredient. But in concocting the elixir the Fairy Queen described and giving it to the fairies, she would certainly be performing magic. The moment her protected status ended, Mendigo would be on her.

That was not an option.

Kendra set the silver bowl on the steps leading up to the gazebo. Then she turned and confronted Mendigo. The puppet was more than half a head taller than her. "I think you work like Hugo. You have no brain and just do what you're told. Is that right, Mendigo?"

The limberjack stood still. Kendra tried not to get creeped out. "I have a feeling you won't obey me, but it's worth a try. Mendigo, go climb a tree and sit up there forever."

Mendigo stood motionless. Kendra walked straight at him. He was trying to lift his arms to grab her, but was unable to carry out the intention. Standing close to him, she reached out a tentative finger and touched his wooden torso. He did not react, except to continue struggling against whatever force prevented him from seizing her.

"You can't touch me. I haven't done anything mean or used any magic. But I can touch you." She gently stroked both of his arms just beneath the shoulders. The limberjack jittered with the effort of trying to grasp her.

"Want to see my second decisive move of the night?" she asked. Mendigo quivered, hooks jingling, but remained powerless to take hold of Kendra. Unconsciously biting her lower lip, she grabbed both arms just below the shoulders, unhooked them, and dashed away from the limberjack. She heard the overgrown puppet chasing her as she raced to the edge of the pond and hurled the wooden arms into the water.

Something clipped Kendra's shoulder and sent her spinning to the ground. A crushing force pressed against her back, pinning her down. She could hardly breathe.

Craning her neck, she saw Mendigo looming over her, using his foot to hold her in place. How could a creature that looked so flimsy be so strong? The spot where he had kicked her stung deep—it would certainly bruise.

Kendra reached for his other leg, hoping to unhook the shin, but the puppet danced out of reach. For a moment Mendigo appeared indecisive. Kendra prepared to roll away in case he charged and tried to kick her again. If she could just unhook a leg!

Instead, Mendigo hurried onto the pier. Both of his arms were floating on the water. One had almost drifted within reach of the pier. Mendigo crouched, balancing carefully on one foot, and stretched out a leg toward the nearest arm.

Just as his toes made contact, a white hand shot out of the water and seized Mendigo by the ankle, yanking him into the pond with a splash. Kendra waited, holding her breath as she watched. The limberjack did not resurface.

She dashed back to the steps and picked up the bowl. Kendra dared not run while holding the tears. Instead she walked swiftly, careful not to waste any of her precious cargo. She walked across the lawn, through the arch, down the path, and onto the road.

Stars continued to fade in the eastern sky. Kendra hurried along the road. She was pretty sure her sheltered status was at an end. But, if mischief had to be done, at least it had felt worthwhile. She had a feeling it would not be her final mischievous act of the night.

CHAPTER EIGHTEEN

Bahumat

By the time Kendra reached the barn, a predawn gray dominated the eastern horizon. Her journey from the pond had been uneventful. Not a drop had spilled from the silver bowl. She went around to the little door Seth had kicked open and ducked inside.

The titanic cow stood munching hay from the loft. Every time Kendra saw Viola, she marveled anew at her enormity. The cow's udder was bloated, nearly as badly as the first time they had milked her.

Kendra had the tears. Now she needed milk and blood. Since the Fairy Queen had been communicating mentally, Kendra trusted her first impressions. The milk would have to be Viola's. And the blood? Her own? The cow's?

Probably both to be safe. Maybe both were required. But first the milk.

Kendra set the silver bowl in a protected corner and retrieved one of the ladders. She intended to steal only a few squirts. There was no time for a proper milking.

Kendra had never tried to collect Viola's milk. She and Seth had simply been relieving pressure for the cow and letting it spill all over the floor. There were plenty of barrels, but trying to dump a barrel into a little silver bowl seemed tricky. And considering that she would be sliding down a teat to get milk out, it seemed like it would be hard to avoid falling in the barrel herself.

She located a large pie tin, the kind Dale used to leave milk around the yard. Perfect. Small enough to dodge, but big enough to catch all the milk she would need. She positioned the tin under the teat, trying to estimate where the milk would squirt.

Kendra climbed the ladder and jumped, embracing the fleshy teat. Milk gushed to the floor. Only a little splashed into the tin. She adjusted the tin, climbed the ladder, and tried again. This time was a direct hit, filling the tin almost to the brim, and she even managed to keep her feet on the landing.

Kendra brought the tin over to the silver bowl. She poured milk until the bowl was three-quarters of the way full. Only blood remained.

Viola mooed thunderously, apparently upset at having

her milking abruptly halted right after it began. "You're going to moo louder than that," Kendra muttered under her breath.

How much blood would she need? The Fairy Queen had not specified quantities. Kendra went through the closets looking for tools. She ended up with a weed digger and another pie tin. Getting enough blood to pour from a pie tin into the bowl would be disgusting, but she was scared that if she tried to put blood from the source directly into the bowl she would end up spilling everything.

"Viola!" Kendra called. "I don't know if you can understand me. I need some of your blood in order to save Fablehaven. This might sting a little, so try to be brave."

The cow gave no sign of comprehension. Kendra returned to the teat she had been milking. It was the one area not protected by fur, so she figured it would be the best place to harvest some blood.

She climbed the ladder only a couple of steps. She wanted to stab the teat low, so it would drip. If she had found a knife, she would have tried to make a cut. The only thing sharp about the weed digger were the points at the end, so she would have to go with a puncture wound.

Up close, as she contemplated stabbing it, the pink teat looked alien. She needed to stab hard. On an animal this big, the skin would be pretty thick. She told herself it would just feel like a thorn to the enormous cow. But would she want somebody jabbing a thorn into her? The cow would probably get upset.

Kendra raised the weed digger, holding the pie tin in her other hand. "Sorry, Viola!" she yelled, plunging the weed digger into the spongy flesh. The tool sank almost to the handle, and Viola made a terrified bellow.

The heavy teat swung into Kendra, slamming her off the ladder. She kept hold of the weed digger, wrenching it free of the wound as she fell. The ladder clattered to the floor beside her.

Viola sidestepped and tossed her head, bellowing again. The barn shook, and Kendra heard timbers splitting. The roof shuddered. The walls swayed and cracked. Kendra covered her head. Gigantic hooves thumped against the floor, and Viola let out a long, plaintive moo. Then the cow settled down.

Kendra looked up. Dust and hay floated down from above. Blood trickled down the teat, already dripping from the tip.

Since Viola had calmed down, and the blood was flowing freely, Kendra cast aside the pie tin and retrieved the silver bowl. Standing under the teat, she started catching drops of blood. She had toured a cave with her family once, and the sight reminded her of water dripping from a stalactite.

Soon the mixture in the bowl turned from white to pink. The flow of blood slowed. The lower side and tip of the teat were stained red. Kendra supposed it was enough.

She went and sat by the little door. Now for her blood. Maybe she could just try the cow blood and see if that worked. No, haste was essential. How would she get blood out? No way was she using the weed digger unless she could sterilize it.

Leaving the bowl, she hunted through the closets again. She noticed a safety pin on a pair of coveralls. She unpinned it and ran back to the bowl.

Holding her hand over the bowl, she hesitated. Kendra had always hated needles, the idea of being fully aware that something was about to hurt but having to endure it calmly. But today was not a day to be squeamish. Gritting her teeth, she stuck her thumb with the pin and then squeezed two drops of blood into the mixture. That would have to do.

Kendra looked at the pie tin. She should probably drink some milk herself, since a new day was beginning. She took a sip. Then she realized that her family would need milk as well when she found them.

There had been bottled water in one of the closets. Kendra hurried to the closet, selected a bottle, unscrewed the cap, dumped the contents, and filled it with milk from the pie tin. The bottle barely fit in her pocket.

Kendra retrieved the small silver bowl. Swirling the solution a bit, she exited the barn. Predawn colors streaked the horizon. Sunrise was approaching.

Now what? There were no fairies in sight. When the Fairy Queen had given instructions, Kendra had felt no doubt that the handmaidens she referred to were the fairies. She was supposed to make a potion for them that would somehow get them to help her.

What would it do? Kendra realized that she had no idea. What could it do? Win their affection? Then what? Lacking other options, she had to trust the reassurance she had felt when the Fairy Queen spoke to her mind.

First she needed to find fairies. She wandered the garden. There was one, clad in orange and black with matching butterfly wings. "Hey, fairy, I have something for you!" she cried.

The fairy darted over to her, looked at the bowl, started chirping in a squeaky voice, and zoomed away. Kendra roamed until she found another fairy, and ended up with an identical reaction. The fairy acted excited and then flew away.

Soon multiple fairies were flying up to Kendra, peeking in the bowl, and then soaring off. They were apparently spreading the news.

Kendra ended up beside the metal statue of Dale. She set the bowl on the ground and backed away, in case her proximity might discourage the fairies. The morning grew brighter. Before long, dozens of fairies hovered around the bowl. They were no longer showing up only to zip away. A crowd was forming. Occasionally one would fly right up to the bowl and peer inside. One even laid a tiny hand on the rim. But none took a drink. Most stayed several feet away.

The crowd swelled to more than a hundred. Still they would not drink. Kendra tried to be patient. She did not want to frighten them away.

Suddenly the sound of a mighty wind interrupted the

quiet morning. Kendra felt no breeze, but she could hear a shrieking gale in the distance. As the sound of the wind tapered off, a ferocious roar echoed across the yard. The fairies scattered.

It could mean only one thing. "Wait, please, you have to drink this! Your queen had me make it for you!" The fairies darted around in confusion. "Hurry, time is running out!"

Whether it was her words or simply that they were no longer startled, the fairies gathered around the bowl again. "Try it," Kendra said. "Have a taste."

None of the fairies took her up on her offer. Kendra dipped a finger into the bowl and sampled the elixir. She tried not to make a disgusted face—it tasted salty and nasty. "Mmmm . . . delicious."

A fairy with raven black hair and bumblebee wings approached the bowl. Mimicking Kendra, she dipped a finger and tasted it. In a whirling shower of sparks the fairy grew to nearly six feet tall. Kendra smelled the fertile aroma that had accompanied the Fairy Queen. The enlarged fairy blinked in astonishment, then glided high into the air.

The other fairies mobbed the bowl. A blizzard of sparks flashed across the yard as the fairies transformed into much larger versions of themselves. Kendra backed away, shielding her eyes from the dazzling pyrotechnics. In moments, she was surrounded by a glorious host of human-sized fairies, some standing on the ground, most hovering.

The fairies were uniformly tall and beautiful, with the lithe musculature of professional ballerinas. They wore vivid, exotic apparel. They still had magnificent wings. They still emitted light, although the gentle twinkle had become a brilliant blaze. The biggest change was in their eyes. Merry mischief had been replaced by something stern and smoldering.

A fairy with lustrous silver wings and short blue hair alighted in front of Kendra. "You have summoned us to war," she announced in a heavy accent. "What is your bidding?"

Kendra swallowed. A hundred human-sized fairies took up much more space than a hundred tiny ones. They used to be so cute. Now they were quite imposing. She would not want to be the enemy of these proud seraphim.

"Can you restore Dale?" Kendra asked.

A pair of fairies crouched over Dale, placed their hands on him, and then helped him to his feet. He regarded Kendra with befuddled wonder, patting himself, as if surprised he was intact. "What's going on?" he asked. "Where's Stan?"

"The fairies healed you," Kendra said. "Grandpa and the others are still in trouble. But I think these fairies will help us."

Kendra returned her gaze to the stunning silver fairy. "Muriel the witch is trying to release a demon named Bahumat."

"The demon is free," the fairy said. "You have but to command."

Kendra pressed her lips together. "We have to lock him up again. The witch, too. And we have to rescue my Grandpa and Grandma Sorenson, and my brother, Seth, and Lena."

The blue-haired fairy nodded and issued instructions in a musical language. Some of the fairies began rummaging in nearby plants. They pulled out weapons. A yellow fairy produced a crystal sword from the soil of a flowerbed. A violet fairy transformed a thorn from a rosebush into a spear. The silver fairy with blue hair changed a snail shell into a beautiful shield. The petal of a pansy became a blazing ax in her other hand.

"This is your will," the silver fairy confirmed.

"Yes," Kendra said firmly.

All together, the fairies took flight. Kendra turned to watch them go. Then a hand grabbed her left arm and another seized her right and she was soaring between two fairies—a slender albino with black eyes and a blue, furry fairy. Kendra recognized the blue one as the downy fountain sprite she had seen in Grandpa's office.

The sudden acceleration took her breath away. They cruised low to the ground, skimming over bushes, dodging tree trunks, and swishing past branches. Flying near the rear, Kendra marveled at the squadron of fairies ahead of her effortlessly weaving through obstacles at such reckless speed.

The exhilaration was overwhelming. The wind of their velocity brought tears to her eyes. The pond with the gazebos streaked by beneath her. At this rate, they would reach the Forgotten Chapel in moments.

But what about when they got there? Bahumat was supposed to be incredibly powerful. Even so, considering the legion of fierce fairies surrounding her, Kendra liked her odds.

Glancing back, Kendra saw no fairies behind her. They had apparently left Dale in the yard.

The mad dash through the forest continued until the fairies ahead swooped skyward. Kendra's escorts followed, rocketing up beyond the treetops. The sudden ascent left her mouth dry and her stomach tingling.

And then she was no longer moving. Kendra and her escorts hovered above the treetops, watching the others plunge toward the Forgotten Chapel. Kendra tried to recover from the thrill of flying and digest what was happening below.

Four winged creatures were rising to meet the fairies. The huge gargoyles were at least ten feet tall, with razor claws and horns like rams. A few fairies broke off from the main group to intercept them. The winged beasts clawed at their smaller opponents, but the fairies adroitly evaded the blows and slashed off their wings, sending the gargoyles hurtling to the ground.

Something flashed in Kendra's eyes. The sun was peeking over the horizon. "Let's go," Kendra said to her escorts.

The fairies dove. Kendra felt her stomach rise to her

throat as they plunged toward the church. Human-sized imps were spilling out of the front doorway, shaking their fists and hissing at the incoming fairies. Many of the fairies cast their weapons aside and soared straight at the imps, catching them in vicious embraces and kissing them on the mouth. In radiant bursts of sparks, every imp that was kissed transformed into a human-sized fairy!

Kendra saw the silver fairy with blue hair plant a kiss on an obese imp. The imp instantly metamorphosed into a plump fairy with coppery wings. As the silver fairy glided away, the plump fairy tackled another imp, forced a kiss, and in a flash the imp became a thin, Asian-looking fairy with hummingbird wings.

The fairies streamed into the church. Most did not bother with the door. They glided through windows or smashed through the corroded roof.

Kendra's escorts held her over a gap in the roof. She saw fairies kissing imps. Other fairies drove back a variety of foul beasts. One fairy used a golden lash to send a toadlike monstrosity crashing through the wall. Another fairy grasped a scabby beast by its mane of white hair and hurled it through a window. A gray fairy with mothlike wings chased a brawny minotaur out the front door with a scalding blast of steam from the end of her rod. Many of the unsavory creatures voluntarily fled before the terrible onslaught.

Others fought back.

A demonic dwarf with a hide of black scales bounded

around the room wreaking havoc with a pair of knives. A rampaging atrocity that looked like a cross between a bear and an octopus battered fairies with its thrashing tentacles. A greasy creature coughed globs of slime into the air. It had the general appearance of a large tortoise without a shell, its body an amoeboid puddle beneath a long neck. Several fairies crashed to the church floor, wings snarled in the goopy substance.

The undaunted fairies counterattacked. The bottom half of the dwarf was turned to stone. Tentacles severed, the octobear retreated. A torrent of water flushed away the greasy creature. Some fairies attended their fallen comrades, healing injuries and washing away slime.

As the room cleared, fairies charged through the door to the basement.

"Take me to the basement!" Kendra said. Her escorts immediately responded, nearly giving Kendra whiplash as they plummeted into the church and glided to the basement door. The fairies had to tuck in their wings to descend the stairs, so Kendra ran down beside the furry fairy and the albino.

The basement had expanded. A massive excavation and renovation had occurred. It was deeper, broader, and longer. The alcove at the far side had grown as well, now completely unfettered by knotted ropes.

The basement was not lighted as brightly as before, although the fairies carried their own luminescence with them. Hideous carvings sneered from the walls. One corner was piled with strange treasures—jade idols, spiked scepters, and jeweled masks.

Kendra scanned the room for her family. The easiest to spot was Seth. He was inside an enormous jar with breathing holes punched in the lid. There were some leaves and branches in it with him. He had grown no taller, but he looked a hundred years old. Saggy wrinkles creased his face, and he had only a few wisps of white hair left atop his head. He placed a pruned palm against the glass.

Kendra guessed that the orangutan chained to the wall was Grandpa. The large catfish swimming in the tank beside him was probably Lena. She saw no sign of Grandma.

Flanked by her fairy escorts, Kendra dashed toward her family. Scores of hideous imps scuffled with fairies. Those fights did not last long as kisses transformed the imps back into their original forms.

Kendra reached the gigantic jar. "Are you all right, Seth?"

Her elderly brother nodded feebly. His smile showed that he had no teeth.

A snarling imp pounced at Kendra. The blue, furry fairy caught the creature in midflight, pinning its arms to its sides. It resembled the same imp that had apprehended her brother earlier. The albino fairy flew up and gave the imp a kiss on the mouth, and it became a striking fairy with fiery red hair and iridescent dragonfly wings.

Seth began tapping on the glass. He was pointing

excitedly at the fairy. Kendra realized that it was the fairy he had unwittingly transformed.

The redheaded fairy approached the jar, shaking a scolding finger at Seth. "I'm sorry," Seth mouthed from inside the container. He clasped his hands and made pleading motions. The fairy regarded him through narrowed eyes. Then she snapped her fingers, and the jar shattered. She leaned forward and kissed Seth on the forehead. His wrinkles smoothed and his hair filled in until he promptly looked like himself again.

Kendra pulled the bottle of milk from her pocket and handed it to Seth. "Save some for Grandma and Grandpa."

"But I can see—"

An earsplitting roar shook the room. A creature who could only have been Bahumat emerged from the alcove. The loathsome demon stood three times as tall as a man and had the head of a dragon crowned by three horns. The demon walked upright, possessing three arms, three legs, and three tails. Oily black scales bristling with barbed spikes covered its grotesque body. Malevolent eyes gleamed with wicked intelligence.

To one side of Bahumat floated the spectral woman Kendra had seen outside her window on Midsummer Eve. Her ebony wrappings flowed unnaturally, as if she were underwater. The unearthly apparition made Kendra think of a negative photograph.

At the other side of Bahumat stood Muriel, now clad

in a gown as black as midnight. She leered at the fairies and glanced confidently at the towering demon.

No imps remained in the room. A crowd of shining fairies faced these final opponents.

Bahumat crouched. Inky darkness gathered around him. The demon sprang forward with a roar like a thousand cannons firing together. A black wall of shadow flowed from Bahumat like a wave of tar. Total darkness engulfed the room. Kendra felt like she had been struck blind. Even with her hands over her ears, the prolonged bellowing of the demon was practically deafening.

There seemed to be no substance to the shadow Bahumat had emitted. It was just darkness. Where were the fairies? Where was their light?

The ground rumbled, and a sound like an avalanche overpowered the demon's roar. Suddenly daylight flooded the room. Looking up, Kendra beheld a blue sky. The slanted rays of the rising sun fell into the basement. The entire church had been hurled aside!

Descending from above, and charging from all directions, fairies swarmed Bahumat. The demon slashed a fairy with one of its tails, raked another with an impossibly quick swipe of its claws. Jaws snapping, the creature swallowed a yellow fairy whole. Many fairies were falling. While the majority attacked, other fairies laid hands on the injured, curing most of them rapidly.

Muriel stood in a theatrical pose chanting spidery words. A pair of fairies near her turned to glass and shattered. She extended a contorted hand, and another fairy turned to ash and disintegrated in a gray cloud.

Long streamers of ebony fabric flowed from the spectral woman, entangling nearby fairies. The ensnared fairies began to lose their luster and wither. The silver fairy appeared, slicing through the fabric with her ax of fire. Other fairies joined her, using gleaming swords to sever the black material.

The fairies swirling around Bahumat now held ropes. They looked like the ropes that had crisscrossed the front of the alcove, except now they appeared to be woven out of gold. Bahumat kept roaring and swinging and biting, but the ropes were beginning to tangle him up. Knots were forming in them. The draconic creature was slowing down. His great jaws clamped shut, tearing off the gauzy wing of a fairy with markings like a ladybug.

The spectral woman turned and drifted away, her ethereal wrappings no longer quite as flowing. The fairies ignored her departure. A pair of fairies had taken hold of Muriel, and they flung her at Bahumat. Soon she was bound to the demon by flaxen cords. She screeched as her body shriveled with age and her gown turned to rags.

Three fairies alighted atop the demon's head. They each grabbed a horn and tore it out. The demon wailed. Dozens of fairies seized the ropes binding the demon and hurled Bahumat back into the alcove. Busily the fairies began threading knotted ropes back and forth over the entrance.

Kendra turned. The blue, furry fairy gestured toward the orangutan, and the shackles binding it to the wall fell apart. Another gesture and a burst of light changed the orangutan into Grandpa Sorenson.

The albino fairy pulled the convulsing catfish from the aquarium and changed her back into Lena. "Where's my grandma?" Kendra cried.

The red-haired fairy who had freed Seth approached the aquarium. She lifted out a small, putrid slug that had been clinging to the side above the water and changed it back into Grandma.

Grandma Sorenson massaged her temples. "And I thought my mind was muddy as a chicken," she muttered. Grandpa hurried over and embraced her.

"Do you need milk?" Kendra asked, holding out the bottle to her grandfather.

He shook his head. "We have not slept, and so the veil has not yet covered our eyes."

A group of fairies gathered near the alcove, extending their arms, palms downward. Soil, clay, and stone began flowing together and piling up until Hugo was reborn. The golem stretched and let out a groan to rival the roars of the banished demon.

The fairies busily healed one another, mending wings and closing wounds. One circle of fairies spread their arms, and fragments of glass skittered together, took the form of a pair of fairies, and came back to life. Several other fairies joined hands and started humming. Particles of ash swirled loosely in their midst, but refused to coalesce. The fairies released one another, and the ash dissipated. Some fairies, it seemed, were beyond rescue.

Several fairies took hold of Hugo and lifted him out of the basement. Others did the same for Grandpa, Grandma, Lena, Seth, and Kendra. Airborne again, Kendra had a view of the destroyed church. The wreckage spread across the clearing for a couple hundred yards. The Forgotten Chapel had not simply been flung aside—it had been obliterated.

The fairies set them down a good distance from the wreckage and the basement. All except Lena. Two fairies were carrying her away. The former naiad was having harsh words with them in a foreign tongue, struggling in their grasp.

Kendra touched Grandpa Sorenson's arm and nodded toward the commotion.

"Nothing to be done about it," he sighed as the fairies hauled Lena away. He had an arm around Grandma, holding her close.

"Hey!" Kendra shouted. "Bring Lena back here!" The fairies holding Lena paid her no heed, passing out of sight into the woods.

The remainder of the fairies assembled above the basement, floating in an enormous ring. They had more than tripled their numbers with all the imps they had reclaimed. Kendra had seen many fairies fall during the battle, but most had been revived and healed by the magic of their comrades.

The radiant fairies raised their arms together and started singing. The music sounded impromptu, full of hundreds of interweaving melodies with almost no harmonies. As they sang, the ground in the clearing began to undulate. The wreckage from the church slid across the field, clattering into the open basement. The ground began to quake. The walls of the basement crumbled. The surrounding area folded in and swallowed it up. The field heaved like a stormy sea.

As the undulations subsided, the basement had been replaced by a low hill. The fairy choir became more shrill. Wildflowers and fruit trees began sprouting throughout the clearing and on the hill, coming to full bloom in a matter of seconds. Flowers blossomed all over Hugo, who offered no reaction. When the singing finally ceased, a cheery hill covered by a fragrant array of brilliant blossoms and mature fruit trees had replaced the Forgotten Chapel.

"They made Hugo look all fruity," Seth complained.

The legion of fairies glided toward them, scooped them up, and carried them on a breakneck flight for home. Kendra relished being part of the mercurial procession, overjoyed at the fortunate ending to the terrible night. Seth whooped the whole way, as if he were riding the coolest roller coaster on the planet.

Finally the fairies deposited them in the yard, where Dale stood waiting. "Now I've seen everything," he said as Grandpa and Grandma Sorenson were set down beside him.

The fairy with short blue hair and silver wings stood before Kendra. "Thank you," Kendra said. "You did wonderfully. We can never repay you."

The silver fairy gave a single nod, eyes glittering.

As if responding to a signal, the fairies crowded Kendra, each in turn giving her a quick kiss. As each kiss was bestowed, the fairy reverted to her former size amid dazzling sparks and darted away. The rapid succession of kisses brought overpowering sensations. Again Kendra smelled the earthy aromas of the Fairy Queen—rich soil and young blossoms. She tasted honey and fruit and berries, all sweet beyond comparison. She heard the music of rainfall, the cry of the wind, and the roar of the sea. She felt as if the warmth of the sun were embracing her, flowing through her. The fairies kissed her eyes, her cheeks, her ears, her brow.

When the last of more than three hundred fairies kissed her, Kendra stumbled backwards and sat down hard on the grass. She felt no pain. In fact, she was mildly surprised that she did not float away, she felt so light and drowsy.

Grandpa and Dale helped Kendra to her feet. "I would wager that this young lady has quite a story to tell," Grandpa said. "And I would also wager that now is not the time. Hugo, attend to your labors."

Dale was helping Kendra to the house. She felt euphoric and distant. She was glad her family was safe. But she felt so inexplicably blissful, and the troubles of the evening seemed so remote, that she began to wonder whether it had all been a surreal dream.

Grandpa was holding hands with Grandma. "I'm sorry it took so long to get you back," he said softly.

"I can guess at the reasons," she said. "We need to talk about you eating my eggs."

"They weren't your eggs," Grandpa protested. "They were the eggs of the hen your mind was inhabiting."

"I'm glad you can be so detached."

"There may still be a couple in the fridge."

Kendra stumbled on her way up the porch steps. Grandpa and Dale helped her onto the porch and into the house. The furniture was back! Nearly all of it had been restored, with some alterations. A couch had been reconstructed as a chair. Some lampshades were made of different material. Jewels had been added to a picture frame.

Could the brownies have worked so fast? Her eyes were drooping. Grandpa was holding Grandma's hand, whispering something in her ear. Seth was chattering, but the words made no sense. Dale held her shoulders, guiding her. They were almost to the stairs, but she could not keep her eyes open. She felt herself falling, and hands catching her, and then consciousness fled.

CHAPTER NINETEEN

Farewell to Fablehaven

K endra and Grandpa reclined in the wagon while
Hugo pulled them down the road at a leisurely
pace. The morning was clear and bright, with a few thin,
high clouds barely clinging to existence, accidental brush
strokes on a blue canvas. The day would be hot, but for
now it was pleasant.

A couple of fairies drifting alongside the wagon waved
at Kendra. She waved back and they sped away, weaving
around one another. The garden now teemed with fairies, and they paid Kendra a lot of special attention. They
seemed pleased whenever she acknowledged them.

"We haven't really gotten to talk since it all happened," Kendra said.

"You were sleeping half of the time," Grandpa replied.

It was true. She had slept for two days and two nights straight after the ordeal—a personal best.

"All those kisses knocked me out," she said.

"You excited to see your parents?" asked Grandpa.

"Yes and no." It was the third day since Kendra had awakened. Her parents were coming to pick them up this afternoon. "Going home will seem bland after all this."

"Well, you'll have fewer demons to worry about."

Kendra smiled. "True."

Grandpa folded his arms. "What you did was so special, I don't know how to speak about it."

"It barely seems real."

"Oh, it was real. You mended an irreparable situation, and saved all of our lives in the process. The fairies have not gone to war for centuries. In that state, their power is virtually unrivaled. Bahumat did not stand a chance. What you did was so brave, and so doomed to failure, I can't think of anyone I know who would have even tried it."

"It felt like my only hope. Why do you think the Fairy Queen helped me?"

"Your guess is as good as mine. Maybe to save the preserve. Maybe she sensed the sincerity of your intentions. Your youth must have helped. I'm sure fairies would much rather follow a little girl into battle than some pompous general. But the truth is, I never would have guessed it would have worked. It was a miracle."

Hugo stopped the cart. Grandpa climbed down and

then helped Kendra. She held the silver bowl that she had taken from the island. They started down a faint path toward an archway in a tall, unkempt hedge.

"Weird how I don't have to drink the milk anymore," Kendra said. On the morning she awoke after the fairy kisses, when she went to the window, she saw fairies fluttering about. It had taken a moment to register that she had not yet consumed any milk that day.

"I'll admit that it worries me somewhat," Grandpa said. "Creatures of whimsy are not solely confined to the preserves. The blindness of mortals can be a blessing. Take care where you look."

"I'd rather see things how they are," Kendra declared. They passed under the archway. A group of satyrs were playing tag with several slender maidens wearing flowers in their hair. The paddleboat was adrift in the middle of the pond. Fairies skimmed the surface of the water and soared among the gazebos.

"I'll be curious to know what other changes the fairies wrought in you," Grandpa said. "I've never heard of such a thing. You'll let me know if you discover any other oddities?"

"Like if I turn Seth back into a walrus?"

"I'm glad you can joke about it, but I'm serious."

They walked up the steps to the nearest pavilion. "Just toss it in?" Kendra asked.

"I think it would be best," Grandpa said. "If the bowl came from that island, you should give it back."

Kendra threw the bowl like a Frisbee. It landed in the water. Almost immediately a hand shot up and snatched it.

"That was quick," Kendra said. "It will probably end up down with Mendigo."

"The naiads respect the Fairy Queen. They'll make sure the bowl ends up where it belongs."

Kendra looked at the pier.

"She may not know you," Grandpa said.

"I just want to say good-bye, whether she gets it or not."

They walked along the boardwalk until they reached the gazebo adjoining the pier. Kendra walked out to the end of the pier. Grandpa stayed a few steps behind her. "Remember, not too close to the water."

"I know," Kendra said. She leaned forward to look down into the pond. It was much clearer than it had been at night. She jumped a little when she realized that the face looking up at her was not her reflection. The naiad looked like a girl of about sixteen, with full lips and a profusion of golden hair swirling about a face shaped like a valentine.

"I want to talk to Lena," Kendra said loudly, over-pronouncing the words.

"She may not come," Grandpa said.

The naiad kept staring up at her. "Get Lena, please," Kendra repeated. The naiad swam away. "She'll come," Kendra asserted.

They waited. Nobody came. Kendra studied the water. She turned her hands into a megaphone around her mouth. "Lena! This is Kendra! I want to speak with you!"

Several minutes passed. Grandpa waited with her patiently. Then a face rose almost to the surface of the water, right at the end of the dock. It was Lena. Her hair was still white with a few black strands. Though she looked no younger, her face had the same ageless quality.

"Lena, hi, it's Kendra, remember?"

Lena smiled. Her face was barely an inch from the surface.

"I just wanted to say good-bye. I really enjoyed our talks. I hope you don't mind being a naiad again. Are you mad at me?"

Lena motioned for Kendra to come closer. She put her hand by her mouth like she wanted to share a secret. Her almond eyes looked mirthful and excited. They did not match the white hair. Kendra bent down a little.

"What?" Kendra asked.

Lena rolled her eyes and motioned for her to come closer. Kendra crouched a little more, and in the same instant that Lena reached up for her, Grandpa Sorenson pulled her back.

"I told you," Grandpa said. "She is no longer the woman she was back at the house."

Kendra leaned forward just enough to peer over the edge again. Lena stuck her tongue out and swam away. "At least she isn't suffering," Kendra said.

Grandpa walked her back to the gazebo in silence. "She told me she would never choose to return to life as a naiad," Kendra said after a while. "She said it more than once."

"I'm sure she meant it," said Grandpa. "From where I stood, it didn't look like she went willingly."

"I noticed the same thing. I worried she might be suffering. I thought maybe she needed us to save her."

"Are you satisfied?" Grandpa asked.

"I'm not even sure she remembered me," Kendra admitted. "At first I thought she did, but I bet she was faking, trying to get me close enough to drown me."

"Probably."

"She doesn't miss being human."

"Not from her current point of view," Grandpa agreed. "Much like how being a naiad did not sound very fulfilling to her from a mortal perspective."

"Why would the fairies do that to her?"

"I don't think they saw it as a punishment. Lena was probably a victim of good intentions."

"But Lena was arguing with them. She didn't want to go."

Grandpa shrugged. "The fairies might have known that once they restored her, she would change her mind. Looks like they were right. Remember, the fairies experience existence like the naiads. From their point of view, Lena was out of her mind wanting to be mortal. They probably thought they were curing her insanity."

"I'm glad they restored everybody else," Kendra said. "They just restored Lena too much."

"Are you sure? She was a naiad to begin with."

"She didn't like the idea of aging. At least she won't die now. Or get any older."

"No, she won't."

"I still think she would rather be human."

Grandpa frowned. "You may be right. Truth be told, if I knew a way to reclaim Lena, I would. I believe once she was mortal again, she would be grateful. But a naiad can only descend to mortality voluntarily. In her current state, I doubt she would make that choice. I am sure she is very disoriented. Perhaps in time she will gain some perspective."

"What's it like for her?"

"No way to be sure. For all I know, this is a unique occurrence. Her memories of mortality are apparently distorted, if she retains them at all."

Kendra unconsciously twisted the sleeve of her shirt, a pained expression on her face. "So we just leave her there?"

"For now. I will do some research and give the matter considerable thought. Don't tear yourself up about it. Lena would not want that. The alternative was being devoured by a demon. She looked all right to me."

They started back toward the wagon. "What about the Society of the Evening Star?" asked Kendra. "Are they still a threat? Muriel said she was in contact with them."

Grandpa pinched his bottom lip. "The Society will be a threat as long as it endures. It is difficult for an uninvited guest to gain access to a preserve—mortal or not. Some would say impossible, but the Society has shown repeated resourcefulness at circumventing so-called impossible obstacles. Fortunately we foiled their attempt to use Muriel to free Bahumat and overthrow the preserve. But we now know they have learned the whereabouts of Fablehaven. We will have to be more vigilant than ever."

"What secret artifact is hidden here?"

"It is unfortunate that your grandmother had to share that secret with you. I realize it was a precaution in case both of us were incapacitated, but the knowledge is a terrible burden to place on children. You must never speak of it. I have tried to impress that idea on Seth as well—heaven help us all. I am the caretaker of Fablehaven, and I know little about the artifact save that it is hidden somewhere on this property. If members of the Society of the Evening Star are aware that the artifact is here, and we have every reason to believe they are, they will stop at nothing to penetrate our defenses and lay their hands on it."

"What will you do?" Kendra said.

"What we always do," Grandpa said. "Consult with our allies and take every measure to ensure that our defenses remain intact. The Society has known the location of dozens of preserves for centuries and yet has failed to infiltrate them. They may pay us extra attention, but unless we let our guard down, there is little they can do."

"What about that ghost lady? The one who escaped while the fairies were trapping Bahumat?"

"I do not know her story, except that she was obviously colluding with our enemies. I have never met many of the dark beings who lurk in the inhospitable corners of Fablehaven."

They reached the wagon. Grandpa boosted Kendra up and then climbed in himself. "Hugo, take us home."

They rode in silence. Kendra considered all they had discussed—the fate of Lena and the impending threat of the Society of the Evening Star. The fateful night that had seemed like the end of her problems was starting to look like the beginning.

Up ahead, off to the side of the road, Dale was chopping a fallen tree into firewood. Drenched in sweat, he swung the ax aggressively. As the wagon rolled by, he glanced up at Kendra. She smiled and waved. Dale gave a tight smile and looked away, returning to his chore.

Kendra frowned. "What's up with Dale lately? Do you think being turned to lead traumatized him?"

"I doubt he felt a thing. He's beating himself up over something else."

"What?"

"Don't say a word about this to him." Grandpa paused, glancing back toward Dale, then went on speaking. "He feels bad that his brother Warren wasn't present when the fairies were curing everybody."

"Grandma said Dale's brother is catatonic. I still haven't met him. Could the fairies have helped?"

Grandpa shrugged. "Considering that they put Lena back in the water, changed imps back into fairies, and remade Hugo out of a pile of rubble, yes, I imagine they could have cured Warren. Theoretically, any magic that can be done can also be undone." Grandpa scratched his cheek. "You have to understand, last week I would have said there was no possible way of curing Warren. Believe me, I have investigated the subject thoroughly. But I've never heard of an imp changing back into a fairy, either. It simply doesn't happen."

"I wish I'd thought of it," Kendra said. "Warren didn't even cross my mind."

"Not your fault in the slightest. Warren just wasn't in the right place at the right time. I'm grateful the rest of us were."

"How did Warren get like that?"

"That, my dear, is part of the problem. We have no idea. He disappeared for three days. On the fourth he returned, white as a sheet. He sat down in the garden, and hasn't said a word or responded to anyone since. He can chew food, and walk if you lead him. He can even do some simple chores if you get him started. But no communication. His mind has flown."

Hugo stopped at the edge of the yard. Grandpa and Kendra climbed down. "Hugo, see to your chores." The golem hauled the cart away.

"I'm going to miss this place," Kendra said, taking in the bright flowers attended by glittering fairies.

"Your grandmother and I have waited a long time to find somebody like you among our posterity," Grandpa said. "Trust me. You'll be back."

* * *

"Kendra," Grandma called up the stairs. "Your folks are here!"

"I'll be right down." Kendra sat alone on her bed in the playroom. Seth was already downstairs. She had packed her bags and helped him with his.

Kendra sighed. When her parents had first dropped her off, she had counted the days until their return. Now she almost felt reluctant to see them. Since they knew nothing about the magical nature of the preserve, there was no way they could possibly relate to what she had experienced. The only person she could share it with was Seth. Anyone else would think she was insane.

Just thinking about it made her feel isolated.

Kendra crossed the room to the painting she had done of the pond. It was a perfect keepsake from her stay—a paint-by-numbers drawn by a naiad depicting the location of the bravest act of her life.

Yet she hesitated to bring it. Would the image stir too many painful memories? Many of her experiences here had been dreadful. She and her family had nearly been killed.

And she had lost a new friend when Lena was returned to the pond.

At the same time, the painting might make her long for the enchanted world of the preserve. So many aspects of Fablehaven were wonderful. Life would seem so dry after the extraordinary events of the past couple of weeks.

Either way, the painting might cause her pain. But of course those memories would persist with or without the picture of the pond. She picked it up.

The rest of her bags were already downstairs. She cast a final glance around the playroom, treasuring up the details, and walked out the door. She went down the stairs, along the hall, and started down the staircase to the entry hall.

Her mom and dad stood in the entry hall smiling up at her. They had notably gained weight, especially Dad—he looked twenty pounds heavier. Seth stood near Dad clutching his painting of the dragon.

"You did a painting too!" Mom exclaimed. "Kendra, it's gorgeous!"

"I had help," she said, reaching the bottom of the stairs. "How was the cruise?"

"We made a lot of memories," Mom said.

"Looks like Dad ate plenty of snails," Seth said.

Dad rubbed his belly. "Nobody warned me about all the desserts."

"You ready, honey?" Mom said, putting an arm around Kendra.

"Aren't you going to look around?" Kendra asked.

"We walked the grounds a bit while you were upstairs, and toured the lower rooms. Was there something in particular you wanted to show us?"

"Not really."

"We should probably get going," Dad said, opening the front door. Not too many days ago that door had been mangled and an arrow had protruded from the frame.

Outside, Dale was loading the last of the bags into the SUV. Grandma and Grandpa waited nearby on the driveway. Dad helped Kendra and Seth load their paintings while Mom thanked Grandma and Grandpa Sorenson profusely.

"It was our pleasure," Grandma said earnestly.

"You'll have to let them visit again sometime soon," Grandpa insisted.

"I'd like that," Kendra said.

"Me too," Seth agreed.

Seth and Kendra hugged their grandparents goodbye and then climbed into the SUV. Grandpa winked at Kendra. Dad started the engine. "You kids have a good time?"

"Yeah," Seth said.

"Amazing," Kendra added.

"Remember how worried you were when we dropped you off?" Mom said as she buckled her seatbelt. "I bet it wasn't half as scary as you imagined."

Kendra and Seth shared a very special look.

Drink the milk.

Acknowledgments

Special thanks to Chris Schoebinger for seeing the potential in this story and making it a reality. Thanks also to Brandon Dorman for his wonderful illustrations; to Emily Watts, whose editorial talents smoothed out the rough edges; and to Richard Erickson, Sheryl Dickert Smith, and Tonya Facemyer, whose design prowess made everything look really cool. My appreciation to the entire Shadow Mountain team for doing a tremendous job.

Thanks go out to the friends who provided feedback on early drafts: Jason and Natalie Conforto, Randy and Rachel Davis, Mike Walton, Lisa Mangum, Tony Benjamin, the Excel crew, Nancy, Liz, Tamara, Bryson and Cherie, Summer, Mary, my dad, my mom, and all the others. See, Ty, you should have read it.

Thanks to Aaron Allen and family for the laptop and the support. Thanks to Tiffany for untying certain knots. Thanks to Ryan Hamilton and Dean Hale for extended encouragement. Thanks to Tuck for the dictionary and the eleventh-hour contributions.

Thanks to my parents for so much more than genetic material, and to my siblings for helping me learn how to tease, and to my extended family for being there more than many would consider normal.

Thanks to all former teachers, schoolmates, associates, dates, friends, acquaintances, comedy troupe members, rivals, enemies, and disinterested third parties. Keep on keeping on.

Thanks to you for reading these acknowledgments and hopefully the rest of the book. And the next. And the next.

Most important, a special acknowledgment to my enchanting wife, Mary, and my beautiful children, Sadie and Chase. Thank you for giving my life something to revolve around besides the sun.

Reading Guide

The following questions may be useful in promoting discussion about some of the themes and ideas found in *Fablehaven*. They are intended as a starting point for interactions in classrooms and with reading groups.

1. There can be great protection from exact obedience. How was this principle reinforced for Seth? For Kendra? How does the principle of obedience function in your life?

2. Kendra was generally a rule keeper, Seth a rule breaker. How did their attitudes evolve over the course of the book? What are advantages to both attitudes? Disadvantages?

3. Consequences serve an essential role for maintaining order and justice and harmony. How do laws help to keep order in Fablehaven? How were Kendra and Seth affected by the consequences of their decisions? How have the consequences of past decisions helped or hindered you?

4. Many of the problems in Fablehaven arose as a result of decisions the characters made, often without bad intentions. Sometimes, what we don't know *can* hurt us. How was that true for Kendra and Seth? Are there similar examples in the world around you?

5. It can be a challenge to find the courage to do what we fear the most. What enabled Kendra to do something

that terrified her? What circumstances do you find most intimidating? How do you find the strength to make it through difficult situations?

6. Circumstances arose where many of the characters in Fablehaven had to risk their lives. Do you think you would risk your life for anything? If so, what?

7. Many of the creatures in Fablehaven have roots in various mythologies, particularly Greek. Can you identify which creatures come from which mythologies? Did you recognize any vocabulary in the book with mythological roots? What are some common words that come from mythologies?

8. Several of the creatures of Fablehaven personified specific attributes. What did the fairies seem to personify? The satyrs? The cliff troll? What are the strengths and weaknesses of those characteristics?

9. Lena spent part of her life as a naiad, in an unchanging state. What aspects of mortality did she like? What did she dislike? How do you think she felt about being returned to the water? Was it fair for the fairies to do that?

10. Fablehaven existed to help protect and conserve vanishing magical species. Why would that be worthwhile? Why do you suppose Grandpa Sorenson even wanted to protect the dangerous creatures? What non-magical plants or animals in our world are in danger of extinction? What are we doing to protect them?

11. There is a promise at the front of the book that none who enter Fablehaven will leave unchanged. How did their experiences at Fablehaven change Seth and Kendra? What do you take from the book?

These are just a few topics to initiate discussion. We would love to hear your discussion topics, your reactions, and your questions on the message board at Fablehaven.com.

To find out more about all things Fablehaven, or to get in touch with the author, be sure to visit Fablehaven.com.

RISE OF THE EVENING STAR

Kendra sat in silence as Dad chauffeured her to the movie theater. She had tried to persuade Alyssa not to go. Alyssa had started to act suspicious that Kendra secretly wanted Case all to herself, and since Kendra could not tell her friend the truth, she had to drop it. In the end, Kendra had decided to join them, concluding that she could not leave her friends alone with a scheming goblin.

"What movie are you seeing?" Dad asked.

"We're going to figure it out when we get there," Kendra said. "Don't worry—nothing racy." Kendra wished she could tell her father about her predicament, but he knew nothing about the magical properties of the preserve Grandpa and Grandma Sorenson managed. He thought it was just a normal estate.

"You're sure that you're ready for finals?"

"I've been keeping up with my assignments all year. It will just take a quick review. I'll ace them." Kendra wished she could talk to her Grandpa Sorenson about the situation. She had tried to call. Unfortunately, the only number her parents had for him repeatedly led to a recorded message informing her that the call could not be completed as dialed. The only other way she knew to contact him was through the mail. So, just in case the phone was out for a while, she had written Grandpa a letter describing the situation, which she planned to mail the next day. It felt good to lay out her predicament to somebody besides Seth, even if it was just on paper. Hopefully she would get through by phone even before the letter arrived.

Dad pulled into the movie theater parking lot. Alyssa and Trina were standing out front. Beside them stood a hideous goblin wearing a T-shirt and khakis.

"How do I know when to pick you up?" Dad asked.

"I told Mom I would call on Alyssa's cell phone."

"Okay. Have fun."

Not very likely, Kendra thought as she stepped out of the SUV.

"Hey, Kendra," Case rasped. She could smell his cologne ten feet away.

"We were getting worried you weren't coming," Alyssa said.

"I'm right on time," Kendra insisted. "You guys were early."

"Let's pick a movie," Trina said.

"What about Brittany?" Kendra asked.

"Her parents wouldn't let her come," Trina said. "They're making her study."

Case clapped his hands together. "So what are we seeing?"

They negotiated for a couple of minutes. Case wanted to see *Medal of Shame*, about a serial killer addicted to terrorizing veterans who had won the Congressional Medal of Honor. He finally relented on watching his action movie when Trina promised to buy him popcorn. The winning movie was *Switching Places*, the story of a nerdy girl who gets to date the guy of her dreams after her mind gets swapped into the body of the most popular girl in school.

Kendra had wanted to catch that movie, but now she worried it would be ruined. Nothing like cuddling up to a bald goblin during a cheesy chick flick.

As she had suspected, Kendra had a tough time focusing on the movie. Trina sat on one side of Case, with Alyssa on the other. Both were vying for his attention. They all shared a jumbo bucket of popcorn. Kendra declined whenever they offered her some. She wanted no part of anything those warty hands had pawed.

By the time the credits were rolling, Case had an arm around Alyssa. The two of them kept whispering and giggling. Trina sat with her arms crossed, wearing a disgruntled expression. Monster or not, when had any good come from multiple girls going out together with a guy they were all interested in?

Case and Alyssa held hands as they exited the theater. Trina's mom was waiting in the parking lot. Trina said a terse good-bye and stalked away.

"Can I use your cell phone?" Kendra asked. "I need to call my dad."

"Sure," Alyssa said, handing it over.

"You want a ride?" Kendra asked as she dialed.

"I'm not that far," Alyssa said. "Case said he would walk me."

The goblin gave Kendra a strange, sly smile. For the first time, she wondered if Case was aware that she knew his true identity. He seemed to be gloating that there was nothing she could do about it.

Kendra tried to keep her expression neutral. Mom answered the phone, and Kendra reported that she needed to be picked up. She handed the phone back to Alyssa. "Isn't that a pretty long walk? You can both have a ride."

Alyssa gave Kendra a look that questioned why she was deliberately trying to ruin something spectacular. Case put an arm around her shoulders, leering.

"Alyssa," Kendra said firmly, taking her hand, "I need to talk to you in private for a second." She tugged Alyssa toward her. "Is that all right, Case?"

"No problem. I need to run and use the rest room anyhow." He went back inside the theater.

"What is your deal?" Alyssa complained.

"Think about it," Kendra said. "We hardly know anything about him. You just met him today. He's not a little guy. Are you sure you want to go walking alone in the dark with him? Girls can get in a lot of trouble that way."

Alyssa gave her an incredulous look. "I can tell he's a nice guy."

"No, you can tell that he's good-looking, and pretty funny. Lots of psychos seem like nice guys at first. That's why you hang out a few times in public places before you spend time alone. Especially when you're fourteen!"

"I hadn't thought of it that way," Alyssa conceded.

"Let my dad give both of you a ride. If you want to talk with him, do it in front of your house. Not on a dark, lonely street."

Alyssa nodded. "Maybe you have a point. It wouldn't hurt to hang out within screaming distance of home."

When Case got back, Alyssa explained the plan, minus the part about him potentially being a psychopath. He resisted at first, saying it was such a nice night that it would be a crime not to walk, but finally consented when Kendra reminded him that it was after nine.

Dad showed up in the SUV a few minutes later, and agreed to give Alyssa and Case a ride. Kendra climbed up front. Alyssa and Case rode in the back, whispering and holding hands. Dad dropped the lovebirds off at Alyssa's house. Case explained that he lived just down the street.

As she drove away, Kendra looked back at them. She was leaving her friend alone with a creepy, conniving goblin. But there was nothing else she could do! At least Alyssa was in front of her house. If something happened she could cry out or run inside. Under the circumstances, that would have to suffice.

"Looks like Alyssa has a boyfriend," Dad remarked.

Kendra leaned her head against the window. "Looks can be deceiving."